MEDUSA

Through the Eyes of the Gorgon

By

Skevi Philippou

CHAPTER ONE

Deep within the vast darkness of Chaos, the ingredients of life emerged.

Atoms, molecules, and chemicals swirled into a primordial mist to create matter and energy.

Chaos was the lone and primal creator, and from her boundless womb came all of existence — that which was... is... and shall be.

First, from Chaos, emerged a female form. She was beautiful and broad-breasted; emanating life's glorious shining light from her body of cosmic carbon dust. This was Gaia, light from darkness. Born lifeless and inert, she fell through the void of Chaos. She fell and fell, for time unimaginable until she woke into awareness of her existence.

When her eyes opened, she saw the emptiness around her and wept. She curled up into a sphere and became the earth. Her tears of hydrogen and oxygen formed condensation. Her skin became the land, her breasts formed the mountains. Her beautiful hair came to be the floor of the sea and at the centre of it all, was her consciousness.

However, Gaia could not bear to unfurl and look above, as there was nothing but darkness all around.

Hence, she opened her eyes and willed her consciousness to fill the seabed, creating Pontus, the ocean, to keep her company. His life-force pulled and tugged through her body, creating rivers, lakes, and streams. Together, they brought many children into being including Nereus, Thaumas, Phorcys, and their sister, Ceto.

Pontus and her children, however, remained in the waters and mists. Thus, she still felt the dark and lifeless void that surrounded her warm body. Oh, how she longed for a heavenly companion to engulf her completely. So she looked up into the void one final time, her desire creating the sky and the heavens: Ouranos. His great, heavenly arms surrounded her with suns and stars, comforting her with his expansive thermal strength and spinning her slowly.

Gaia had found the perfect companion in Ouranos, no more would she have to peer into the darkness alone.

A new cyclical force emerged from this union and from it, Chaos provided the missing ingredient: *love*. Eros was born from Chaos and was entrusted to Gaia's care.

Eros and Gaia were one-half of the cycle: the light and the love. And Chaos, seeing the need for balance, created Nyx, ruler of the night, and Erebus, the darkness and shadows. During the day, Eros flew through the air igniting energy between Gaia and Ouranos, while Nyx united them at night time. And when Gaia joined with Ouranos, the Titans were born: Cronus, Coeus, Crius, Hyperion, Iapetus, Theia, Rhea, Themis, Mnemosyne, Phoebe, Tethys, and Oceanus.

Thus, the symmetry of the Universe began — light and dark. Erebus took Nyx as his wife and their union bore, amongst others, the righteous anger called Nemesis.

Phorcys, the Immortal Old One of the sea born of Gaia, ruled the seas with his wife and sister, Ceto. Ceto bore frightful daughters. The first, Scylla, was a grotesque monster. Her next offspring, the Graeae, the Aged Ones, were sisters three, Deino (Dread), Enyo (Horror), and Pemphredo (Alarm). They were implicitly connected to each other — their hair grey from birth, with only one eye and one tooth which they were forced to share.

So it was, that these protogonei inhabited the earth and oceans, whilst mortals slowly evolved from the protein remnants of Gaia and Ouranos, crawling from the seas onto the land. As the eons passed, humankind began to walk on two legs and developed the ability to speak. Seeing the greatness of Gaia and Ouranos though, people began to fear them.

Soon after, Ceto then bore the Gorgon sisters, born of the same egg: Euryale (She, of the Bellowing Cries) and Stheno (the Forceful). Birthed within the deepest caverns beneath Mount Olympus, their clanking brass hands with claws of sharpened steel and hair writhing of venomous snakes, made them the Queens of the Underworld. Their dreadful forms became the nightmares of mortal men as their voluptuous female figures with enticing curves, seductively lured men to come just a bit closer — shyly, coyly, with eyes lowered in coquettish charm. But, once their prey stepped closer, their slithery manes would violently spew and hiss and the shine of gold beneath their unfurling blackened wings tantalized their powerless victims into submission. They were at their core monstrous demons who would lick their victims with venomous, lolling tongues, paralyzing them; then (depending on their mood) they would rip these men apart with sharpened fangs or turn them to stone with a single, mesmerizing gaze.

Though valiant mortals soon gained knowledge of the Gorgons' formidable powers and tried to destroy them, all attempts were in vain. For the power of Gorgon essence lay in their seductive charm; the irresistible desire to meet their eyes could not be controlled. It was said that for one brief moment, the victim would be captivated in the light of their beautiful, albeit mesmerizing eyes before the stone paralysis began to creep from the legs, to the heart, then to the mind.

These were the children whom Ceto bore from the seed of Phorcys. All monstrous and strong, all powerful and immortal. However, none were blessed with the beauty and goodness of their grandmother, Gaia. None had the light within, to compete with Gaia's grace. And so it was, that Ceto contemplated that perhaps she might lose favour with her mother as other offspring of Gaia had borne at least one child of grace in her honour.

Now came the time to make amends and honour Gaia as Ceto was again with child. She wanted this child to be blessed with gifts that her other children did not possess. So, rising up from the sea, her squid like tentacles carried her with great speed, up to the highest peak of the highest mountain to appeal to Gaia for her favour so that her last child might be blessed with a distinct destiny. Standing in her half aquatic form, she bow down in supplication, lips nearly touching the ground, she closed her ocean-green eyes and carefully spoke:

"Great Mother of all Creation, I come to you today to beseech your blessing. Here where the silence carries my words to you — let your grace and ultimate majesty guide my request to fulfilment. The child I now carry will be my last. I ask that you help this child become as wise and beautiful as her grandmother. If you please, Gaia, help this child's destiny be one of greatness."

From within the great mountain, Gaia's serene response came at once.

"Ceto, my daughter of the sea, you have pleased me with your request. Long have I yearned for the pure light of the heavens to shine within your spawn. But, altering the destiny of mortal or god is not such a simple task. The rules of this universe are complex and everything in creation has its purpose and place. However, if it should be that this child's destiny be changed by the holder of all destinies, then it shall be done. Go first to Anangke."

Inspired by Gaia's promise, Ceto opened her arms and faced the skies above. With soft breath, she called the name of her sister, Anangke, the Goddess of Destiny, Necessity, and Fate. An all-powerful entity worshipped by men and gods alike, Anangke held the fate of every being in her hands. Transported then to a world of light and cloud, Ceto's tentacles formed her legs and stood pure and naked before a great throne of shining crystallite. Fluid and almost translucent from the greatness of the light, the figure stood tall before Ceto as she called out "Sister, I—".

A booming harmony of voices replied at once. "Ceto! My sister, as Goddess of Fate I know your purpose here! This desire can indeed be accomplished and inevitability, must be served! Your child must be born a human mortal; she must live a human mortal life, with human mortal parents. This will be her form for many years. Only in this way may she choose her own path. With no influence whatsoever, only her given soul to guide her, she must go to the mortals."

Ceto's tears began to rain from her scaly grey cheeks as she realized that her child's life, that of a daughter, would be far removed from her own.

"This is the time that your child will not be your own. She will be a human; she will live, eat, and act as a human. She will be happy, brave, beautiful, and wise. But, hear me now, Ceto! Medusa's life as a human will be cut short. Her human life will end by the actions of a god. On the eve of a day of worship, Medusa's true form will surface."

From the shining throne, a lucent female image materialized, tall and beautiful. Anangke approached her sister and closed her eyes by a cylinder of white light. Suddenly, Ceto was thrown into Chaos where her body floated in an ocean of darkness. Gaia pulled her down into her depth, entering Ceto's womb to craft the child in her own image, reforming the golden life-strands of the gods into earthly elements and the double-helixes of all mortal creatures.

She chose for the child, the gifts of beauty, grace, intelligence, and love — just as Anangke had said. She carefully wove within the rudiments of the mortal blood the gift of prophecy and true discernment. Finally, deep inside the child's heart, Gaia placed a seed from her Tree of Life—the seed of the knowledge of the immortals; the primacy of the gods.

As eternity is as swift as a blink of an eye for the gods, so it is as deep and lonely as solitude everlasting for the mortals. Ceto slithered down the hills and back into the deep foreboding sea, to find her husband Phorcys and wait for the night when her child would come into being.

CHAPTER TWO

When the fig trees were in full bloom and began to yield their tender fruit, Ceto's child was born.

Beautiful and innocent, the child had the appearance of a human mortal, with the limitations and weaknesses of any new-born. After, a brief moment in her gentle arms, Ceto, in joy and sorrow, lovingly handed the child to Gaia, who had already chosen a mortal couple for the special girl.

Before the sun rose above the purple peaks to the east, Gaia placed the infant near a path; the very path Petros (the righteous) and his wife, Agathi (the pure of heart) traversed daily. Gaia knew all who lived across her lands and so knew well this humble, loving family. Although Petros was only a simple dirt farmer and greater in years, he was very wise. His wife, whose tender and nurturing nature set her apart from all other women of this town, was the Great Mother's choice to take the infant to her loving bosom and nurture her as if her own.

This day, like every day, Petros and Agathi's passage began over the first hill, past the old, twisted olive tree with many carved initials. It was on the downhill slope, normally a welcome relief for the two daybreak travellers, that Agathi spotted movement amongst the weeds beside the road.

"Petros — look!"

Petros furrowed the dark, sun-worn skin of his brow with interest and because his curiosity always begged caution, he motioned for Agathi to stand to one side so that he might investigate further. Slowly, he stepped towards the shifting grass reeds, gently poking the ground with his walking staff. The creature there mewled in protest. In disbelief, Petros stepped back, and his wife grabbed his arm.

"A child, Petros!"

Agathi rushed forward without a moment's hesitation as her husband shouted "*Wait!*" in vain. There, Agathi, mother of three fine daughters, found the babe lying in the soft patch of grass, covered with nothing more than a simple white linen wrap. Tears streamed down her face as she reached to pick up the child.

"*No*, woman! Do not *touch* the child!" Petros apprehensively looked around, cautioning, "This may be bait for a trap! It is not our child! Leave it be! Someone will come for it in due course!" He seized Agathi's arm, intent on lifting her away from the babe.

"Nonsense!" she shouted, pulling free of his grip. "This infant will surely perish without our help!"

Trembling nervously, she picked up the bundled child, carefully cradling and examining it. Now pacified, the infant ceased its cries, permitting Agathi to examine more closely. Soon enough, the mother's experienced hand hit upon a strange bump.

"There is something within this cloth," she said, a troubled look appearing on her gentle face. Searching inside, she carefully pulled out a delicate golden chain. Attached to the end of the chain was a golden ring set with a large, flat, green stone. Taken aback, she handed it to her husband.

Petros turned the glistening item in both calloused hands and whispered, "*Gold.*" Eyes of concern and awe met each other; their gaze was only broken by the baby's renewed cries.

"This must belong to a powerful person — a *very* powerful person," he stated authoritatively. "Pure *gold…*" his voice trailed off as he adjusted the object for his aging vision to better focus. "Wait… there is something written inside… an inscription."

"Well, what does it read?" Agathi exclaimed, her curiosity reaching its peak.

Stroking his grey beard pensively, Petros read, "M.E.Δ.O.Y.Σ.A."

Agathi smiled at the child, caressing her few small golden locks and cooing a mother's hymn. Unsure of what to do next, her husband shuffled forward to peer into the infant's bright green eyes.

"This is a *gift*, Petros. Surely, a gift from the *Gods!*"

Sceptically scratching his head, he questioned, "Can it be? A gift from the Gods? But, we already have three lovely daughters of our own — why another? For what reason would this child be given to us?"

With a snort, Agathi ignored his male reasoning, supported the child purposefully in the crook of her arm and began to walk towards home, content with her blessed gift. Petros, shaking his head, could only follow.

Petros and Agathi lived on the outskirts of a small village called Avernae, which lay to the east. It was so close to the sea, that the smell of its free spirit roused the inhabitants from their sleep each morning. Farmers and fishermen, traders and artisans, all met daily at the *Agora,* the town's heart, to sell their catch, produce, cloth, and crafts. The farmers' fields were many, with vast caverns and high cliffs keeping the land safe from the ocean's briny water below, where fisherman brought in their daily catches as they had for time immemorial. The hustle and bustle of traders and craftsmen, provided an almost circus-like atmosphere to the otherwise placid village.

They kept the baby under wraps, so as not to arouse unwanted attention from curious townspeople they might encounter as they made their way back home. Agathi entered the courtyard of their home first, where her two eldest daughters, Dorkas and Elpis, sat weaving baskets for market. Their grandmother thoughtfully watched over them, making sure they were mastering the craft to perfection. With peals of surprise at seeing their mother's unexpected return, the girls hastily dropped their projects and rushed to see what she was clutching so gingerly in her arms.

"Daughter, why have you come home so soon? What is that you cradle so lovingly in your arms?" the old woman asked over the din of the girls' enthusiastic chatter.

Agathi smiled at her excited brood, "Alright! Alright! *Shoosh!*" She sat on her favourite milking stool and said, "Now, come see. *Carefully!*"

"A baby!" the sisters exclaimed in unison; each touching the new-born's skin and hair. The youngest child, Hagne, now drawn to the excitement screeched, "A little baby!" in such a high-pitch that she almost startled the child.

The old woman beckoned Petros, suspicion looming in her gesture.

"*What is this?*"

"As you can see, mother… It is a baby," Petros replied, somewhat forcing his usual casual tone, then sighing, "She thinks it is a gift from the *Gods*— a daughter—a miracle baby given to us by the immortals! She is completely enamoured and does not care what anyone thinks! She has determined that it is her duty to help fulfil this child's destiny!" Shoulders shrugged, he acknowledged the futility of opposing his wife's mind when made up.

"Well… what shall you call her?" the ever-persistent grandmother asked.

Without hesitation, Agathi said, "*Medusa.*"

That first day, clear signs that Medusa was no ordinary child, began to emerge. After sleeping soundly for several hours, Agathi, like any mother with a new-born, fretted over the decision to wake and feed her. She anxiously checked on her every few moments, waiting for her to stir. Then finally, past noon, she resigned herself that the infant certainly needed nourishment, and so she peeked into the hastily-contrived bed, where she discovered a Black Whip snake coiled upon the child's tiny chest. Without hesitation, she grabbed the serpent, tossed it out the window, and quickly hoisted up the baby (linens and all) and held her closely to her breast. At first she protested but Medusa soon acquiesced to her new mother's embrace. Agathi thought it best to mention nothing of this to her family. No need to alarm them unduly, she decided.

The next day, however, when Agathi walked into her new baby's room to tend to her, she again found the mysterious snake lying on her foundling's chest. This time, when she approached, it raised its brown head and set its golden eyes, defiantly meeting Agathi's concerned gaze. *Is this an omen? It looks as if it wants to guard her. A bad omen, surely!* Hesitatingly, she seized the snake in her two hands and tossed it out the window as before, again, telling no one. She prayed to the Gods that this mysterious event would occur no more.

The next day however, just past noon, as before, she found that the snake had indeed returned, positioning itself on Medusa's chest. This time, its warning was clear, it raised its head and rippled its blue-black scales, hissing vehemently as Agathi approached. In tears, she ran screaming for Petros:

"Petros, Petros, come quickly! A *snake* in Medusa's bed, Petros! A Black Whip snake in her bed!"

Hearing her cries, the grandmother suddenly burst into the room, grabbed the spitting serpent and carried it to the edge of the garden. Lifting the creature to the noonday sun she raised her head to the sky and shouted, "ANATHEMA SE! Damn you to Hades!" Then she tossed the snake on the ground. With one look back at the old woman, the snake quickly slithered into the thickets and disappeared.

Running with hoe in hand, Petros appeared a moment later, breathless.

"A snake in Medusa's bed?!"

"Yes, and not the first time! But, I... I was afraid it was..." Agathi tried to explain, "That it could have been..."

"Sent by the Gods?". No sooner than the grandmother finished her sentence did the sound of thunder roar in from the clashing seas in the distance. Feeling uneasy, they moved into the doorway of their home.

"Yes, Mother, sent by the Gods! Perhaps... perhaps I should not have judged so hastily," she said, holding Medusa closer to her heart, "but..."

"You did as any mother would," the wise grandmother said, eyeing the path the snake had taken.

"Let us just hope the Gods do not take offense at our ignorance," Petros offered, putting his arms around wife and child.

The years went by with no more interference from the snake and Medusa grew into a happy, healthy child. Her parents proved to be most loving and nurturing and her siblings, Dorkas (the beautiful), Elpis (the thoughtful), and Hagne (the quiet) all adored the young one, they called sister. Still, they could not easily ignore Medusa's *differentness*, for the child exhibited extraordinary gifts even from a very young age.

By the time Medusa was four, she could speak as proficiently as any adult and her ability to read and understand complex ideas was astonishing. She even surpassed the educated male youth of the town. Most remarkably, she could explain the actions of the Gods far beyond any other child of her years. Those abilities, along with a profound gift of prophesy, that only became more pronounced with time, quickly set her apart from everyone else in Avernae.

For Medusa, predicting the next day's weather became… *child's* play. Announcing the approach of visitor's hours in advance came to be expected and her family came to rely upon her ability to divine the whims of the Fates. "The scythe will have a will of its own today, Father. Careful that it does not cut into you." "Mother, a dark-skinned merchant from Libya will buy thirty of your baskets today at market. Be sure to bring many of the dark red reed. He will prefer those and pay you well." However, there was also a dark and disturbing side to her predictions. That troubled her family deeply and others, as word got out.

Being the closest in age, Medusa and Hagne often played together, having developed a special, sisterly bond. One day as Medusa and Hagne played peacefully in the courtyard with dolls made of cloth and filled with hay, Medusa abruptly threw her doll to the ground and screamed as if in agony, greatly disturbing Hagne's otherwise quiet play.

Hearing her scream, the grandmother came running outside enquiring, "Medusa, what is wrong?! Hagne! What happened?"

"I do not know, Grandmother!" Hagne said, looking confused and frightened.

"My doll fell into a deep cavern! It is stuck!" cried Medusa, piling tiny pebbles on top of it.

Reaching for the doll the grandmother said with a smile trying to appease the child, "But see we can easily rescue your doll! There is no need to fret!"

"No! No one can hear his cries! He will die alone and his blood will stain the stones forever!"

Why would such a small child have such a disturbing imagination? The grandmother asked herself.

"Medusa — *enough*! *Enough*, child! Come along, now, let us go inside." She motioned for Hagne to bring the doll and scatter the pile of stones.

If this is a prophecy, the grandmother thought, *I need not know any more of it*. She told no one of this day, cautioning Hagne as well. Fate must never be altered in any way. *Ever*.

As Medusa grew, so too did her reputation as an exceptional child. Her prophetic dreams and acumen were things of on-going curiosity amongst the townspeople. Many of them however, were secretly cautious, naturally wary of offending the Gods. Many thought it best to direct their children away from her. They need not have worried since the children of the town had already begun shying away from Medusa as they discovered gradually that she did not enjoy playing the same games as they did. Her interests were drawn elsewhere.

One day, Medusa wandered alone through the agora as her father stopped to buy some new tools. Busy as ever, the centre bustled with traders, pilgrims, religious adepts, soldiers, deviants, philosophers and of course, children. The children helped their parents earn a living. Hence, they generally kept busy and stayed out of the adults' way, but they also tended to avoid the strange little girl.

Medusa, although acutely aware of this, did not mind since she used this time to explore. Soon, she found her way to the philosophers and seers quarter. She began to listen to their theories, their notions, and their bright, new ideas on everything; from the meaning of life and how to live it properly, to mathematics and the meaning of the movement of the planets. On this particular afternoon, the topic of discussion was the Gods; *Zeus* to be precise and his position as supreme ruler and the ethical analysis of his many acts.

One philosopher argued that Zeus was just and fair; after all, he had acquired his throne as King of the Gods by bravery and cunning. His reasoning was that anything Zeus wanted, Zeus obtained, by one means or another, and all were blessed to be a part of his creation on this world. Another, insisted that the acts of Zeus were nothing more than human fable; the fabrication of simple men wishing themselves as free and powerful as a God —mere reflections of their lustful desires and nothing more. A loud discussion had ensued, with the men waving wrinkled scrolls and pointing provocatively towards the heavens.

In the midst of this heated discourse, a small but clear voice could be heard ringing out amongst the others. "Men argue only what they cannot prove," Medusa announced. "This does not make them right nor wrong as they are, believers in their own thoughts."

One elderly man peered down with his one remaining eye and asked,

"Little girl, where did you find such wise words?"

"Wisdom is not found, but brought with you upon this earth," she said.

The men all smiled curiously, as they allayed their own views to examine this child closer. "Well, young one, it appears that *you* are also a believer in your own thoughts!" he said, considering himself clever.

"My thoughts are not of things I *believe*, but of things, I *know*...." Medusa calmly replied.

"*Indeed!*" one of them said, dubiously. "Reveal to us more of what is it is, that you *know* then, child!" All the other men drew in closer now, listening intently.

"I know that this world is but a small shadow of the vast universe that birthed the great Gods of Olympus; and that the rational and wisdom that spurred the deeds of almighty Zeus, hidden at birth on Mount Aegeum in order to escape being devoured by his own father Cronus, are far beyond that which mortal man can comprehend."

The men all began to murmur amongst themselves. Never before had a female — not even a grown woman — spoken so candidly in this way.

"Simple fabrication!" declared the one called Erastos the Elder.

"Fertile imagination and nothing more!"

"Fabrication? And if the mighty Zeus had not defeated Cronus from Mount Olympus? If he had not filled the heavens with holy bolts of lightning to end his father's dark reign of terror? What then of mortals? If he had not caused the heavens to tremble and groan and the earth to quake, then what of humankind? Would they now exist?!" Medusa's clear and passionate rebuttal echoed through the forum.

Taken aback, several of the men nodded in agreement, others murmured unsurely.

"It is not for mere mortals to question the deeds of Zeus but, to hold him in reverence for their very existence!" Medusa told them with certainty.

"Perhaps you have a point, young one... But nothing is set in stone. Times change, ideas change. What once was, will not be forever."

Medusa sat silent in thought for a moment, contemplating the wise man's words.

"It is perhaps only a thought of an unknowing child; however, I cannot help but feel that.... That things are already changing. There is an energy, an invisible force, something that binds us all together, yet is capable of taring us all apart within the blink of an eye. It feels like it is time, time to make a change in what we hold as truth. Time to look further, beyond what we hold as knowledge.

The wise men were silenced by this child's words. Each deep in thought, none felt the need to take this further for the time being.

"Wise words, all," the one-eyed man said, nodding.

"Perhaps she knows of what she speaks!" voiced another.

Medusa merely smiled.

Thus began, a curious friendship from that day forward, between herself and the town's wise men. Still, her behaviour continued to provide the townspeople with fodder for discussion at suppertime or gossip about the hedonistic goings-on at the agora:

"Agathi's girl, Medusa, has been telling strange tales again! Of meeting monsters in her dreams. Monsters that were still there when she awoke!" a woman at the date vendor's stall was heard saying.

"So what is so special about that? Every child fears creatures lurking in the night!" stated the vender dismissively.

"No, you do not understand! Medusa does not *fear* them, she speaks of *befriending* them! Calling them *brother* and *friend*! It is not natural for a child to have such a dark imagination! Why, in my day—"

Another woman who loved a good embellishment exclaimed "I heard Medusa believes that the Gods speak directly to her! She is a strange little child, indeed, speaking to the sea at night… calling the caves *home*. My children will have nothing to do with her!"

While most came to view Medusa as a strange child possessing a dangerously fruitful imagination, there were others who were wise enough to see Medusa for the exceptional child that she was. One such individual was a boy named Iasonnas.

Iasonnas was the son of the village mayor, from a prominent and much respected family. Unlike other boys his age, who were only interested in staging imaginary battles with Cyclopes or pretending to be one of the Gods of Olympus, Iasonnas was a thoughtful, sensitive boy, often seen scurrying about town, paying visits on the infirmed and aged. Tall for a boy his age, his long, curly black locks could often be seen streaming in the breeze, as he made his way, to bring magical charms, herbal concoctions, or just a well wish, to those in need of comfort. He had many friends and the entire town treated him well.

One day as Iasonnas passed by the common well in the town square, he chanced upon the bottom half of a young girl sticking out of the well. One leg pointed precariously into the air, the other barely toeing the ground. Intrigued by this most humorous sight, he approached the well and leaned over, discovering a reddened-face Medusa.

"Hello, there! What are you doing down here?" he asked with a giggle.

"The water sprite! She went down the well! I need to tell her something! Please help me find her!" Medusa cried, her fingers reaching dangerously close to the water below.

Though intrigued by her strange exclamations and precarious predicament, being the practical young man that he was, Iasonnas wrapped his arms around her waist and forcefully pulled her out before she could most certainly fall in. Holding her tightly as he stood her on the ground she angrily spat, "Get your hands off of me, *boy*! The sprite! I have lost her now for certain and it is all your fault!"

Iasonnas was very amused by her anger, however, he composed himself and calmly, held her tighter still and whispered, "If you promise to forget about the well, I will take you to where the sprites *live*."

"Well… I do not believe *you* would know of such a place!" Medusa said adamantly, wiggling out of his grasp and straightening her clothes.

Concerned that she may take to the well again when no one would be there to rescue her, Iasonnas quickly determined a course of action to satisfy them both. "Well, just follow me and I will *prove* it!"

Medusa hesitated, but knowing that sprites travel all the waterways, she felt he might — just *might* — know of what he speaks. *I mustn't under any circumstances miss an opportunity to deliver my message*, she reminded herself. And besides, this boy did not seem like all the others of the village. His eyes, the colour of Heliopora coral danced with intelligence, patience, and mirth. She nodded her head and he led the way.

Iasonnas took Medusa deep into the forest to the west of town, down a steep, winding path where the air suddenly grew thick and the temperature became much warmer than in the rest of the forest's cool glade. Medusa glanced at the boy as they walked further down the darkening path. *His energy seems pure. From when he grasped my waist I felt sweet calmness.* As she contemplated quietly while looking ahead, she saw a shadowy figure of a man standing calmly before them. Iasonnas walked by the apparition, as if it was not there. Medusa looked up at this handsome tall stranger, whose placid expression would calm a stampeding wildebeest. His stone white appearance invoked much emotion, stirring deep in the young Medusa. As she walked by, not an eyelash did he flutter, nor a breath did he exhale. Leaving him in the distance, she turned to see that at the end of this long and dark path, was a pool of cool water fed by a trickling stream that stretched far to the north and out of sight. A gentle falls replenished the pool and gave the atmosphere a somewhat *magical* air. The water seemed to breathe life, jumping and splashing, creating little droplets of silver. Its shimmering gleam shone in the children's eyes and captivated their imaginations. Towering above, ancient embracing cedars with branches, entwined and reached high into the sky, arching into a great, dense canopy. Like a page out of a great hero's legend, a stillness hung thick and sweet in the air as if time was suspended. In awe, Medusa turned to Iasonnas and exclaimed in wonder, "No one has ever shown me such a place! It all looks so… *beautiful!* This *is* where the sprites live, I can feel it!"

Iasonnas smiled at her reverence for this special place, which mirrored his own. "And you are the first I have ever shown it."

She looked deeply into his eyes. "The *first?*"

He just smiled. His warmth and sincerity emanated through his eyes. This touched Medusa as she had never met any other child in the town who seemed genuinely interested in befriending her. This led her to ask:

"Well… why *me?*"

"I… I do not know. Something told me that you were… *deserving.* A girl who would risk her life to bring a message to the sprites must know something others do not. Somehow, I just *knew.*"

Their smiles broadened. Medusa suddenly knew she had made a friend like no other. From that moment on, Medusa had someone who would try to understand her, and someone she could trust.

Reaching down to the water's edge, the children rested on the stones, their fingers catching small silver droplets of water as they spoke of sprites and trolls.

Medusa reached into her sandal and pulled out a small rolled parchment, wrapped in a red string no larger than her small finger. She smiled proudly as she explained to Iasonnas. "This is what I must tell the sprite named Eosphera. She will need this information to protect against the harsh coming winter." Iasonnas looked on as she carefully placed the small parchment on the water and pushed it towards the splashing falls, where it was taken underwater and disappeared.

Content in her completed mission Medusa smiled silently as she gazed into the crystal waters, seeing Iasonnas' reflection smiling back at her, their eyes made contact. Not one to shy away, she stared at his placid smile; her mind travelling far, his image began to shift and change to that of a grown man with a golden brown beard. Within a blink of an eye, Iasonnas' reflection was back to his youthful self.

Medusa turned and looked at him curiously "You will be a handsome man someday Iasonnas."

Iasonnas raised his brows in confusion as Medusa got to her feet and began the journey back into town, passing the haunting but tranquil apparition once more, still standing in the exact spot she originally saw him. This time, though as placid as before, his stone white appearance seemed cracked and aged; His beautiful blue eyes glazed white, his lips ever so slightly apart, he stood alone once more, as the children passed by and faded from the sight of the path.

Soon a flutter of small sparkling silver and green wings appeared out of the darkness. The size of a sparrow, it fluttered up the path, a perfectly formed female being with a silver fish tail, giving it the appearance of a tiny mermaid. It dipped and fluttered in the air, gripping in its arms the parchment, trying to stabilize, whilst holding this great weight.

The sprite paused in mid-air and upon seeing that the children had gone already, turned to the apparition which was visible to all, but human eyes. Hovering over his stone white face, the sprite touched his nose with the tip of her tail and flew back away as the sound of cracking began to emanate from his core. Crumbling to the ground in a sudden thunder, white powder flew up as the sprite held the parchment tight as cover. As the dust settled, she peeked to see the rubble of stone on the floor, with only the handsome face still intact as a death mask memento.

Looking out into the sunlight the sprite flew swiftly back into the shelter of the woods, hoping that Medusa's message was one of hope for a light winter ahead.

CHAPTER THREE

By the age of eight, Medusa had proven herself to be a supremely gifted young girl, excelling in every academic activity she attempted. Although not encouraged in any way by her family, she could not resist the urge to satisfy her curiosity and constantly expand her knowledge of everything.

Spending long hours alone pouring over every scroll that crossed her path, she taught herself how to read and write many forms of the Greek language, as fluently as any scholar. Through the Gnomic poetry of Phocylides, she even gained a unique eight-year-old's respect for the principles of honour and justice. While mathematics was not a field of study taught to the young women of Greece, Medusa spent many quiet nights trying to solve Pythagorean equations by lamplight that she had copied from Iasonnas' wax tablet.

Iasonnas welcomed her interest, much to Agathi's dismay, since Medusa would disappear for hours. She would search high and low for the girl, sending out her other daughters to find Medusa and bring her back home. Once found her mother would say to her:

"Medusa, child why do you waste your time on things that do not concern you. Would not you rather be learning the skills a young girl will need? Cooking, cleaning, and keeping the house and the fields." "Mother, I have done my chores, I have cleaned the animal's troves and I have weaved baskets for market tomorrow. This is what I need to do now."

Agathi would shake her head and smile, "My love if it makes you happy then carry on. However, do not expect the young men to be happy marrying an educated woman."

Her grandmother, who had an eye for match-making would always suggest Iasonnas as the boy of interest.

"That son of the mayor. He will be a fine catch for our Medusa. Do you not see how they spend hours together?"

In response to this chatter, Medusa would roll her eyes, pack up her parchments and head off elsewhere. *How could they even think for a moment that I will marry that boy? He is a friend and will be nothing more!*

Medusa also found herself drawn to many other scholarly topics, from astronomy to alchemy, philosophy to calligraphy, though she could never let her full interests be known because proper young women of Greece focused their efforts only on the *womanly* arts that would best serve them as daughters, wives, and mothers. Other studies which did not pertain to the practical practices necessary to those of her gender were expressly forbidden. However, Medusa had already set her sights on a much higher calling.

While her insatiable desire to learn occupied much of her waking hours, Medusa always found the time to feed and care for the family's one and only horse, Hippos. Despite having been given the rather simple name meaning "horse," the rustic, red creature was a special gift from the State to Petros, presented for his heroism in the wars against the Persian Empire. Once a great and beautiful stallion with a flowing ivory mane, he was now a proud but aging steed content to nibble from his petite care-taker's hand. Medusa loved him like no other creature on earth.

"Good morning, my noble friend," she greeted as she opened the gate to his stall. Hippos brought his muzzle to her chest and rubbed up and down affectionately, snorting an acknowledging puff. "Shall it be a big, tasty carrot or a sweet, red apple, this morning?" she said, presenting one in each tiny hand. As Hippos chose the apple, Medusa gleefully exclaimed, "Ah, then it shall be the apple for you and the carrot for me!" Hippos nodded in agreement.

They both chewed while she ran her hand lovingly over his coarse, white-whiskered snout and fondled his ears. "Tell me, dear Hippos, shall we ride this afternoon? A walk along the path?" Hippos nodded. "Very well, then that is just what we shall do! A nice, long walk along the old trail down to the sea. I think you love the sea as much as I do!" She scratched him lovingly behind the ears and headed out of the stable. As she did, she accidentally pushed against one of her father's many toolboxes nearby, scattering the tools in the straw. Dutifully, she began picking up the handcrafted items, some as tiny as her fingernail, carefully pressing her little hand into the straw to separate the miniscule instruments from the chaff. While doing this arduous task, she saw some splintered planks of wood beneath the straw. Curious, she began brushing away the spire and sand and discovered more planks of wood — one of which moved to the touch. Lifting it, there in the dust, she spotted a bundle about a meter in length wrapped in old fleece and tied with coarse string. She started to pull out the bundle, when Hippos snorted and hoofed the stable floor.

"Do you know what this is, Hippos?

Hippos nodded as if in agreement.

"Perhaps I should not remove it. Father has hidden it here I am sure. I should certainly cover it back up!"

Again, Hippos snorted, leaving her to decide for herself.

Thoughtfully chewing her lip, Medusa sighed, "Well, I *could* always just take a peek! I can just put it right back again!"

Her mind made up, she removed the package carefully, untying the delicately knotted cord. Un-swaddling it, she discovered a fine lightwood hunting bow. Her heart pounding excitedly, she picked it up and ran her fingers down its smooth contours, stopping at a tarnished, silver talisman fixed to its grip. "The stag of Artemis, the mighty huntress!" she exclaimed breathlessly to a stoic Hippos. She looked up at him. "The spoils of war, perhaps. Father was a great soldier, you know." Then, she reverently placed the bow back inside its hidden crypt, but not before removing the talisman and slipping it into the folds of her tunic. This, she decided, she would keep for herself. Delighted with her discovery (despite knowing her father would not be pleased to discover that she had disturbed his hidden treasure), she mentioned the find to no one. However, from that day on, the desire to use the bow came to obsess her.

In the stable-yard, Medusa loved to play imaginary wars where she, the 'Archer Queen,' defeated every foe — no matter the size of their army — with her golden bow. When she was certain no one was watching, she would fasten the talisman to her wrist to derive its mystical powers. Her fantasy arrows flew through the air, sometimes ten at a time, while she galloped on her trusty red steed en route to her enchanted fortress atop Mount Parnassus. Hippos, her lone confidante, observed her fabrications, contently chewing oats and hay from his feed bin. After all the skills and knowledge she had already come to master, her most pervasive desire now, was to learn the art of the archer.

As part of the children's regular household chores, they were often sent into the nearby woods to gather berries and mushrooms for the supper table. How Medusa loved this adventure when she,

Dorkas, Elpis, and Hagne would all set out for the forest. Despite her sisters' faithful admonitions, they came to expect Medusa to invariably stray off on her own. She never seemed to be able to follow the well-beaten path, always managing to find the darkest and most secluded patches of the lush vegetation of the forest. This day was to be no different.

As her sisters busied themselves scouring the sprawling ferns for mushrooms, Medusa wandered off the trail, making her way towards the heart of the forest where the ancient trees reached for the sun and strange animals called from within the darkness, hooting, grunting, and howling; the wind whistled an eerie tune while fairies frolicked. The cool darkness and mysterious sounds that would unnerve most grown men were quite comforting to Medusa. They would fuel her imagination with what lay beyond her eyes' sight, and she would pretend to be a creature of the forest, growling and prancing through the twisted paths seeking others of her kind.

On this day, Medusa happened upon the oldest part of the forest where the most ancient tree of all stood, whose glorious stature effused the very centre of existence. A timeless and majestic fir, like those used for centuries for boat building, the tree was tall and spiralling; its bark thick and knurled and the highest needles swayed with the winds persuasion, seeming to swirl and dance with a consciousness of its own. Finding that she became dizzy trying to see the very top, she lay down on the needled blanket beneath her. Gradually, all sound faded away. Reaching inside her peplos, she removed her prized talisman and secured it to her wrist.

Her peaceful silence was abruptly broken however by a loud whirring and a *thud*. Sitting up quickly, she scanned her surroundings. Then, the sound came a second time — this time to her right. *Whoosh — thud.*

Jumping to her feet, she scuttled away from the tree, noticing two remarkably beautiful arrows embedded in the ancient trunk.

Fascinated, she freed one dark and smooth wooden shaft, admiring its strength and flexibility. She traced the flawless, shining bronze arrowhead secured with golden cord at its tip. Then, she ran her tender fingers through the white fletching at the tail of the arrow. She stopped, as a shiver crept through her body, feeling a presence behind her.

Quickly turning, she found a beautiful white buck standing on a rise, intently observing her movements. His majestic antlers were outlined by the faint light that broke through the dappled foliage, making them appear to be on fire; its dark, round eyes were fixed upon Medusa. Then, from the shadows and into streaked sunlight a tall woman emerged dressed in all white raiment, holding a curved bow that shone and sparkled in the beaming light; Alive with gold gilding, it gleamed with glorious splendour. It drew Medusa's attention from the woman when it caught her eye.

"You discovered my arrows," the graceful woman said with a smile. "Beautiful, are they not, Medusa?"

She knows my name? Remaining calm, though her heart raced, Medusa held out both arrows. "How do you know who I am, huntress?"

The woman carefully returned the arrows to her pearlescent white quiver (adorned with small shards of antler and other animal bone) and replied, "This is my home. I know all who enter."

"You live *here?* In the *forest?*" asked Medusa.

"I go wherever I am most needed," the woman smiled. With one outstretched arm, she beckoned the stag; it serenely came to her hand, taking its place at her side. "Wherever the creatures of the forest call me, wherever hunters of pure heart need me, I am there."

Medusa absently touched the talisman tied to her wrist. "Did *I* call you here? With *this?*" She raised her arm to show the silver stag of Athena.

The woman smiled and nodded, "You wish to be one with the bow, do you not?" Medusa's gaze moved to the woman's shining bow, bespeaking both her eagerness and curiosity.

"Would you like me to teach you how to use it?" Intrigued by the elegant woman and her most timely offer, Medusa eagerly nodded.

"Come, then," the woman said, leading her to a clearing in the forest not far from the ancient tree.

"The secret to controlling the bow, Medusa, is controlling your heartbeat." She placed the bow in Medusa's left hand and set her stance. Then she took an arrow and placed it to the bow shelf, slightly drawing out the tension of the string.

"Do you see that pomegranate tree across the way?" Medusa nodded, her eyes keenly focused on her target. "Aim for a single fruit on that tree. Raise the bow up like this." From behind the girl's shoulders, the huntress held the bow so that the arrow aligned with Medusa's sight. "Good. Now remember, control your heart beat. Breathe calmly and evenly, so that you feel the wind and see only your target. Think: *There is nothing in existence, only the target.* Use these elements to guide the arrow to that fruit." The woman's hypnotic instructions instantly became ingrained in her mind: *Breathe. Feel. See.*

With a large, deep red fruit in her sights, Medusa aimed and released…

… Just as the arrow neared the target, she heard Dorkas calling in the distance.

"Medusa! Medusa! Where are you, sister?"

Startled, she turned toward her sister's voice. However, when she turned back again, she found herself alone; standing at the base of the old pine tree. Still clutching the bow in her hand, all signs of the woman vanished.

"Medusa, come! It is time to go home now!" Dorkas shouted.

"Thank you, my Goddess," Medusa whispered, though not at all certain the huntress had really been there. "I will remember what you have taught me and will learn the art of the bow well." Removing the talisman, she slipped it back into the folds of her garment and quickly hid the bow inside a cleft in the ancient pine.

True to her promise, as Medusa grew tall and strong, so too grew her skill with the bow. Rarely did a day pass, that she did not wander off to practice in secret, drawing on her boundless determination and natural abilities to become its master. Her poise and aptitude soon evidenced extraordinary expertise, no longer missing her targets; hitting each squarely, dead-centre and without fail. Of course, she kept this skill hidden from everyone; everyone but Iasonnas. Iasonnas was bemused by her interest but terrified as he was often used as a moving target. He was forced to hold a small target on a stick as he ran through the hills while Medusa fired her shots. After she destroyed the target with her arrows, he would collapse on the ground and shout "A woman's place is in the home!!!"

After all, it was not a woman's place to learn the art of the hunter. Conversely, to her mother's joy, she demonstrated an equally remarkable talent for embroidering wondrous designs. Designs of such detail, that like her other remarkable talents, soon set her apart from everyone else in the village. By the age of nine, Medusa had learned to embroider masterful images on fine linen. Avernae was quite renowned for its weaving of strong yet delicate cloth and Medusa had become a regular face at the local cloth-makers workshop. Hagne would walk with Medusa into town where she would ask for their left-over scraps, which the weavers were only too happy to provide. They were glad to see the unwanted pieces put to good use. Still, she made her selections most carefully, scrutinizing each piece with a critical eye, holding each up to the light.

The weavers simply smiled at the artistic whims of the young girl known for her peculiar ways.

"Blessings of the Gods, kind weavers," she always said most politely. "May I trouble you for a few small scraps of your fine cloth?"

"Indeed you may, young lady," one of the weavers would always reply. "Choose freely from the leftover pile. They are small, but, of the finest quality."

"This I know well," would be her reply. "None finer in the whole of Greece, I am certain."

Though few had seen the fruits of her artistic labours, it was widely known that her talent was captivating; her images, more vivid than anyone could ever imagine. They were pleased to help such a gracious young lady bring her creativity to life in such a *sociable* fashion. Once at home, Medusa would set the irregular fragments into the small wooden stretcher her grandmother had given her and carefully trim off the excess; the very stretcher her grandmother had herself used as a child. Then she would search through her little wooden box of silk threads her father had brought back from his trips to Athens, searching for just the right colour; deep, earthy red was her favourite. However, she also used black or sometimes rich indigo. In the end, each embroidered cloth told a story, shared a dream, or brought a fantastic fable vibrantly to life.

Her first artistic endeavours had been simple interpretations of Greek letters or ancient symbols. However, as her creative nature grew, so did her aesthetic and methodology, more frequently drawing from a place deep within her unconscious mind. This day, like most others, there was a certain sense of urgency in her work, as though her mind was pushing the work out before she was ready to give it. After stretching and trimming the cloth, she meditated on the blank canvas before her, allowing the image to materialize. It flashed in her mind over and over again until she could see it vividly embossed upon the cloth. Then, she feverishly began to capture the image on the fabric before it faded from view.

Sometimes the work took hours, sometimes only a few minutes. However, she always knew when it was complete. She always knew when the story was told. Now, hers were stories never before told: dreams with cryptic meanings no one could accurately decipher, though Iasonnas often tried. Epic battles, mighty warriors and fantastic cave-dwelling monsters from distant lands appeared on the finely woven linen.

This is a powerful message, but, missing something! she thought on this day as she examined the emerging form. Turning to her supplies, she mixed ground dandelion root with water and clay in a small glazed mortar to create a pasty, red paint she would apply with her hands. Frantically dipping her nimble fingertips into the mixture, she daubed the paste over the taut linen as her vision came to life. Today, the clash of sword and arrow unfolded, crossed as if in heated battle. *There will be a battle between the swordsman and the archer.* From the sword emerged a battered shield and a crimson-red crescent moon. *A battle at night, with only one protected. Bloodshed.*

Her needle then created a branch of wormwood and an arachnid.

Injustice is at its core and the victory results from treachery. Finally, entwined amongst all of the other images appeared a snake shedding its skin. *Yet, there will be rebirth.* Now complete, she sat back, exhausted. "I must take this to the sage ones," she decided. Her most intricate and emotional works were always given to the wise ones; the philosophers and mystics of the village. The effect on the human soul, she had discovered, captivated, intrigued, but also unsettled anyone else who viewed them.

Like all mystics of the East, the seers of Avernae had long used magical, geometric drawings to aid in their spiritual quests. They had discovered centuries before that, certain images can somehow transcend time and space; Priests and Oracles of Attica had long sought the most inspiring images to induce trance and help them see into the future. From the first time the elders set eyes on Medusa's visionary needlework, they knew hers were more powerful than any they had ever known. Mystics, who had performed their magic while viewing her linens, claimed to have witnessed the birth of creation and travelled eons into the future and re-lived great moments in time. So she willingly traded her cloths to the scholars and wise ones for the chance to borrow from among their precious, ancient scrolls. Their scrolls had expanded her mind in dimensions she had never imagined. Now, they welcomed her arrival and the visions her embroidery provided them.

"And what have you brought us today, young one?" the elder called Diodorus asked. Medusa held out the red and black image, the aged sage taking it carefully from her hand. As he did, lightning flashed across his eyes; swords and arrows jumped from the cloth — two warriors locked in mortal combat.

"Medusa, child, the Gods have truly bestowed upon you a rare gift," Diodorus often told her. A gift many mystics thought beyond the reach of any mortal.

Back home while the sun was setting and the Cicada bugs sang their repetitive melody, Medusa and the women of her family sat in cool evening breeze of the yard. Medusa's grandmother, while watching over her granddaughters, began to question the girl over her embroidery works.

"Child, what does this mean?" pointing to a red flower on the cloth.

"That's a poppy flower grandmother. It symbolizes, sleep, the God of dreams Morpheus."

"And why does he make an appearance in this story?" her grandmother enquired inquisitively.

"He is calling someone to a dream. I am not sure who she is, but she has a mission to fulfil and Morpheus is aiding Hermes in his work by calling her."

"Do you know what her mission is?" her grandmother persisted.

"To comfort the souls of the lost... She was chosen for her kindness and love; a sensitive soul, who cares for all and sorrows for the loss for innocence. She was charged with finding and guiding the souls to Hermes."

Agathi, who sat across the way listening while splitting peas, yelled out:

"Child, why don't you ever embroider something nice? I saw the flower and the male and female figures and thought it pretty until you explained its meaning!"

"Daughter leave the child be, she has a mission which is not yet revealed to us, remember that!" with that, her grandmother tapped Medusa's her shoulder as if to say *do not fret, continue.*

From the dusk that emerged so gently, a flutter of feathers flew by just as unnoticed by the females. A white owl settled firmly upon the notched branches of an ancient olive tree that sat in dim light beside the walls of the enclosed yard where the family now discussed the wedding of the eldest daughter Dorkas.

Medusa's mother stated "Alkisti of Cumae, she has a son. Only one year older than our Dorkas. His father is a blacksmith; he must be learning the family trade."

The grandmother squinted one eye and shook her pointed finger suspiciously,

"That boy... There is something about that boy that I don't like."

Ever as pure of heart, Agathi replied honestly, "Oh mother, that boy needs some softening up that's all. He has spent his young life in fires and smouldering metals. He is like a soldier hardened in battle. I am sure he will be sensitive to his wife when the time comes."

"Huh..." huffed the old woman unconvinced, "We will watch his path and see."

While listening to the conversation, Medusa huddled near the burning light of the night oil to complete her work. Concentrating intensely over her story, she thought she smelled the sweet scent of burning olive leaves. Alerted by this sudden sensation, she quietly left her work on the ground and followed the scent; she walked past the chattering women and followed a faint glow that appeared in the tree, outside the walls.

Grabbing Hagne's arm gently, she asked:

"Sister, do you see a light beyond the wall?"

Hagne arched an eyebrow

"No Medusa, the sun went down."

"Do you not smell the burning scent of a votive offering?"

Hagne shook her head as she slipped away from her sister's grip and walked away.

Medusa's curiosity beckoned her outside, where she witnessed the glorious white bird's silent presence. Staring intensely from its unwavering stance, its eyes twinkling bright in the moons haze, Medusa curiously watched on, at this bird of the night, with eyes of a conscientious being who sat unruffled.

The bird, as if it had a message to convey, pierced the silence of the night by unfolding its pristine wings and lifting them wide apart. With two mighty flaps, it flew up high in the starry sky and without neither hesitance nor warning, bolted down and just barely missing Medusa head, it lifted up and vanished into the night air.

Medusa stood to attention, strangely unafraid by the sudden actions of the mysterious bird. Her mind a buzz with questions, she stared curiously into the empty sky; she felt a sense of intrigue as to what omen might had been brought forth by this creature of the night.

—Eyes that sparkle as true and clear as the day, snow white feathers that shows the purity within, the smell of burning olive leaves, a votive to the Queen of Wisdom… Reaching the heavens and anointing my head; Am I the chosen few? So pure I will stay, until I have my answer from her righteous council.

To the city I must go…

Medusa knew now what she had to do…

CHAPTER FOUR

Medusa had witnessed the Arkteia coming-of-age rites that took place each year at the Brauronia festival many years before. When the *arktoi*, the "She-bears" of the Cult of Artemis, danced through the streets in their magnificent saffron robes, imitating bears. It was a glorious event that drew spectators from villages and cities all across Attica. The *arktoi*, would move in syncopation to musical accompaniment, sing, and run foot races in honour of Artemis to mark their transition into womanhood and their new status as Holy Priestesses. The ceremonies were such a spectacular sight that for many, it was the highlight of the year's events.

To become an *arktoi* of the Cult of Artemis held great prestige and privilege for any young girl hopeful of becoming a Priestess of the Temple of Athena. A true mark of distinction, only girls from the finest families could be considered for entry into the Sanctuary of Brauron, with only nine chosen. Brauron provided girls their first experiences of holy life; lessons- that honour can only be attained through humility and selfless acts of sacrifice; that patience and seclusion is the one and only true path to spiritual purity.

However, before any girl could be accepted into the Sanctuary, it was imperative that she was educated in certain rites and ancient rituals. It was a prerequisite that she knew prayers and hymns specific to each God, as well as appropriate chants and evocations. Most importantly, the chosen had to possess the inner strength to persevere against any obstacle set in her path. The life of a priestess-in-training was austere, well-ordered, and resolutely solemn. This was not a life path for just any young woman.

As it had been done for centuries, the girls entered the Sanctuary of Brauron at the age of twelve and worked their way up through the ranks of the "She-bear" Cult of Artemis. Their tender age meant for easier grooming into the Priestesshood. First, becoming an *arrhephoros* (sacred basket carrier) at the end of their first year. Proceeding to *aletris* (miller of corn) the following year; then, reaching the much coveted rank of full *arktoi* (She-bear) at the end of their third year. Finally, trading their bearskin for the cherished saffron robe at the conclusion of their fourth year. This final transition was celebrated by the Arkteia festival and set them on their way to becoming Holy Priestesses of the Temple of Athena in Athens.

According to ancient legend, the spring at Brauron had for eons been sacred to Artemis Brauronia, visited by countless religious pilgrims each year from the far corners of the earth. However, as the telling goes — the Greeks had offended Artemis by not offering her proper sacrifice. As chastisement for their impudence, she would not send a favourable wind to allow the Greek navy to join the fighting at Troy. So, in order to appease her, the Greeks decided to sacrifice Iphigeneia, the daughter of King Agamemnon, leader of the Greek armies. However, when Artemis discovered their plan, she promptly intervened. She whisked Iphigeneia away to Scythian Tauris, leaving in her place a brown bear. Iphigeneia then became a Priestess of the Artemis Cult at the court of King Thoas of the land of Tauris, near the Black Sea; where it was her job to sacrifice foreigners landing on the shore.

Many years later, Iphigeneia's brother, Orestes, went to the city of Tauris. He intended to steal the Cult statue of Artemis, having been ordered to do by the Sibyl, the Oracle of Apollo. The Scythians, however, caught Orestes in the act and planned to sacrifice him to the

Goddess. Iphigeneia came to her brother's rescue and the two of them then stole the statue together. When Athena discovered what they had done, she told them to take the statue to Greece and set up two cult sites in honour of Artemis. The first site was located at Halae Araphenides, the second at Brauron. Orestes set the Taurian statue up at Halae in a temple dedicated to Artemis Tauropolos, while Iphigeneia established a cult dedicated to Artemis Brauronia at Brauron. Now, the Brauronia festival, which began each year with the ritual sacrifice of a goat (rather than the sacred bear), was established by the Cult of Artemis to honour the Goddess' grace, generosity, and fair judgment. Through the years, it became the training centre for the Athenian Priesthood, and the priestesses' primary hurtle. Every daughter of Greece knew well, the ancient legend of Artemis and Athena and longed to dedicate their lives to the Goddesses. However, none had their hearts set higher than Medusa.

As they stood watching the splendour and pageantry of the magnificent parade, a very old woman standing near Medusa caught sight of the brilliant light in the child's eyes. She smiled kindly at Agathi, "Your girls seem quite enchanted by all this."

"Yes, quite so! Medusa has always held a fascination with holy life."

The old woman's sweet and gentle blue eyes twinkled as she leaned down to speak to Medusa, "Is that so, child? Would you like to grow up to join the Cult of Artemis… to become a Priestess of the Temple of Athena?"

Medusa nodded, then turned back to follow the procession, not wanting to miss a single moment of the ceremony. Hagne stood to the other side of her mother, caught up in the spectacle of it all.

The old woman spoke with Agathi and Petros who were both dressed in their finest, explaining about the Cult of the Arktoi and how Medusa might one day enter the Temple to serve if that was her desire. "It is not easy to be accepted; many girls attempt, but, few are accepted. Preparation and dedication can only take you so far. You must have a special gift. Something distinctive for them to allow you entrance."

"Thank you so much for your kindness, dear woman. Please tell me how is it, that, you know so much about these matters," Agathi asked, full of intrigue.

"I was a Priestess once myself," she sighed, looking wistfully at the young acolytes parading by. "But, certain circumstances stole me away from all that."

After the procession passed from sight and the newly-conse-crated Priestesses were on their way to Athens, Agathi invited the old woman to join the family for the simple meal she prepared for the event. They sat by the cart and ate in a quiet green corner of the town, beneath a sprawling olive tree rich with fruit. Medusa presented Hippos with a fresh, ripe pomegranate she had brought along just for him. With a quick kiss and crust of bread, Petros smiled and made his way to the men's quarter.

"*Please*," urged Agathi, pouring homemade wine into earthen cups, "share your story with us."

"Well, if you would really want to hear it, perhaps it would be a good lesson for your two fine, young girls."

Medusa and Hagne sat closer and put their food aside to give their full attention.

"I was born to a wealthy Athenian family, one of eight daughters. But, I was the only one with the spirit and desire to become a Priestess. My parents did not deny me my wish, and were, in fact, proud of my choice and let the whole of Athens high society know of it. And upon facing the trials at Brauron, I was accepted to the Cult of Artemis, later becoming a full She-bear. I then followed the road of holy glory, becoming a Priestess of the Temple of Athena.

"After many years of loyal service to the Temple, one day I was attending a meeting of the Senate when I caught sight of somebody newly seated. He was a tall and strong young man with the body and face of a warrior. The scars on his face and body spoke of many glorious battles he had seen. He wore a rough, short beard and had the blackest hair I had ever seen. He had the most soulful blue eyes one can imagine. He looked at me as I took my place and something stirred inside me when he did. Of course, I tried to ignore him, however, throughout the meeting, his eyes never left mine. It felt as if he could see inside me.

"I came to find out that he was an outsider. His father was a wealthy nobleman of Athens — which, of course, granted him a place in the Senate. However, his mother was from a prominent family of Sparta. A city we had fought many wars with, in the past. This made him a rogue, an undesirable. Nevertheless, he attended each affair of State.

"The sight of him made me nervous. My heart leapt each time I looked at him! That meeting seemed to last forever. So finally, I had to get *out*." The old woman stopped to sip some wine, clearly troubled by the telling. She took a deep breath and continued.

"Once the meeting ended, I quickly made my way out of the Forum and headed straight to the great library where I was needed that day. I know he watched as I left, and felt him following me through the crowd, though when I turned back, I could not see him. I went inside the library and continued my duties until dusk."

"The streets are seldom quiet in Athens, but that night as I made my way home, I felt only the stars and the moon speak to me. I thought to go back to the Temple... but, I could not. My mind was a muddle. How could this man move me this way? After twenty-seven years of chastity, why did I desire him? Why *him?* I am sorry to speak so openly, but at my age, you learn to say the things that must be said."

"No need to worry," said Agathi, "I have held no knowledge from my daughters. Hagne is wise to the ways of the world and Medusa is mature and wise beyond her years."

The old woman drank more wine and continued.

"I was consumed by him. He filled my mind! The next day, I foolishly deserted my duties at the Temple and walked instead past the Forum hoping to see him, knowing full well that I should not. I had *never* done such a foolish thing before. Then, just as I turned to leave — resigned to end this before it was too late — He saw me! Taking me by the hand, he led me into a darkened alleyway. Pressing me against the wall, he held me there and looked deep into my eyes. And that was *all*. I knew then that I could never go back to the Temple. I left with him that very night. We fled to Sparta and were wed the next morning." She closed her eyes and sighed. "Life with him gave me so much happiness. However, I still carry tremendous guilt for abandoning my vows to Athena, my family, and to Athens. He became my world. My night and my day, my every thought and breath."

The four were silent for a moment. Then, Medusa spoke,

"Pardon me for asking. How did you come to return to Athens?"

With a knowing smile, the old woman replied, "Life, I have learned, is above all, unpredictable. One never knows what the

Fates have in store for you. After only two seasons, he left for war with a neighbouring city…"

"And he did not return?" Agathi asked — her heart on her chest.

"No, my dear, he returned. But, he came back upon his shield. He died, as he had lived, without fear or regret. But, with him now gone, there was nothing left for me in Sparta. I was, after all, an Athenian. I had no choice but to return to Athens and my family. However, sadly, they could not find it within their hearts to forgive me and the shame I had brought upon them. I was renounced and asked to leave their house. My mother followed later with a sack of gold coins. That was the last time I ever saw her. She died three seasons later of the sleeping sickness and I have only seen my brothers and sisters from afar."

The three sat silent, moved by this old woman's sad tale. Agathi put her hand on the woman's. "Thank you for sharing your story."

"Thank you for listening. People today are always too busy to care about an old woman's memories. Who would guess that I was once as young and free as they?!" She turned to Medusa and Hagne, "Now you see, girls, what a man can do to a woman? Choose your path and keep to it no matter what may come and you will be happy! Let no man keep you from your true destiny."

Medusa's eyes opened wide as she slowly nodded.

With the sun now arching in the west, Petros was returning with the broadest of smiles across his lips. "The wine, no doubt!" Agathi and the old woman shared a knowing chuckle.

"Greetings wife, daughters, kindly old woman! I, Petros of Avernae have returned!"

"And I think I shall take the reins, tonight," Agathi whispered to the old woman. Turning to her wine-happy husband, she said, "Petros, it is time to load our things. We should try to make Avernae by nightfall."

"Yes, my love, anything you desire!"

Agathi hugged the old woman. "Why do you not come home with us? There could be no reason for you to stay here any longer."

"I knew you had a kind heart, my dear, but I must decline your most generous offer."

Agathi looked on confused, "We have plenty of room for you… if only you …"

"That is most generous of you but this is my home. I could not dream of dying any, place else. I sit, I watch the people come and go, I have a small, humble room where I am safe and have enough to eat.

Having your company today has made me a very happy old woman and I thank you greatly for allowing me to share my story with you!" They hugged as Agathi turned to climb into the cart.

"Oh, we cannot leave without at least knowing your name!"

The old lady smiled, her eyes shining brightly as she gazed upon the family. "Dione Athinei Plutaho."

"We shall remember you, Dione. Always."

The ride home was a silent one, the events of the day kept Medusa's mind swimming.

Agathi let Hippos lead them back home as Petros dosed off and Hagne re-lived the wonderful excitement of the day over and over in her mind.

While Medusa had enjoyed the festivities immensely, she could not forget the old woman's story or her face as she told it.

Though she had always known she could never be admitted to the Temple Priesthood, (hearing the words that only a girl from a noble family could be considered, wounded Medusa deeply), in her heart, she felt that her true destiny lied within the temple walls.

"What is that on your face, girl? A frown… a look of worry?" asked Petros as they neared home.

"I shall never be a She-bear Father, and never become a Priestess of the Temple of Athena," she said with sadness in her eyes.

"Yet, I feel that is where I truly belong."

Petros looked at his wife and winked. "Oh, never say never, Medusa, for no man knows what the Fates have in store for him. Or perhaps, no little girl knows what *gift* her father has arranged for her!"

Medusa's eyes opened wide in anticipation. "*Gift*, Father?"

Agathi turned toward Medusa and quickly back to Petros, a critical look on her tired face.

"What are you saying, Petros? Did it work? Did he agree?"

Suddenly, Medusa saw images flash before her eyes: an old man tall and rugged, beardless, lines cut deeply into his sun-parched skin. He was clutching Petros' hand in his two and smiling warmly. Her vision was broken by her father's call — "Medusa, are you listening to me... *Medusa?*"

"Y-Yes, Father?"

Petros looked straight into his daughter's eyes. "Medusa, my child, you *will* have the chance to enter the Sanctuary at Brauron, after all," he said with a broad smile. "All has been arranged."

"How... *how*, Father? We — *I* am not of noble blood."

He took her small hands in his. "Listen carefully to what I now tell you. This is most important. I must tell you about a man named General Klietonas."

"Yes, Father."

Petros held onto her hands and began.

"General Klietonas came from a long line of military leaders. Like his father and his father before him, all the men of his family were great warriors known for their valour, loyalty, and courage in battle. This gave each son a higher burden to bear that they might surpass their father's distinction and bring honour to their family. Klietonas was a man of great determination and ambition who learned his lessons early, and never made the same mistake twice."

"It was on a campaign to defend the higher settlements in the south-eastern state of Pelion that he happened to meet a young and spirited soldier who had just entered the army. They were both part of an effort to protect Eastern Attica from the Median army who had waged war to gain control of Greek soil. The battle was bloody and their opponents fierce. The number of wounded and dead rose quickly as it seemed the attack would continue until every last man was dead."

"Near the end of the battle, the young soldier was badly wounded and left for dead by his fellow soldiers. When he finally gained consciousness, he managed to drag himself into a nearby cave while most of the other men ran into the forests and hills, fearful for their lives. The Median army followed the soldiers as they retreated, hacking their way through what remained of the Hellenic army."

"Over the noise of fighting, the soldier heard a voice call his name. Weak and bleeding badly from his leg, the soldier found the strength to answer the voice. 'Where are you? Call out again!' he said.

"'Over here! *Hurry…* I am wounded and trapped…' the voice said, then faded as the soldier frantically tried to catch sight of him. Spotting the bright blue of a Greek uniform near another nearby cave, the soldier crawled his way over and discovered his General, Klietonas, propped up against the wall, barely conscious, with an arrow piercing his chest and several large rocks covering his left leg."

"'General!' the soldier said, worried at how deeply the arrow was buried in the General's chest.

"'My horse… my horse threw me when I was hit! I cannot feel my leg!' the General said.

"Fearing that the enemy might spot them at any moment, the soldier pushed the rocks aside and dragged the General into the cave. Once inside, he prepared to do what he knew he had to do — pull out the arrow. Just as he took hold, the General grabbed his hand and said,

'Soldier, you must push it *through* me. Use... both... hands,' he said, looking directly into the soldier's eyes. He then put his leather belt between his teeth and nodded to begin."

"By this time, the soldier's own loss of blood had greatly weakened him. He was not even sure he had the strength to do as the General asked. Knowing though, it was the only way to save him, he locked eyes with the General and gave a great push. The arrow's head plunged through the General's back and came out through the other side, causing Klietonas to lose consciousness from the pain. The soldier then carefully pulled the rest of the arrow through and tried to stop the bleeding."

Medusa's eyes grew large; hanging onto to her father's every word.

"The General was bleeding very badly. The soldier knew he just needed to stop the bleeding long enough for the enemy soldiers to leave the area, and then find his own men. However, every attempt to stop the blood failed, and he could see the life draining out of the General by the moment. Then he remembered: '*Yarrow* — I need *yarrow*,' the soldier thought *that will stop the bleeding! But, how will I get it?* Speaking to the unconscious General, the soldier laid out his plan: 'I'm going to have to leave you to go out and find yarrow to stop the bleeding. Then when I return, I will bind your wound.' Then he made a splint from his leg armour and binding his wounds with strips of cloth from his tunic, he removed his xiphos and hid it in a crack in the cave. After this, he crawled into the woods where fifty or more of the enemy were still searching for any of the Hellenic army who had survived."

"Such a brave man, this soldier!" Medusa said.

Her father nodded.

"So, by the end of the first day, the soldier had tended to both their wounds. But, now they were in need of food. And by the end of the second day, the hunger hurt far worse than the soldier's wounds and he knew the General would not survive another day without nourishment to rebuild his strength. So, he waited until the moon was high in the night sky and the enemy soldiers would most likely be too drunk to notice. He crawled into the woods and began collecting fungi and berries he had spotted while searching for yarrow.

"As he searched, he heard the flapping of wings overhead. When he looked up, he saw that the fruit trees were teaming with bats. So, he picked up a rock about the size of his fist and flung it at the nearest one. To his amazement, although it sent the rest shrieking into the night, one dazed bat fell fluttering to the ground almost at his feet! He quickly killed it and took back it to the cave. So, that night, the two ate raw bat meat, berries and tree fungus.

"The next morning, General Klietonas said he felt strong enough to attempt an escape. By this time, most of the Median army had moved on, but they could still hear the screams of their men in the distance, begging caution for the two. So, they waited until the sun reached its highest point in the sky. Its burning beams struck the pale sun-bleached ground and reflected blindingly into the eyes of the enemy. With this opportunity, General Klietonas and his soldier made their way along the tree line, trying to blend in. Unfortunately, they had not travelled for more than half a stadion when they were spotted by five enemy soldiers on patrol."

"What happened next, Father?!" Medusa asked excitedly. "What happened next?"

"Well, my sweet, a battle began for life or death! The soldier defended his General as best he could, but the five enemy soldiers soon got the best of him. Just as one of the soldiers charged at him with his sword drawn, the soldier leaped over his head and drove his xiphos into the side of an enemy officer who had come charging in on horseback — which *enraged* the other enemy soldiers! And though he fought with all his skill and might, he suddenly felt the cold metal of a bronze short sword slice deep into his arm, knocking him to the ground, and nearly unconscious!"

"Oh, no!" Medusa said, holding Hagne's hand tightly.

"All was not lost though! Just as he opened his eyes, he saw all six of the men lying face down on the ground with arrows sticking from their backs! The Hellenic army and reformed just in time and General Klietonas and the young soldier were saved! The invaders were completely defeated in just two days and all the men were sent home with honors."

"Amazing, Father! Just amazing!"

"Wow!" Hagne whispered beneath her breath.

"Well, a grand ceremony was held in honour of the brave men who fought and died in that battle. General Klietonas stood before the whole legion and spoke of the young soldier who had saved his life. He said, 'Young man, your act of selflessness and courage, saved my life. You could have saved yourself and left me there to die, but, you did not! You stood bravely by your General and not only brought him back from the brink of death, you also fought valiantly and with honor at his side. You are a fine warrior and a son of Greece I am proud to call my *friend*. I am forever indebted to you! And if ever I can repay this debt, you need only ask. I am your humble servant.'"

"That is a fantastic story, Father! A tale fit for the Gods of Olympus!"

"Now, the General is a nobleman and a powerful politician of Athens, known all across Hellas."

"But, what of the brave young soldier, Father? What became of him?"

Petros raised his sleeve and presented his badly scarred arm. "I am that solder, Medusa."

"Oh, Father! You are a great hero! I am so proud of you!" She thought a moment. "And... and I am to be the repayment of that debt?!"

"Indeed, my daughter," he said with a broad and proud smile. "Indeed you are."

CHAPTER FIVE

It was a warm, spring day and Medusa's family was busy preparing for the arrival of Nikias, the son of a blacksmith from Cumae, who had been chosen years before by Medusa's mother and grandmother as a match for Dorkas. Their wedding would take place in two days, and Dorkas, now eighteen years of age, would move away to start a new life with her betrothed.

With just three months before the trials at Brauron, Medusa had been freed of her household chores to focus on her devotional studies, readying for the austere duties of the Priestesshood. She now spent most of her time in quietude, reciting prayers and chants and practicing the rituals befitting a God.

Medusa had only seen him once before several years ago, However, she remembered Nikias as *layered*; a person within a person. Much as how she had come to think of herself. Nikias had coarse, dark red hair and a bristly beard, and while not especially tall (a bit shorter than Dorkas, in fact), he had a very robust body brought on by many years of forging metal. He rarely spoke, and when he did, his voice carried a harsh, demanding tone. Though everyone thought of him as plain-spoken and hardworking, Medusa sensed a darkness about him. Secretly she had hoped this day would never come.

When the day finally arrived, Medusa's parents, grandmother, and sisters Dorkas and Elpis were excitedly waiting outside the front gate to greet them, leaving Medusa and Hagne alone in the courtyard. Medusa focused intently on reciting her chants and prayers, while Hagne sat quietly near-by, cherishing the time remaining before her little sister would leave her life, perhaps forever. When Medusa heard the chatter of their arrival, a sudden cold shiver raced up her spine, breaking her concentration.

"You have a wonderful farm, here, Petros, fine fields," said Nikias' father cordially, the two gazing out over the barley and grape arbours. "You have done quite well for yourself!" As they entered the courtyard, Medusa and Hagne stood proudly to pay their respects.

"As you may remember, these are my two youngest daughters, Hagne and Medusa," Petros said.

"Yes, a pleasure to see you girls again," said Nikias' mother with a smile.

Medusa and Hagne smiled graciously in return. From behind the father, stepped Nikias, with a sour and unfriendly expression covering his red face. Medusa felt another cold shiver as his coal black, soulless eyes met hers. Her father turned, addressing Nikias

"This, children, is Nikias. He is training to become a blacksmith and after the big day, will become one of our family. Nikias... say hello to Hagne and Medusa." Nikias looked only at Hagne, mumbling something beneath his breath. Medusa and Hagne backed up against the stone wall to allow the guests to enter the house.

As the boy passed, Medusa saw disturbing images flash before her eyes: She saw Nikias as a grown man, hammering metal in a dark, sweltering room while sparks and hot cinders flew about, burning his skin and singeing his filthy clothes. She saw him drinking slovenly from large vats of wine; his grimy, black hands pawing her sister and shoving her to the ground. She held Hagne's hand tightly as they proceeded inside. She knew Nikias had sensed her uneasiness for just as he ducked inside, he glared back coldly.

After a light repast, Petros took the men on a tour of his orchards while the women sat to chat in the courtyard. Medusa was about to venture into the nearby woods to collect what she needed for a ritual of thanksgiving when Iasonnas appeared at the front gate. Despite the distraction he presented, he was nonetheless a welcome sight. Knowing she must soon leave her best friend, Medusa had tried to make exceptions for Iasonnas, allowing him to sometimes tag along, though many were the times he followed her into the forest only to mock, chatter and try to break her concentration. She knew he had made up his mind to dissuade her from becoming a Priestess; she also knew all his attempts were in vain. Nothing could break the commitment she had made with destiny.

"Medusa, would you like to go into town and visit the cloth makers?" he asked hopefully. "Or, we could go practice archery? You know, I am getting pretty good, too! Not as good as you, but, *still!*

My father's pomegranate groves have some nice, ripe fruit we can shoot at!"

She shook her head. "Iasonnas I need to collect elements from the woods to perform a special ritual. You are welcome to come along, but you must promise not to distract me. You must stay silent."

She headed out the gate.

"Medusa! Medusa! Wait a minute! Wait for me!" Iasonnas called, running along behind her.

Into the forest, Medusa walked until she found just the right oak tree, one with mistletoe in bloom. She ceremoniously cut off a small, green branch and shaped it. Carrying the wand in her right hand, she found a spot in a clearing and scribed a circle where she would make her makeshift altar. Iasonnas picked up the roots she had placed on the ground and held them to his nose and sniffed loudly.

"What are *these* for?" he asked.

Medusa took the roots from his hands and began carefully preparing them while chanting aloud. Crushing them in a stone mortar, she added berries and saffron and then mixed them together using the wide end of the oak branch.

"You are not planning to *eat* that, are you?!" Ignoring his attempts to break her meditation, she dumped the mixture into a censor and then opened a small leather pouch containing black powder. She sprinkled in a good amount of the pungent ingredient.

"You know, my father is trying to make me marry *Chloe*, the daughter of Amiandas the brick maker?" he said, lowering his awkward, gangly frame to the ground. "Silly thought. I do not even *know* the girl! And what he does not seem to understand is that after my studies are through, I intend to ask the girl I *love* to marry me. And, that would *not* be Chloe!" He paused, peering cautiously through his long, black curls.

Medusa got on her knees and began to strike two small black stones together over the censor.

"Do you want to know her name? I mean, the girl I *love*? I know you must be *curious*."

Medusa continued with her task, paying no attention to Iasonnas.

With a hard strike, the flint sent a spark to the burner, setting the contents alight. Then she stood and offered the smoke to the elements of the four cardinal directions.

"That stings my eyes! Medusa… are you even listening to me?" he coughed.

Medusa sat down and closed her eyes, softly pronouncing beneath her breath an invocation; the words of which Iasonnas could not understand. Attempting to gain her attention, he stood and took a step into the circle — causing Medusa to strike his foot with her oaken staff. "*Stooop thaaattt! Stayyy out of the cirrrrcle,*" she sang in rhythm to her chants. "Have you no respect for the rites of the Gods?!"

"Oh, well… of *course* I do!" he resigned, plunking himself down hard on the ground beside her. Sitting quietly and just watching, he was beginning to realize that there was nothing he could do, to draw her attention away. For the first time, he knew he would have to try much harder to make the future he had planned come true.

The next day, all the women were up before the sun, preparing food and decorating the house and courtyard for the big event. As a veritable feast was prepared, including a lamb ceremoniously slaughtered in honour of Nikias' parents, half of the town's people were expected to attend to witness this happy union.

By noon, the couple were joined as husband and wife, with the town's people showering them with fine bedding, tools, and household Goods. Everything a newlywed couple would need to begin a new life together. And while the dancing, festivities and wine would flow well into the night, as per custom, the couple climbed into Nikias' single-horse-drawn cart to hurry on to the little cottage he and his father had built next to his family home. His parents would follow along later, in their own time.

As all gathered around to wish them well, each taking their turn to share an embrace, Dorkas took Medusa in her arms and whispered, "Take care of yourself, little one, and know that I love you with all my heart. Stay the course the Fates have set for you and you will find your happiness. I know that you will make a fine Priestess!" Medusa kissed her sister and then held her face in her two hands, saying, "My dear sister, please be most careful. If this new life does not prove to be what you expect, remember that you can always come back home."

Dorkas saw words unspoken in Medusa's worried eyes. "Fear not, my sister. I will be fine now that I have a good husband to love me." With teary eyes, she turned to go. As they pulled away, Nikias turned to face Medusa with an icy leer that again sent shivers up her spine. Suddenly, her eyes flashed ahead to a weary Dorkas, now ripe with child, being welcomed with open arms through her parents' front gate.

The big day finally arrived when Medusa was to leave for Brauron. Before sunrise, she and her mother and father set out by horse-drawn cart. After a long, sleepless night practicing prayers and invocations, she was anxious to show the Priestesses how very much she belonged amongst them. As she had expected, standing in the darkness at the side of the old dirt road, was Iasonnas. With nothing more than a hopeful gaze, he watched as Medusa passed. Covered in the customary white linen shroud, with only her beautiful green eyes showing, Medusa felt the sorrow of leaving her best and most trusted friend behind. However, each had their own destinies. He stared forlorn at the cart until it vanished from sight and pledged aloud to wait for Medusa's return when he would make it his mission to keep her home for good.

Medusa's arrival at Brauron marked a very special step in her initiation into the life of a Priestess. That day, they rode up the hill southeast of the Sanctuary where a walled city surrounding a wondrous natural spring and garden had once flourished, it was now an empty echo of its former grandeur; with the ancient wind whistling mournfully through the cracks in its now crumbling walls. Medusa stared through the cracks as they passed, seeing mysterious figures moving about and beyond, shuffling aimlessly through its broken, cobblestone streets.

"Perhaps this was not the best path to take," said Petros with a worried look. He beckoned Hippos to run a little faster as he saw the dishevelled figures now following the cart.

As they began to descend the hill at a faster trot, Medusa looked back at the group of scavengers trailing behind them, staring hungrily. She felt a lonely presence about them, seeing images of them being shunned and spurned — outcast and banished; tears of separation as the flesh rotted off their living bodies. She quickly picked up one of the many small wooden crates filled with food her mother had packed, and tossed it off the back of the cart.

"Medusa! What are you doing, child?!" cried Agathi.

"You always bring more food than we can eat, Mother. They need it. They are hungrier than we are." Agathi brought the back of her hand to her brow and smiled, proud of the thoughtful and generous young woman her daughter had become. The beggars scurried along, collecting the food as the crate broke into pieces and its contents spread down the hill. One beggar picked up a small flatbread and clutched it tightly to his chest, eyeing Medusa gratefully as they rode off toward the Sanctuary.

As they drew near the violet blue ocean where the Sanctuary stood, the salt of the sea air comforted Medusa, as she was for the first time about to leave the loving protection of her family. Petros stopped the cart a short distance from the Temple, taking advantage of a small tree-laden outcropping to hide their presence.

"Now, my daughter, this is *your* time. You need not fear a thing. You will go inside and they will ask your name. You will say, 'Medusa of Athens.' Give them this letter." Petros handed his daughter a small papyrus scroll, a letter of introduction from the General asking that Medusa be considered for entry.

"We will remain here, child, in the unlikely event that you are not chosen," Agathi intervened anxiously, tears welling up in her wise, old eyes. "However, if you are chosen, be certain to keep your belongings close to you. And always remember — never lose faith in your abilities! You are a bright and gifted child! And above all, my daughter, if you lose your will to stay — please, *please* come back to us. With us you will always have a home. You need only send word and we will be here." Agathi pulled Medusa close, picking her up from her seat and squeezing her tightly.

Though Medusa had been tutored for months that she might remember the details of her "new" family, Petros now reviewed one final time what she must say:

"One last thing…" her father said seriously.

"Your father's name?"

"Klietonas of Athena. *Klieton the Major.*"

"Your mother?"

"Sophronia Athenae."

"What siblings do you have?"

"Two brothers and one sister, Klieton *the Minor*, Sangrotis, and Evanthia."

"And where do you reside?"

"My family recently moved from Marathon to Athens, to a large white house on the left fork in the east road out of the city."

"Good, my daughter, you are ready." He placed his calloused hands lightly on her shoulders. "You will do fine."

Medusa embraced her father and uttered thanks to the Gods that she had a family who loved her so dearly. She knew she would miss them and her home, but reminded herself that the Gods had set a glorious path before her; one of supreme importance and prestige. With her gentle, old hands trembling, Agathi unwrapped a tiny package and removed a shining gold ring with a flat, green stone attached. "Take this, Medusa, and keep it always close to your heart. Take it now and know that we are always with you."

Medusa turned to her father. "Father, there is something I must tell you… about the golden *talisman*… the Stag of Artemis, I… "

"I know, my daughter," he said with a warm, understanding grin. "I have known for a long while now. You were clever enough to find it, so now it is yours to do with as you choose. May it bring you comfort and strength," Petros said, a slight catch in his usually clear and commanding voice.

They all stood at the side of the cart as Petros unloaded her small, round leather bag and one small pouch of special dried fruits her mother had prepared. Her parents drew in the beautiful vision of their most special daughter — their little gift from the Gods — as she clutched her belongings and prepared to say good-bye. Tears came to Petros' eyes as he pulled his daughter close one last time. "The years will pass quickly, Medusa. Do not worry! If you leave us today, we will see you on the day of graduation. Look for us here amongst the faces in the crowd!"

Medusa nodded, fighting back the tears. "Good-bye, my noble, old friend," she whispered into Hippos' ear, rubbing her face on his. "I will miss you." He nuzzled against her. With a brave smile she went forth to join the other girls who were arriving on the main path to the Temple. She gave one final glance back as her parents held each other tightly, watching their little girl vanish from their lives.

One by one the candidates were stopped at the great stone entrance to the Sanctuary by two resident Priestesses in dark brown robes. Towering limestone columns stretched above and ominously towards the heavens, forming a commanding colonnade leading from the street to the Temple doors. Medusa, like all the other girls arriving, was much too nervous to notice.

"Your name, child?" asked one Priestess.

"Medusa of Athena," she replied, proudly presenting the letter.

"*Hmmm*, so your father is General Klietonas? Very well, enter the Temple. Give your offering and then proceed directly to the meeting place outside in the courtyard. Do *not* stray off the path."

Medusa nodded and went in to find the walls of the Temple inner sanctum painted with colourful, larger-then-life motifs depicting Artemis in her many magnificent adventures. She could smell burning oils of storax and myrrh, the gum resins that sweetened the dense air inside the Temple's ominous shadows. Respectfully approaching the marble likeness of Artemis who stood with open arms as if to welcome all who entered, Medusa placed a sprig of eucalyptus at her feet, bowed. She then followed the other girls into the Spartan courtyard where a semi-circle of stone benches awaited the eager aspirants.

Medusa sat quietly next to the other girls, placing her belongings at her feet. She was already wearing the pristine white robe that was customary for a novice, however, some girls had yet to don theirs. An excited young She-bear helped the girls line their eyes with black paint to help them feel more a part of the ritualized setting. Medusa already felt as if she belonged.

The girls, thirty in all, now dressed in their ceremonial white robes and dramatically-painted eyes of black, stood in a straight row as a Priestess emerged from the Temple. Meanwhile, all the parents waited eagerly in a shelter beyond the Sanctuary walls, to learn whose daughter would have the honour of being accepted and whose daughter would be turned away. All, of course, but Medusa's. Unable to make their lowly presence known, they waited alone, sitting patiently in the grove where they would wait until nightfall. Each young woman now stood waiting for the trials to begin and the chance to prove their worthiness. As Medusa looked down the row of girls, the silence was disturbed by the sound of shuffling feet. A moment later, a Priestess stood before them and began her formal address.

"I bid you welcome, all young maidens of Greece, to the holy and auspicious Sanctuary of Artemis Brauronia. As you know, this has been the sacred sanctuary of the Goddess since long before recorded time. And we are here today to invite some of you to join the She-bear Cult of Artemis in loyal service to the Goddess. *Sacred be the name of Artemis, chaste and mighty.*" The girls all bowed, prostrating themselves on the cool, stone-inlaid ground. "You may be seated." Each girl took her seat, most nervously holding her breath.

"Many, are the hopefuls I see before me today. However, only nine of you will be chosen to honour the mighty Goddess for a full four seasons as little She-bears." The girls could not help but look to their left and right, trying to gauge who looked *worthy* to pass such tests and who did not. Medusa smoothed her robe and checked the bag at her feet, her mind raced with prayers and chants she had been rehearsing for months. Though she could not be certain she would be among those chosen, she was confident that no one knew the rituals better than she. And no one's desire to serve the Goddess was greater.

"It is now time for the Sanctuary Guardians to take you one by one inside the Temple where your trials will begin. High Priestess Evangelia Philippon will judge your abilities. Do not address the High Priestess unless asked to do so." The Priestess picked up her heavy staff and struck the large brass gong behind her to signify that the year's trials had officially begun.

Medusa knew she would have to greatly impress the High Priestess to gain entry, and hoped that her gifts and talents would be enough to encourage her choice. But, seeing so many girls of noble blood — those, perhaps, more worthy — she felt somewhat an outcast.

How can I, the daughter of a simple farmer, pass for a noble? I must not make a single mistake lest my identity become suspect and all my dreams come to an end.

Two Guardians, (third-year initiates of the She-bear Cult), emerged from the shadows dressed in bearskins. The hoods of their robes were crafted from the heads of great brown bears, their curved claws magically catching the eye of every young hopeful. They approached the first girl and extended their hands. The girl nervously accepted and was led into the shadows of the Temple for the very first trial of the year.

The other girls waited nervously as time passed most slowly; some busily rehearsed prayers and chants, others regretted their parents' choice to enter them into the Cult. Indeed, there were those amongst them, driven more by their family's desires than their own. Others were dreaming of the glory and power they would one day possess as Priestesses of the Temple of Athena.

Medusa kept her mind focused and sat calmly clutching one of her finely-embroidered cloths, ready to reveal the stories she saw in her mind's eye. She watched the other girls, now sensing their energies that manifested as colours and rays of light shooting from their heads as their heads raced with thoughts. Sensing more deeply now, she began to hear them:

To the God of Sun and Light, may he protect us by day, in his domain we may flourish...

I will not cry. I will not giggle. Prayers!

"The energy of the Temple is most powerful," she whispered beneath her breath. "Ten thousand prayers have brought the Gods' blessing here." A sea of thoughts and images washed over her like a warm ocean wave.

At long last, the Guardians came for Medusa. Eyes wide, she folded neatly her cloth and slipped it into her belt, she picked up her possessions, and took their hands. They led her inside the Temple greeting room where the High Priestess waited. She proudly walked forward through the Temple's elaborately embossed, giant bronze doors, catching a whiff of sweet cedar. Inside, a splendid pure white room bordered with a marble frieze of Artemis' eternal glory and might, mistress of the woodland creatures, huntress and guardian, greeted her warmly.

At the far end of the room was a raised stone platform with a throne fashioned from exotic animal horns and tusks. Upon the throne the High Priestess, Evangelia Philippon sat majestically, adorned in a heavy purple robe cinched with a bronze cloth belt. Medusa's eyes wandered from this illustrious figure to a stone statue of Artemis towering above, bow and quiver in hand. At her side, a regal stag stood. She recalled the vision she had had many years before when the mysterious huntress had introduced her to the art of the bow. "*Artemis*

"… My Goddess," Medusa whispered.

Evangelia motioned for Medusa to come closer, her deep and clear voice rich with authority, "Child! Come forth!" Medusa set her belongings on the floor and stepped forward, bowing gracefully. Looking up, she saw a beautiful woman not more than thirty years of age, artfully poised with each arm gently resting on either side of the imposing throne. Her deep brown eyes framed with black paint seemed to smile. *She is so young! Much younger than I thought. And so beautiful!* "It is my honor to welcome you to the Sacred Sanctuary of Artemis Brauronia. Rise child and come closer. Do not fear me." Evangelia's pronouncement reverberated throughout the room, a hypnotic alto.

Medusa stepped closer, her eyes drawn to a scroll the priestess had laid out on a wooden table beside her.

"You are Medusa, daughter of Klietonas of Athens. We have heard wondrous things about you, young one."

Medusa bowed humbly.

"As you are aware, we are here today to select the young women we believe will become the greatest assets to our Cult. It is essential that you understand how important it is for us to be absolutely certain of the few who will remain with us for the turning of each season."

Medusa nodded, keeping one eye on the scroll, trying to read as much as she could.

"The scroll interests you?"

Though hesitant to speak openly, Medusa found the voice to say, "Yes, Excellency."

"What about it interests you, Medusa?"

"The *secrets* it holds, Excellency."

"*Secrets?*" The High Priestess was intrigued. "Come. Take a closer look."

Medusa unrolled the edges of the scroll and examined it closer. She saw that it was written in an ancient form of the Greek language no longer in use. However, she could easily decipher one extract. The High Priestess watched her face light up as she began to translate. "This speaks of the first Priestesses of the Cult — before the building of the Temple!"

"You can read this ancient text, Medusa?" she asked in disbelief.

"Yes, Priestess. And this panel speaks of the Loyal Cult's first Holy Orders — the Oath of Artemis."

The High Priestess could hardly believe what she was witnessing. She rose from her throne and slowly approached Medusa. "Medusa, do you often have the opportunity to read such scriptures?"

"No, not as often as I would like, Excellency. Sometimes, I trade my embroidered linens to the village Priests for a chance to look at their sacred scrolls, but none are as old or fine as this."

"I see... And what do you make of this?" she said, reaching into a hollow space beneath the table, retrieving an inscribed clay tablet.

Medusa examined it closely. She turned it towards the flickering lamp light. "This is much older, and more cryptic than the scroll... more... *symbolic*. Each word inscribed here has a... *hummm*... double meaning waiting to be revealed by whoever has the ability to glean the message within the message. It holds great power, no doubt!"

"And, do you possess the ability to reveal this *great power*, Medusa?"

"Yes, Priestess. I am certain I do. I can understand many old scripts."

Returning to her throne, the High Priestess sat pensively for a moment. "Medusa, I must make certain that you fully understand the life you will lead if you choose to stay with us on this sacred path."

Medusa looked up into the discerning brown gaze of the Priestess. "I believe I see in you, the promise to honour our Sacred Cult. As well as the unwavering strength needed, to give your life in the name of the Gods."

Medusa smiled, as these were the words she longed to hear.

"Priestess, I believe it is what I was created to do. It is my destiny."

"Come, stand here before me, child." Medusa approach and stood at her side. Evangelia reached out and placed her hand on the girl's brow and closed her eyes, invoking her own special gift of discernment. Medusa's aura came alive, and after a moment, the High Priestess pulled away. "You have extraordinarily powerful energy, Medusa. Among the most powerful I have ever encountered! However, I also sense something *else* within you, something I cannot quite explain. A *rogue* force that you have not yet come to know."

Why does this energy follow me? I feel it too!

Sensing apprehension in the child, she took Medusa's face in her two hands and spoke tenderly. "But, you need not concern yourself with events that may never come to pass, child," she reassured. "No one can know what the Fates has in stall." Medusa gave a sheepish smile and nodded. The priestess then noticed the cloth folded in Medusa's belt. "And what is that you have there, child?"

"One of my visions, Your Excellency."

"And is it for me to see?"

"Yes, Excellency, I have brought it to show you," she said, presenting it.

The Priestess took the linen cloth in her hands and held it up to the light emanating from the large brass basin to her left. Her eyes widened as she recognized many of the symbols. Then she rose slowly and walked back to the entrance of another chamber where she showed the linen to someone in the shadows. Medusa felt a strong presence coming from the darkness. *What does she see in my visions? Please, Goddess, do not allow them to dismiss me for what I see!* She watched curiously as the High Priestess returned and took her place on her throne.

"My girl, you are quite certain that this is the future you would choose for yourself?"

"Yes, your Excellency. It is the only life I have ever imagined for myself."

Evangelia smiled. "Thank you, Medusa. You may take your place among the other girls now."

Medusa slowly walked out, guided back to the courtyard. She watched as one by one the other girls filed in and came back out, eyes wide, some in tears. One girl ran away crying just as she was being led into the Temple, another, fled before her name was even called. Finally, the last girl to be summoned re-emerged through the Temple's great doors and it was time for the chosen to be announced.

As the names were proclaimed, the chosen were asked to take two steps forward, at which time they were presented with their coveted bearskins, the first acknowledgement of their membership into the Cult. Second to last, they called out, "Medusa of Klietonas of Athens!" Medusa's eyes lit up as she tried to control her smile for the sake of those who had not been chosen. As she stepped forward, two Priestesses smiled excitedly and placed a soft bearskin over her head.

It is not as heavy as I thought it would be! And, it smells so... powerful! She reveled in the moment, allowing her joy and anticipation to fill her entire being.

All those not chosen left the Sanctuary; some disappointed and in tears, others relieved they that would not have to bear the hardships of the Priestesshood and could blissfully go back to their ordinary lives. Medusa's parents watched from their hidden spot, as one by one the rejected left the sanctuary. Long after the last girl had left, they waited in guilty hopefulness of spotting their daughter. However, Medusa did not appear and so their hearts were filled with a mixture of pride and sadness as they knew now, their little girl was set on the path to her true destiny.

CHAPTER SIX

Medusa was in her twelfth month now upon acceptance into the Holy Cult of Artemis Brauronia. Her spirit fresh, strong, and vibrant; ready to take on life with goodwill towards all her Sisters, she quickly became quite popular, be-friended by both students and teachers. There were, however, those who were jealous of her beauty, natural aptitude for the Priestesshood and her gift of prophecy. One such girl was called Melissa. Thus began, her turbulent relationship with Melissa Glaukos of Athens, a young girl who would test Medusa's patience and personal resolve.

The only daughter of a prominent doctor and surgeon known all across Attica, Melissa began to focus her jealousy into spiteful attempts to stir Medusa's emotions, pushing her to react, often beginning in the early morning hours even before Medusa woke. Melissa took pleasure in soiling Medusa's robes with mud from the river, hiding her stylus and wax tablet and accidentally bumping into her in the dining hall, causing her to spill her food on herself. Medusa was also certain it was Melissa who had taken her cherished the Stag of Artemis talisman. Most cruelly, she felt joy in interrupting Medusa's chants with rude noises and desecrating the icons of her sacred altar.

For weeks, Medusa ignored the harassment as best she could, choosing the more gracious path; refusing to be provoked. However, as Medusa became more and more focused on her religious commitments, she began to tire of Melissa's constant inconsideration.

Why can she not leave me well enough alone! What a waste of life to spend it hindering others!

Finally, after one particularly mortifying ordeal when she found urine in her ceramics project, Medusa could tolerate no more. Throwing her clay bowl to the floor, she stormed at Melissa, pressing the insufferable girl against the wall — with a roomful of her sisters as witnesses, she proclaimed:

"Listen and listen well, Melissa! We are Sisters — not *opponents*! I have endured your childish torment long enough! Leave me be or by the Gods, I will end this *my* way!"

Eyes filled with contempt, Melissa's jaw dropped. She had never imagined the fair Medusa capable of such a reaction. When Medusa finally released her hold on the quaking girl, she simply nodded and sauntered out of the room with two of her minions in tow. Medusa kept her eyes fixed on Melissa, following her out of the room as all the other girls watched and whispered. Xenophoni, Medusa's closest friend, placed a calming hand on her shoulder, "Do not be concerned Medusa. Now that she knows you will not stand for it, she will not bother you again. I am sure."

"No, this is not over," Medusa said, her heart pounding. "I saw into her mind."

Shocked at the rage she discovered in herself that day, Medusa had to fight to control her emotions as Melissa's voice could be heard floating haughtily down the hall, "Who does she think she *is*?! A daughter of a common General who has spent her life in the war camps! *Humm*! She is no *socialite*! She does not even *belong* here! She is not one of *us*!"

As Medusa had foretold, the torment was far from over. Rather than attack Medusa head-on, Melissa turned her attention to bullying the other girls at the Sanctuary; targeting Medusa's friends. Far less fearful of what they might do, she would find them alone and make threatening demands. "Have you prepared my prayers for me yet? Where are they? I swear, if you are late again, I will tell the High Priestess you sneak out at night to be with boys. And you *know* she will believe me!"

The bullying was troublesome and bothered Medusa. Though it seldom occurred in her presence, she could sense the fear in the other girls. More than once, she had had flashes of Melissa cornering one of the girls with her demands and issuing threats. With each passing day, Medusa's tolerance and patience became more brittle. Her heart pounded at the mere thought of Melissa and her stomach turned to acid when she heard her shrill, demanding voice in the room. Finally, the day arrived when Melissa went too far.

It was the day of Medusa's thirteenth birthday, and she had awoken for the ninth morning straight, in a cold sweat. With womanhood quickly approaching, her prophetic visions were more and more vivid often turning towards the dark and frightening than mere prophetic. For over a week now, she had found herself transported every night to another existence; a place of twisted images and ghostly impressions beyond anything she had ever experienced before. A place where her inner rage would reach the critical point and threaten to explode out of control. Most frighteningly, within this other plane of existence, she felt as if she were trapped in a body not her own; she found herself moving slowly and purposefully like a predator; a wild beast whose body pulsed like molten lava about to erupt. Her eyes were narrow and her teeth razor sharp and she felt as if she would go mad if she could not sink her teeth into flesh.

Before awakening this morning, she had found herself prowling through narrow, dark corridors made entirely of polished black stone. She had entered a room sparsely lit with rancid torches where a maze of stone soldiers stood frozen in mid-motion. Archers, swordsmen, even one on horseback, were all turned to stone; their anguished souls trapped within — screaming to be released — their eyes frozen in terror. *Is it me they fear?* She circled the statues and licked their cold torsos hungrily. *What is happening to me?!* Then she heard someone whisper, "***Monster!***"

Jolted awake, she bolted upright in her bed, soaked to the skin. As she brushed the sweat-soaked hair from her face, she felt a sudden, gripping pain in her belly, a stabbing wound in her gut that became more unbearable with each passing second. Pulling down her woollen cover, she found bright red blood soaking her bed. Rising quickly, she quietly took the soiled sheets and stole away to the river to wash them and refresh herself. There, the sun shone brightly, welcoming her — offering to purify her. She now knew, her transformation into womanhood had begun.

As she walked through the Sanctuary, the other girls were just waking. Clutching her wet sheets tightly in her arms, she climbed the wooden stairs to the sleeping quarters. Melissa, on her way down, bumped into her, sending the sheets down the dusty stairs, soiled once again.

"Oh, I apologize, Sister Medusa!" Melissa chimed sarcastically, her smirk belying any vestige of purity in thought. The other girls with her, giggled snarkilly. Medusa's eyes rose from the sheets to the contorted smile of her pretentious sister in Priesshood. *You have no power over me you pathetic child,* Medusa said to herself. With measured grace, Medusa reached down and retrieved the sheets without a word, quickly erasing the grin from Melissa's face. But, Melissa had sensed the new surge of energy in Medusa. Medusa was hiding something. And Melissa took it upon herself to discover what.

Throughout the morning, Melissa repeatedly tried to unnerve Medusa. Taunting, "Wonder where Medusa was returning from so early this morning?" she said just loud enough for Medusa and all her sisters to hear. "Maybe she has a boyfriend she meets down by the river!" Medusa resisted the pressing urge; Even as anger swelled within her, she resigned herself not to let it show. *Willpower can be a powerful quality*, she reminded herself. *And there is no limit to what my willpower can do.*

The girls were well into their daily tasks, cleaning and preparing for the mid-year feast to be held that evening. Four girls in particular, were busy in the garden picking and uprooting vegetables; Three others, were feeding the breakfast scraps to the hogs, a precarious task requiring the girls to stand on a fabricated, rickety wooden perch positioned over the pen. Medusa was tending to the chickens as Melissa stood by the pig pen gawking, ostensibly helping. It was then, that Melissa did the unthinkable. She shoved the plank over the pig pen with her foot, sending the three girls into the muck and ankle-deep in the excrement below. Everyone heard the commotion and came running.

Finding the girls struggling in the filth, they all rushed to help… until they saw how funny they looked with their faces covered with mud and hog waste. Some began to laugh as the three slipped in the slime and crawled on hands and knees through the sty, crying from embarrassment. Four of the girls, still giggling, tried to help the girls out, but taking care not to risk falling in themselves. Melissa laughed in sheer delight at their humiliation, chanting, "Pig-girls, pig-girls! Come see the filthy pig-girls!"

Witnessing this awful humiliation, the blood started pounding in Medusa's ears and her eyes glowered, becoming an eerie, phantasmal shade of pearlescent green as rage began to build inside her. Medusa had now had enough. Throwing the pail of chicken feed to the ground, Medusa marched towards at the giggling Melissa, her fists clinched. With just an inch from Melissa's face, Medusa shrieked, "*Leave us! Leave **now**, you wretched little girl before I remove you!*"

Melissa blanched deathly white as the blood drained from her cheeks, her hollow, frightened eyes now meeting piercing green filled with rage beyond anything she had thought possible of Medusa.

"Oh, just having some fun, *Meddie*," Melissa said nervously, taking several steps backwards. "No need to lose your temper! The girls are fine. Right, girls?!"

Without a thought, Medusa grabbed Melissa by the cowl of her tunic and began squeezing and twisting. "*Apologize*," she said, through clenched teeth. "Apologize ***now*** — or by the *Gods I will —!*"

Melissa let out a gasp, and looked to the other girls to come to her rescue. But, no one dared interfere. The horror of Medusa's rage dominated the air. Gasping for breath, Melissa grudgingly recited, "I apologize, *girls*, for any... *embarrassment* my *playfulness* may have caused you! I did not mean any ill will towards you! It was just... meant in jest!"

Medusa slowly loosened her grip and backed away, trying to calm herself as the blood pounded in her ears, she turned. Melissa though, now angered at being bested, refused to let it go. No more than five steps had Medusa taken, before Melissa picked up a rotten egg from the pigs' trough and took aim at Medusa. The stinking egg struck squarely on the back of her head; with this,

Medusa spun around — the stench and ooze dripping down her hair, seething with anger, the world turned red; there were no clear thoughts in her mind.

Medusa hurled herself at Melissa, flames seeming to consume her from within. Quickly losing her mordant grin, Melissa ran as Medusa gave chase through the pig-pens, around the hens' coop, and down to the Erasinos River below. Hoping to escape, Melissa dove in the water. However, it did not take long for Medusa to catch up and drag her out of the water by her long hair, while she was flailing her arms and screaming.

Though Melissa was older and taller, Medusa quickly threw her face-first onto the river bank, and began grinding her face into the mud. As the girls all ran to get a closer look — gasping in shock Medusa viciously flipped Melissa onto her back, heaving her around as if to unhinge her head from her squirming body. Fingers tightly wrapped around the girl's neck, Medusa pushed her thumbs into Melissa's throat as she ground her teeth in rage. Melissa's face grew purple as she tried to pull loose from Medusa's grip; she could only gasp for air and stamp her feet on the ground.

"*Medusa*!" shouted Xenophoni, fearing that it had gone too far. She desperately began to scream at Medusa to stop. Melissa had stopped moving, but Medusa refused to loosen her grip. Only by the grace of the gods did three temple priestesses arrive in time to keep Medusa from strangling the life out of Melissa. They pulled Medusa off, as the other checked to see if Melissa was still breathing. Xenophoni remained frozen in place, her eyes red with tears. Medusa turned to her, her green eyes bright and wild with blood-thirsty rage and Xenophoni began to shake with fear. Melissa soon came to. Her hands over her red neck, she did not dare look towards Medusa's direction.

Spewing mud and blood, Melissa and Medusa were marched

off to see the High Priestess Evangelia, to face the consequences of their barbaric actions.

In the flickering lamplight of the Temple, the High Priestess sat looking down upon the two girls, who looked so small amongst the majesty of the temple. They stood before her, mud turning to clay on their tender skin. Melissa, ever the martyr when it suited her, rubbed her neck and whimpered as the imprints of Medusa's hands burned into her flesh. Without a hint of mercy in her voice, the Priestess spoke.

"I am *appalled*! Absolutely *appalled*! Where do you two think you are? The gladiators' academy?" She rose to her feet and shouted, "You are priestesses in training! She-bears of the Loyal Cult of Artemis the chaste and noble and soon to be Priestesses of the Holy Temple of Athena!" The girls stood quietly, heads bowed, mortified with shame.

"You are both amongst my very best candidates for Athens… Do you not realize what could have happened here today? Did we err in choosing you two as candidates?" Exasperated, she sat back down; neither girl dared speak.

The High Priestess brought her hand to her right temple as a young Priestess rushed in and whispered something in her ear. She glanced back at the girls, both displeased and relieved. "Melissa, you will remain here with me. Medusa, the Oracle has commanded your presence. Priestess Phyllis will take you to her." As Medusa followed behind the Priestess, Evangelia called after her, "Medusa, you will do well to listen to what the Oracle says and act accordingly."

As far as Medusa knew, the Oracle had never sent for any girl before. It was well known that she was a very, very old woman who prominent people relied upon for words of advice before making important decisions. Be it in war, or love, the Oracle would direct them to the path they should follow. Though she had only mentioned it to Xenophoni, Medusa was certain the Oracle secretly visited the Sanctuary, coming down through a secret passage to monitor the girls' progress. Apphia had said she once saw a wall mysteriously move in the Temple library, but she was always such a fearful girl that everyone, including herself, had dismissed this strange mysterious happening as merely the over- active imagination of a nervous mind.

The Oracle's solitary abode was set atop the mountain peak, on a ridge high above the Sanctuary. The mountain was splotched with sparse, sprawling growth of stunted juniper trees beneath which snakes, spiders, and other reclusive creatures hid from the sun's scorching heat. Although it was much cooler at this height, the afternoon sun was much more brutal than at lower altitudes. The path was rocky and crooked, meandering up the mountainside, only half a meter wide, in places. The Priestess leading the way for Medusa, grabbed the occasional tree branch or rock edge when her feet became unsteady on the stony path.

The closer they drew to the Oracle's cavern, the stronger the pungent odour of burning myrrh and sulphur became. Medusa lowered her eyes and suddenly felt weakened, as if the fumes were somehow attempting to reach inside her mind. At the entrance, the Priestess left Medusa standing, telling her she would return when it was time to escort her back. Attempting to brush away the mud and clay still caked on her arms and face, Medusa entered the darkened cave where she found a plain oaken panel standing. This, she assumed, separated her from the brilliance of the Oracle.

Dark yellow smoke twirled and danced throughout the cave, its bearing seemingly conscious. Medusa noticed a tall-standing, wooden table set to the right of the screen with glowing oil lamps upon it. All around, great, climbing walls of white limestone met beams of ancient acacia entwined with sweet terebinth bearing living, glossy red petals. Somewhere far off, the sound of trickling water brought the entire space to life with an eerie, ethereal quality. A few minutes passed in reigning silence.

Medusa did not feel brave enough to call out, so she stood examining the room as the vapours seemed to penetrate her thoughts. Feeling drowsier by the moment, she now recalled the rage that had erupted from within her just a short time before. She sat on the cold, stone floor feeling sad and disappointed in herself. Never had she imagined that she had such anger inside her and she wondered where it had come from. It frightened her, to think how quickly things had escalated to such a deadly point.

I could have killed her!

Why did I not let her go when I saw the life draining from her eyes?

What is happening to me?

Perhaps this is what the Oracle was planning to tell her. She placed her hand on her tender belly and rubbed gently to relieve the painful twinge that had returned.

I am so sleepy, and these vapours are making me feel so weak....

A swirl of smoke came to rest on her right shoulder, a strange enticing curl to its movement. Glancing at the table, she now noticed something that just moments before was not there. Rising and looking more closely, she realized it was one of her embroideries; one that she had entrusted to the seers back home.

How did this get here? Does the Oracle know this belongs to me?

She carefully unfolded it to see which story it foretold. As always, a strange sparkling energy radiated from the symbols, her mind flashed to the vision it conveyed. Then, she heard her name being called softly from behind the wooden wall. With her concentration broken, she quickly returned the linen to its place and cautiously approached the wall. After a moment, she placed her hands to it. Polished cedar, sweetly aromatic and cool to the touch, the wall was rough and cracked with age. Shaken but, curious, Medusa called out to the Oracle: "Yes? Oracle, do you call me?"

There was no answer.

I know she is there. Why does she not reveal herself to me?

"I… I see that you… you have my embroidery. May I ask, how you got it? Did one of the wise men of the village bring it to you?"

Still the Oracle did not answer.

Confused and growing impatient, Medusa began to search for a crack in the wood so she might look beyond, to see if it was indeed the Oracle who stood silently behind that wall.

I know she is behind this wall. Why does she not speak when it was she, who summoned me here? Has this something to do with my linen? My visions?

Probing with fingertips, she found a tiny fracture in the ancient screen, and placed her eye to it; she could see nothing but darkness beyond. Unbeknownst to her, the Oracle could see everything. High above, an aged and tarnished bronze mirror about the size and shape of a small battle shield, hung nearly undetectable in the corner. Though only a palm-sized portion in of the middle remained polished, it was enough for the Oracle to see all.

With this mirror, the Oracle could see the young girl's face still covered in white clay and clumps of mud. With this mirror, the Oracle could see the angry light in the girl's radiant green eyes; through this tarnished bronze window, the Oracle could clearly see beyond what stood before her — the dark future, lurking behind those most revealing emerald eyes.

Medusa clinched her jaw and sat down once again on the cold floor, waiting for something, *anything* to happen. "Is this to be my punishment, today? Is it my test? Is she watching me now to see what I will do? I want to ask about my linen but, I cannot if she will not acknowledge my presence," she said out loud.

As dusk began to fall and the inner light began to dim, Medusa now paced the length of the room, weary and restless, replaying the events of the day over and over in her mind as the mysterious fumes emitting from within, overtook her senses. Sometimes, she traced imaginary designs on the wooden wall; at other times, she would sit and hold her knees to her head. Finally, she broke the silence once again: "The clay burns me. May I go and wash it off now? I promise to return."

She waited.

She is not going to answer. Perhaps, she has now gone.

Ah, my belly aches again, the blood is flowing stronger now.

I just want to lie in my bed. This is the worst day of my life! I wonder if this will be my final day as a She-bear?!

Just then, she heard the sound of wood sliding against the stone floor. She turned to see a small panel at the base of the wooden wall open. Through the dark opening, a shining bronze bowl appeared. Grateful that her wishes had been answered, she got down on her knees to retrieve the warm water and cloth. "Thank you. You are most generous."

"The mirror above will help you see to cleanse yourself," said a feeble old voice. Relieved to finally have the silence broken, Medusa did as the voice said without question. Placing the bowl on the table near her linen, she looked up and began to wipe away the clay and mud caked to her hands, arms, and legs. The water smelled surprisingly sweet, like orange blossoms mixed with honey; it felt soothing to her burning skin. She stared up into her hazy reflection as she wiped the clay from her neck and face. The mixture of scents intoxicated her, and she began to sway — yet she could not pull her eyes away from her own reflection. Gradually everything began to spin, bend and blur.

As she stared into the mirror, her reflection began to distort; her eyes becoming more and more green... then greener still. They began to burn like embers of coal. But still she could not look away, fascinated with the power she now realized they held. They began to glow with an effervescent radiance that soon spread into her face and hair. Her hair suddenly appeared more vibrant than it ever had before.

"My eyes... they are so... *hypnotizing*," she said with a smile of amazement. "And, my hair moves so beautifully... as if it were alive!"

In a flash, a second image appeared in the mirror. It was the Oracle staring back from Medusa's reflection. She spoke:

"There is balance for all that exists in this universe, a light and a darkness; an equal reaction for every action," came the ancient voice from beneath a white-hooded robe. "What will be your tipping point Medusa? What action will push you to your edge? What action will cause you to lose your balance and make you fall from grace?"

Medusa stared deeper into her own eyes, seeing terrible images now: blood... unthinkable cruelty... malevolent shadows... conspiracies and secret alliances of treachery and back-stabbing. The power of the rage within her seemed to reach out and engulf her like a bottomless, black wave, pulling her down into the dark depths. She felt herself losing consciousness, melting into the images she saw so vividly before her.

Pulling back from her waking nightmare, she turned to see a shadow of a woman standing before her. It was the goddess Artemis. She held out her hand and beckoned Medusa towards her. The image of Artemis was darkened and distorted, as if she were existing between two plains at once. Medusa approached in awe at the vision of her beloved goddess before her once more. Looking down at Artemis' open palm, she saw her talisman waiting for her.

Artemis' muffled voice could barely be heard, "Medusa my child, do not stray into anger and hatred. Keep on the truest path and you shall be vindicated." She motioned for Medusa to take her talisman and as she did, the goddess vanished into thin air. Her intense eyes, the last thing that Medusa remembered of the goddess' apparition.

Looking around, she found herself alone.

It was the dead of night and only a single lamp now burned. Time had passed, however, she could not ascertain how much time she had lost.

She looked to the table. The linen was gone.

She felt drained and disorientated.

"Medusa," a voice echoed. She turned to find the Temple Priestess waiting to escort her back.

Then abruptly, the Oracle was standing right in front of her. She put her hands to Medusa's brow in a gesture both commanding and of blessing, "Follow your Fate and never look back, child. Your task in time is a burdened one and one you must consider well. *Now, go!*" Suddenly, the sole oil lamp extinguished and the cave grew dark and cold. The voice, the white robes, the essence of myrrh and sulphur, vanished into the darkness. The atmosphere turned hollow and desolate.

An unsettling shiver climbed up Medusa's spine.

Dazed and confused, the priestess carefully led her out of the Oracle's cavern, holding high the travelling lamp as they silently began their descent down the mountain through the darkness.

To her deep dismay, Medusa's visit to the Oracle spawned a whole new realm of disturbing; it was as though the oracle had unlocked everything that was once dormant. She experienced, with greater frequency, terrifying visions that now began to seep through her dreams and into her waking life. Images so stark in clarity, she could *feel* them as if they were reality. She now found herself transported through space and time to places far beyond her darkest nightmares. And for the first time, she began to ask herself, *who am I that I see what others do not? Are my visions trying to reveal to me, some deep, dark secret? Or, am I losing my own mind?*

After her first real act of violence, it was a tarrying and sensibly decided that it was for greater good, that she distance herself from the other girls. Though solitude brought Medusa the stillness of thought to ponder where her life was leading her, that stillness was broken by terrifying, unnatural voices from the shadows that beckoned her to join them. When the noise of the world turned off and she was alone with just her thoughts, reality began to crack, and through the silence came the images and sorrowful beckoning shrieks that penetrated her being. Not even in her solitude did she have solace, as now she was a slave to her waking nightmares. Her sisters in the Cult began to see strange behaviour emerge.

"What should we do? She is beginning to frighten me!"

"*Shh!* She will hear you! Come further out into the trees…"

"I cannot sleep with her in our room! The *sounds* she makes!"

"She is up all night pacing the floor! I do not think she ever sleeps!"

The cautious whispers resounded from the shadows as the smell of fear followed Medusa through the long halls of the Sanctuary. Her sisters no longer delighted in sharing her company, which increasingly was becoming more and more unsettling. Xenophoni alone, stayed by her side, sharing in their chores whenever possible. However, even Xenophoni feared what might happen the next time Medusa lost control if no one was there to stop her. Weakened and powerless to control the onslaught of startling images that flashed through her open and vulnerable mind, Medusa grew pale; dark rings now encircled her sunken eyes. Helplessness, pride, bitterness and fury constantly gnawed at her soul; her lost, desperate eyes now seeing only empty space stared back from the mirror. The Sanctuary Priestesses began to see the change in their once-bright acolyte and began to fear the worst. Indeed, not all young girls who entered the Sanctuary of Brauron were meant for the Priestesshood after all.

As the days passed, her visions only became more troubling. She now began to feel as if her life had become part of someone else's dreams; a helpless spectator inhabiting a hollow apparition's body. Pulled into this being's world, Medusa felt her soul entwine with that of a faceless woman. A tall and elegant woman, cold and discoloured, with pale, harsh skin and a golden ring on the index finger of her right hand.

Who is this woman? What has she to do with me?

Never set in the sunlight, these visions were illuminated only by the cold, glaring light of the Moon. Ghastly shadows of foreboding black branches reflected on jagged rocks moving and swirling into images of creatures scrambling to escape the stones' pointed grip. She desperately questioned constantly: *what does it all mean?* Because there was not any one in the world that could help her understand. She decided she would have to explore it in greater depth in order to find the answers.

With each return to this other world, this dark and dismal existence, it began to feel like it was her *true* world. There, where black skies covered the land in a blanket of perpetual gloom. Movement within it began to feel more natural as she gained control of the body not her own. Though frightened that she may one day enter this world and never find her way back out, it was the mysterious female, (and the intimate understanding that had evolved between them) which frightened her most. Medusa could hear the woman's thoughts. Dark and sad, lonely and horribly bitter. Worst of all, she emoted a hatred that Medusa was now beginning to understand. So many dark and grievous energies filled her mind that she began to feel herself entombed in a world without the hope of escape. What is worse, she feared she felt herself losing the desire to escape.

CHAPTER SEVEN

The fourth year of training came to a close, which meant that it was time for the She-bears to trade their bearskins for the coveted robes of saffron. Now they would enact the final rituals and lead the grand Arkteia procession from Brauron to Athens where they would join the Priestesshood of the Temple of Athena.

It was early morning and the sun had barely cracked the sky, however, the acolytes were already busy practicing their "She-bear" dance with great excitement, and preparing for the footraces and games that would take place during this day-long festival in Brauron, and then later in Athens. It was the final days of summer and the evenings were beginning to cool as light grey clouds began to roll in with Notus (the southern wind) and collect on the far horizon just after sunset. Subtle seasonal changes were on the wind.

The young women sat in the Temple courtyard and helped each other neatly apply makeup of charcoal and olive oil to their twinkling eyes. They wanted to look their most dignified for the hundreds of people who would be watching their every move with great envy, during the parade. A thick paste of oil and ochre brightened lips that would glisten in the afternoon sun like ripened pomegranate. More than just a way to intensify their natural beauty, the makeup served to empower them; to demonstrate their transition from aspirants to mature women who were just one step away from the Priesthood.

Medusa stole away from the group and walked alone in the faint light of early morning to face the ocean alone. The chilled sea breeze grew stronger as she approached land's end, the waves lapping onto the shore with vitality. She had come to find great solace in the sea, finding there, the inner strength to contain the visions that not long ago had come to control her every waking moment. Though her dreams still brought potent and often frightening images, she had learned to temper their visits. They were now such an intimate part of her being that she could not imagine her life without them. Barefoot, she stood on the grassy cliff's edge, peering out into the mist-laden sea, arms crossed against the cold. Her tranquillity was interrupted by Xenophoni's arrival.

"Medusa, the girls are preparing to leave. I placed your belongings with mine."

"Thank you, Xenophoni. How do you feel? This is *it,* you know! The final step into womanhood!"

"Well, I believe we have amply prepared for it. Far more than *some* girls," she said, embracing her friend.

"Athens and the Priesthood of the Temple of Athena await us, then."

Xenophoni smiled. "Yes, it does, and I am honoured that you will continue to be my Sister in Athens." She clutched Medusa's hand warmly.

"Will your parents be among the spectators, today?" Xenophoni asked.

"No, I think not. I am certain they will be busy preparing for my arrival."

"I see. Well, I am sure a man as important as your father has many important responsibilities."

Medusa just nodded. The two walked back arm-in-arm to bid farewell to their sanctuary and home of the past four years and take their rightful place at the head of the grand procession.

The crowds were loud and boisterous, the atmosphere was magical, with all the vibrant colours of the rainbow strewn across the streets and walls. The people of the procession, young or old, tried hard to keep their excitement to themselves as the time to begin drew nearer. A gust of wind twilled the pigmented sands across the people, making their faces dirty with greens and blues and reds. The people did not care, it actually caused them to cheer louder as the cow skinned drums began to beat harder.

The young women held onto their short saffron dresses as they fluttered in the wind; the honey-coloured pleats folding and unfolding in the impish air. Medusa glanced back with dark-lined eyes at the ocean as they set out towards the ancient city. While the ocean had been her true sanctuary, the Temple had been her home. And for four years she had dedicated her life to the Mistress of that home. Breaking from the line, Medusa hurried back into the Temple and stood at the foot of Artemis, bowing respectfully. "If you ever need me, my Goddess, you need only summon. I will come."

The procession was set to make one final victorious pass through the narrow streets of Brauron before proceeding on to glorious Athens. There they would be met by hundreds of cheering spectators attending the ceremony to honour the nine young women who would be the newest additions to the Temple's Priestesses. Younger aspirants of the Temple, dressed in plain white tunics, would pass among the crowd with baskets of green wild fig, a symbol of sexual maturity, which was given to the people of Athens as proof that the girls before them were now mature women. Other girls, dressed in long, brown peplos, sang beautiful hymns in honour of Athena and re-enacted scenes from her many fantastic adventures. Each year the proceedings became more magnificent, the crowds, more energized.

Throughout the afternoon, the nine young women took part in special rituals, ran races, and danced in honour of Artemis and Athena. A few, including Medusa, demonstrated their prowess with the bow and arrow. However, the highlight of the parade was when the nine assumed the persona of She-bears for the final time, performing the dance known as The Arkteia, a choreographed performance made up of slow, solemn steps meant to imitate the somewhat cumbersome movements of a bear, performed to a lively melody played by a line of *diaulos* (double flute) players. While the meaning of the gestures had been lost to time, it was generally understood that each movement symbolized devotion to Artemis in return for her ever-vigilant guidance of the young girls on their way to maturity and the Sacred Priestesshood. Their short, yellow chiton dresses were meant to represent the bear skins they *shed* during the final ritual at Brauron, symbolizing the participants' shedding of their old selves, revealing the new. These would be traded for formal white robes of the Athena Priestesshood.

Among the great throng of people lining the way to Athens were two kindly, old faces eagerly searching the procession for their little girl who had now grown up far from their loving arms. With Elpis and Hagne now married and building lives of their own, Agathi and Petros had arrived with Dorkas and her young son, (who as Medusa had envisioned, had returned home to stay). The family had arrived before sunrise so that they might have the best chance of seeing their daughter and sister on this most glorious day. As the procession passed by, they finally caught sight of her in all her splendour. No longer a child, their beautiful little girl was now a lovely young woman whose long legs tapped methodically to the lively rhythm of the flutes. Her beautiful heart-shaped face and mesmerizing green eyes caught the adoring smiles of many in the crowd, but she only had eyes for three souls. Raising her head in the slow She-bear dance, she spotted her parents and sister staring proudly, her mother holding tightly to her father as tears streamed down both their faces. Medusa's eyes saddened as she danced, "Mother, Father, sister... I love you," she whispered beneath her breath. Petros dared to call her name, "*Medusa!*"

Medusa heard her father calling, but could not call back, she simply held a helpless stare for as long as she could, trying her best to communicate her love and gratitude to her family for the life they had given her. The sacrifice they had made was enormous and Medusa's heart both sank in sorrow and soared from the love her family's hearts emitted.

At sunset, the day-long ceremony ended and the streets of Brauron soon emptied of visitors, some of who made the journey to Athens to continue the festivities. Most, made their way to one of the many open-air taverns or to friends' houses to end the celebration with free-flowing wine and specially prepared food. Xenophoni, like Medusa, would be living in Athens, staying with her uncle, a wealthy Athenian Senator. She drew close to her best friend, clasping arms.

"So Medusa, we are officially mature women now."

"Yes, that is what they say, Xenophoni, however, I feel no different."

"Well, we will see how you feel after you have entered the Temple of Athena. Then you will feel like a woman... you will see! Taking on such important tasks and spending time in the presence of such great God..." Medusa just smiled. With their few possessions slung over their shoulders, Xenophoni and Medusa walked together towards their new homes.

"So, tell me about your family, then. Your father — a General! You must be so proud!"

Medusa stopped, deciding it was time to share the truth with the one friend who had stayed by her side when everyone else pulled away in fear. "Xenophoni, there is a story I must tell you."

"A story?"

"Yes, a story about my family. About my father."

"I would like that! A great and glorious story of battle, no doubt!"

Medusa looked directly into her eyes. "My *real* father."

"*Real* father?" She looked perplexed.

"Yes, my *real* father. And it begins with a man called Petros…"

Medusa began at the very beginning and recalled for her friend, the story her father had told her as the two made their way through the quieting streets of Athens. Each detail she could remember, she told the excited Xenophoni who hung onto her every word and as they neared the fork in the road at the edge of the city, Medusa explained, ". . . and now, the General is a nobleman and an important politician here in Athens. His debt to my father was never forgotten. This life that I now live is the repayment of that debt."

"That is an amazing story, Medusa! My cousins will love me re-telling it!"

"Oh, no, Xenophoni! You must never whisper a word of this to *anyone*. If my secret is ever to be discovered…"

"Yes, I understand. Do not worry my friend, I will only tell the story of your kind and generous father, the great General Klietonas!" she said with a wink.

"*Kind and generous…?*"

"Something wrong? He *is* a kind and generous man, is he not?"

"I… I am sure he is, Xeno. But the truth is, I have never even met him!"

"Well, I am quite certain he will take to you just fine, Medusa. You know, you are a very smart and pretty gir- uh, *young woman*! I only wish *I* had your eyes and your hair..." she sighed, dramatically.

Her sidelong glance made the girls burst into welcome giggles, as Xenophoni's auburn tresses and grey eyes were a vision to behold.

Medusa smiled and hugged her friend goodbye as the two young women were anxious to reach their new homes and settle in before nightfall.

Taking the left fork in the road, Medusa nervously walked until she found the magnificent white house where her generous new family waited for her; the place she would call home for perhaps the rest of her life. As she wandered closer, she could feel a sense of familiarity in the air. The house, although grand and extravagant as opposed to her own family home, gave an air of love and safety, as her own home did.

Standing before the threshold she felt a phantom tapping of her shoulder; a persuasive invitation to look over her shoulder. As she did, her eyes met with two more. It was her father, he had followed and waited in the shadows, to ensure the safety of his dear daughter, in the alien Athenian streets.

Medusa's heart panged with a lonely aching as she immediately ran towards her father. Petros shook with nerves and excitement, he embraced his loving daughter, tightly.

"Father, I have missed you so... Mother too, and my sisters, my dear sisters..." Medusa exclaimed with tears in her eyes.

"Oh my child, my dear Medusa, we have missed you too. Now let me look at you, you are so beautiful my darling, all grown up." Petros eyes swelled with tears of bittersweet happiness.

"Father, I have learned so much, you received all of my letters did you not?"

"Yes my daughter, but it was unsafe for you to risk your future, for the sake of holding on to your past."

"Never say that father, you are not my past, you are will forever be a part of me, you are my family, and that is everything I need in my life."

Petros and Medusa could not hold back the tears as they simply held each other and cried; with shaky hands, Petros held Medusa back. "Go child, let your life flourish, and know, that we will forever be with you."

"I love you all. I will continue to send you news of my happenings. Until we meet again. I love you."

Medusa wiped the tears from her eyes and walked back towards the threshold of her new home.

She gave the great wooden door two soft taps. Immediately, a woman with upswept hair, dressed in beautiful white satin robes lined with golden floral designs, opened the door. Smiling kindly she spoke with soft voice,

"Welcome home, daughter," and embraced Medusa warmly. She then led Medusa in from the darkening street into the welcoming honey-coloured light of her new home.

Petros sank into the darkness, tears falling from his face. Once again he had to muster all his soldier's courage and will to walk away from his daughter.

CHAPTER EIGHT

Upon completion of his studies at the boys' school at Avernae, Iasonnas' father arranged entry for his son into the most exclusive gymnasium in the coastal city of Sounion to the east. There, Iasonnas studied the law, philosophy, mathematics and horticulture and all the other important fields of study prescribed to a young Greek boy on his way to manhood. Sounion, a beautiful and sprawling city with a bustling Agora and busy trade routes, had a glorious temple dedicated to the sea-god Poseidon, its patron protector. However, now with just two months before graduation with scholastic honours, Iasonnas' mind was as far from his studies. All he could think about was Medusa; wondering if she had yet returned home.

Finding it more and more difficult to keep his mind on his studies, Iasonnas found himself spending long hours fantasizing about Medusa as his wife, working the land together on the wonderful farm he envisioned in his mind. Deep down, he knew that after four long years away, his stubborn sweetheart would not come back on her own. She would surely need gentle persuasion. He knew she would never confess her love for him until he had proven how completely he loved and adored her. So his daydreams had turned from Medusa leaving the Priestesshood and rushing home to his waiting arms, to his venturing off alone to Athens to demand her consideration.

Sitting in his dormitory alone, the harsh realities of his academic responsibilities were now scattered before him in multiple telltale piles. But, ancient scrolls and scholarly treatises meant nothing to Iasonnas. He had tried his best to be a dutiful son to the kind and generous man who had provided and cared for him all through his life. However, his passion for the land, something his father had hoped would be liberated through studious discipline, now dominated his hopes, dreams, and plans. Though his father had spoken often of the hardships of farming the rocky, unforgiving land which experienced constant droughts and plagues, Iasonnas believed he was more than prepared to take on these responsibilities. He was certain his father's land would provide him the future he longed for. Once he had the support of a strong young woman, a woman intellectually, physically, emotionally and spiritually sound, nothing could stop him. To Iasonnas, no one fitted that role better than his fair Medusa. Hence, with mere weeks between him and the fulfilment of his dreams, Iasonnas began planning his journey to Athens, his journey of love.

Though he was not an overtly religious boy, knowing of Medusa's love of the sea, he began to find solace in the Temple of Poseidon. Standing inside the great expanse guarded by the omnipresent God of the Deep, the days seemed to pass quicker and somehow made Medusa feel nearer. After visiting the shrine on several occasions, Iasonnas began to reach out to the great God of Olympus with his feelings of love.

It became his ritual.

He would steal away from the library during the day and casually wander into the dark stone temple, his heart and mind aburst with anticipation. Then, he would wait for the moment when the Temple was empty and he would begin to pour out his heart to the gigantic bronze statue standing there with intimidating trident jutting forward; his expression one of adamant resolve. It gave Iasonnas the strength to endure another day without his beloved near. He came to feel the very presence of the God as the towering figure glowed in the dim light reflected off pitch-black Temple walls.

Starting from the beginning, Iasonnas described for Poseidon the first time he saw Medusa, dangling comically out of the village well. Speaking out commandingly in the Temple became easier as he paced back and forth before the image, describing the many adventures they had shared growing up, of the strange things she had said or done, and how she had probably blossomed into the most beautiful young woman in the universe. His stories always ended with the wonderful life he had in store for Medusa and himself.

Occasionally, a Priest would pass through the Temple's grand chamber to the rear and smile as he listened to Iasonnas speak of his youthful desires, knowing well that what Iasonnas was doing was hardly an uncommon act of love in Greece. In truth, many young men and women frequented the temples of Attica to find divine assistance in matters of the unbridled heart, often beseeching the Gods for divine intervention on their behalf. However, such desires were usually addressed to Aphrodite, the Goddess of Love, not to a male God such as Poseidon. Iasonnas was acutely aware of this as well but to him, Medusa's love of the sea made it seem only right.

With each visit, Iasonnas felt the God's presence growing ever stronger; an energy surrounding the grand chamber that seemed to pull him in and urge him to push out the words of his emotions. Late night visits, detailing his most explicit desires, often made the waiting easier because he could express his love and frustration. Sometimes though, it made the anticipation unbearable, his unrequited love acutely and excruciatingly painful; sometimes it made his longing erupt like molten lava, leaving him breathless on the Temple floor. Some nights he would abandon his pleas and leave before his passions consumed him.

On one such night, as he lay on the cold stone floor opposite the great God's omnipotent gaze, he sipped from a dark red jug of pomegranate wine stolen from the academy's winery. With just five days until graduation, he closed his eyes and allowed himself to envision Medusa standing there before him; her flowing gown alight with holy radiance. His mind dancing from too much drink, he reached out and touched her smooth white cheek. Then he pulled her near and tenderly kissed her beautiful face as he looked into her bottomless, green eyes. These had been the seeds of his many dreams and plans.

To his drunken dismay though, Medusa began to *snicker* causing Iasonnas to abruptly wake.

He shook his head and to his horror found an old beggar woman kneeling over him laughing insanely. Jumping to his feet and spilling wine all over himself, he pushed the woman aside and stumbled out of the Temple, embarrassed and shocked. Looking back, he watched as the old woman picked up the bottle and brought it to her anxious mouth. He vowed never again to let undiluted wine touch his lips.

After staying clear of the Temple for the next two days, he woke in the night to the sound of a deep voice whispering in his head, *"Come to the Temple. Your dreams will be fulfilled."* The words echoed in his mind the entire morning; the mysterious summons spinning round his mind until he felt dizzy and half crazed.

Reluctantly, he abandoned his room and stole away to the Temple. As he approached, something seemed to grab hold of him, cautioning him to stay out. His senses heightened, almost as if he awoke from a daze, he took control of his own thoughts and turned around abruptly, never entering. Disturbed by the strangeness of the night, he lost the need of sleep and instead sat on the window ledge of his room, gazing out at the slumbering city below, imagining Medusa in his arms. His fantasies were interrupted by the voice, which called again. *"Come to the Temple. Your dreams will be fulfilled."* Iasonnas was not a man who would shy away from the mysterious and so he decided that this time, he would return to the temple and enter as the voice commanded.

Cautiously entering the Temple, he saw the night ritual fires dancing across the black walls behind Poseidon's imposing image, his unclothed figure standing commandingly at the Temple's heart. He stood before the great statue and dropped to his knees, "Poseidon, I heard you calling me. Why do you persist in beckoning me here? Do you feel my pain? Can you truly fulfil my dreams?"

At first he heard nothing. Disappointed in the silence which met his desperate pleas, Iasonnas gave up, rose to his feet and just as he turned to leave, a voice spoke to him. "Do not leave, Iasonnas, for I have heard your longing and I am here to end your suffering."

Though not yet trusting his ears, Iasonnas replied, "I am here, Lord! Please tell me more!"

"Iasonnas, I know of your suffering," the voice said. "I feel your yearning. I can make your dreams come true."

Iasonnas looked up at the motionless statue. "You can bring me Medusa? She is the object of my dreams! Can you bring her to me?"

"Come. Come closer to the priest's chamber that you shall know the object of your dreams."

Iasonnas looked toward the darkened entrance of the Priest's preparation chamber. Slowly approaching, he saw thick smoke emerge from within. It spiralled upward towards the high, wooden beams in dark green clouds and hung above. He began to inhale the sweet essence as he neared the chamber. His heart pounded and his head grew dizzy. He saw a hazy figure move through the mist.

"Come closer, my boy. Stand at the wooden doors you see before you."

Iasonnas was now completely intoxicated by the strange fumes that thickly coated the air. His mind grew freer and lighter; his strong sense of logic and judgement was slighted. Clumsily stepping forward, Iasonnas followed the voice he now trusted. "Bring me Medusa," he said anxiously, "I beg you! Bring me the one I desire!"

"Step closer."

Now at ease with the hazy apparition, Iasonnas stood before the heavy wooden doors and found the two lower panels now open. Here, Priests would enter and cleanse their bodies and souls with holy water and purifying smoke before performing rituals. A pair of delicate, pale white hands appeared as the smoke filled his lungs. The hands reached tenderly beneath his tunic and began to caress his thighs.

"Great Poseidon, you whose powers know no limits, have you brought my sweet Medusa to me in a vision? My dear Medusa, is that you?" His sight and mind a blur, he stood with eyes closed as the woman knelt beneath his tunic and began to pleasure him. His raging desires and the peace of mind, brought on by the mysterious green smoke, gave Iasonnas no reason to doubt that the figure before him was his beloved Medusa.

His senses heightened, his pulse raced and his heart pounded faster and faster in his ears until the ecstasy drove him breathless to the cool, stone floor. Gasping and nervously laughing, he lifted his spinning head to find a hazy image of a woman kneeling before him, smiling sweetly. Iasonnas raised his hand to stroke her hair. As he did, his eyes suddenly came into focus. He now realized he was deceived, as he saw, kneeling before him, a pale man in priestly robes, looking up at him in fear.

Quickly pulling down his tunic, he stumbled to his feet as the old man scurried back across the floor and quickly closed the wooden doors. Standing there panting, a look of confusion and horror washed across Iasonnas' face.

"What have I done?!" he screamed. "Oh, by the Gods, what have I done?! I have betrayed her! I have betrayed the woman I love!" Thinking to run to the shore and plunge his soiled body into the frigid water of the sea to scrub his body clean of the desecration, he fled the Temple. As he did, he heard a deep, booming voice laughing,

"She will **never** have you now, **boy**! You can never wash away the sin of **betrayal**! Medusa will **never** have you **now**!"

Iasonnas mind fluttered uncontrollably as he stumbled and fell about; he fled the temple. All that he saw through the pale moonlight appeared shadowed and evil. His mind a blur with broken images that flashed before him, his weak legs aimlessly stumbled across the cold stone ground. By chance he found the sea which through his intoxication appeared for the first time unwelcoming and sordid. Through warn salty eyes, he saw the sea turn blood red, as if the sins of a thousand whores were being cleansed right before him. In his disgust, he turned to scurry away, slipping in the process and landing in the crimson waters which now covered him wholly.

Flailing through the waters, his senses were awakened enough for him to fight the heavy waters, which pulled him to their depths.

Escaping certain death, he experienced a sudden reawakening, which gave him the strength and courage to diminish his fears and carry on along the path to his beloved, Medusa.

"There will be no end to my persistence, Medusa my love, I will come for you."

CHAPTER NINE

The glorious Temple of Athena *the Victorious* set high atop a rocky outcrop on the Acropolis of Athens. Built to convey Athens' powerful ambitions to be victorious against Sparta and take their place as a world power, it was positioned so that the people of Athens could always keep the Goddess of Victory in sight and thus worship, to assure a prosperous Fate by her good graces.

While Medusa had seen the Temple many times in the past during her trips to Athens with her father, she now understood for the first time, what it meant to stand in the radiant light of its holy grandeur; to bask in its sacred emanations. Although the Sanctuary at Brauron had instilled in her a sense of dedication and spiritual devotion to the Gods, the Priesshood of the Temple of Athena now gave her life meaning and solidified purpose. More than just the dreams of a child come true, it was destiny manifest through the Fates.

Built of hand-hewn white marble, brought from the distant quarries of Paros Marathi, its four great columns upheld the Temple's protective parapet; colonnaded porticoes in both front and back, provided a covered walkway for visitors, pilgrims and of course, the constant passage of Temple Priestesses, Priests, and aspiring adepts. Three sides of the parapet were adorned with exquisitely carved relief sculptures, showing the mighty and virtuous Goddess and all her celebrated accomplishments next to scenes depicting the Greek cavalry in glorious battle: their illustrious victory over the Medians at the Battle of Plataea and an assembly of the Gods Most High: Athena, Zeus, and Poseidon. More than just homage to the Goddess, the Temple announced to whomever stood before it, the Athenian reverence for their creators and their innate belief in the concept of cosmic order.

Inside, at its centre of the Temple stood the likeness of Athena Nike (the "wingless"), holding her battle helmet in her left hand and a ripe pomegranate (her symbol of fertility) in the right. Athena, the great Olympian Goddess of Wise Counsel, War, Heroism, Weaving and other crafts, was always depicted crowned with a crested helm, armed with a battle shield and a spear and wearing a snake-trimmed cloak wrapped around her chest and arm, with one ample breast exposed. As the Patron God of Athens, she was revered as its greatest defender.

As legend describes, Athena sprang from the head of the almighty Zeus, born fully-grown and completely armoured for battle. The Founding Fathers of Athens were greatly indebted to her for intervening on their behalf eons before when Poseidon had tried to extend his domain of power over the people of Athens. A momentous and heroic battle took place during which Athena produced the first olive tree as a sign of her power and desire to preserve life; while Poseidon countered by creating the first horse. Now essential to Athens' continued power and prosperity, Athena was revered for bestowing both the olive and horse upon the people of Athens. As the daughter of Zeus, the most powerful of the Gods, and Metis, the wisest of the Gods, Athena was seen as a joining of the two; a Goddess in whom power and wisdom were harmoniously blended. Now eternally seated at Zeus' left hand as his primary advisor, she was regaled for everything within, that gives the State strength and prosperity and everything without, that preserves and protects it from dark, invading forces.

The walls, the Temple, the fortress, and the harbours were now always under her watchful eye. And one of the primary responsibilities for Medusa and the other Priestesses of the Temple of Athena was to sing hymns to her glory throughout the day. Each morning, as the sun burst through the east portico, Medusa and her Sisters sang, "Of Pallas Athena, Guardian of the City, I begin to sing. Dread is she, and with Ares she loves the deeds of war, the sack of cities and the shouting and the battle. It is she who saves the people as they go to war and come back. Hail, Goddess, and give us good fortune and happiness!"

Life as a Priestess of the Temple of Athena was far more glorious than Medusa had ever envisioned. She relished her daily duties that now included the maintenance of the holy votive candles on the Temple's Sacred Altar, the offering of fresh fruit and flowers to Athena four times daily, visiting the agora each morning to buy fresh food and Temple supplies and seeing to the needs of religious pilgrims and adepts who flocked to the Temple both day and night. This left plenty of time for prayer, meditation, and personal reflection.

Although fits of uncontrollable rage no longer threatened her resolve to devote herself to spiritual life, her visions had only become more powerful and vivid with time. She was now keenly aware that another being resided within her and that perhaps, it always had. Medusa's gift of prophecy had quickly become known to her Sisters of the Temple. Her ability to hear their thoughts and know in advance the course of the day's events both captivated and troubled them. Still, many, including the High Priestess Soteria, began seeking her counsel in matters of Temple importance. Some began thinking of Medusa as somehow divinely chosen as a messenger of the Gods. Some even thought that her rightful place was that of an Oracle. However, none, not even Xenophoni, knew of the dark secrets she kept to herself.

With summer passing into autumn, the Temple Sisters were now busy preparing for Athens' most important celebration, the Panathenaea. Observed every four years in mid-August, it commemorated the birth of Athena with a variety of activities taking place all over the city in which thousands of visitors — religious acolytes, and followers of the Cult of Athena would flock to Athens to take part in. Boat races, musical competitions, as well as gymnastic, equestrian, literary and charioteering contests always provided a joyous atmosphere that spectators and participants would talk about for seasons to come.

It was the responsibility of the elder Temple Priestesses to enact an ancient ritual of blessing and thanksgiving for the year's harvest to launch the festivities, during which the novice Priestesses would sing hymns of joy to Zeus and Metis for creating Athena. At the close of the event, High Priestess Soteria would lead a procession of the game victors with their wives and daughters, through the streets of Athens while citizens would honour them with flower petals strewn in their path. The procession would pass through the agora to the Eleusinian (centre of the Elysian Mystery Cult) at the east end of the Acropolis, then continue north until it reached the Gateway of Propylaea. There, Temple Priestesses would perform a symbolic sacrifice to Athena while commoners made offerings and recited prayers. Then, upon entering the Acropolis (which only lawful Athenians were permitted to do) cattle was slaughtered to honour Athena and burned on the large marble altar on the eastern side of the Acropolis. According to ancient rite, the flesh was given to a select number of Athenians who had displayed the most spiritual piety in recent years, along with bread and sweet cakes.

On this most prosperous day of the year for Athens' vendors and craftsmen, great amounts of gold and silver would change hands as special foods were purchased, horses and chariots were primed, greased and polished, and lodgings for countless visitors were prepared. Many Athenian families let out rooms in their houses for this special occasion for revenue that would last throughout the coming year. Initially a one-day event, the popularity of the festival had made it grow to no fewer than three days.

For the Priestesses of the Temple of Athena, the grand climax of the opening procession was the adorning of the statue of Athena with a newly-woven peplos. A private ritual would take place attended only by Temple Priestesses during which the likeness of Athena would be disrobed and then ceremoniously redressed with new finery. A garland of dried flowers would be placed upon her head and another would be draped across her shield. Considering her amazing ability to embroider extraordinary works of art (a common topic of discussion amongst the Sisters) Medusa was, of course, chosen as one of three to complete this most coveted task. With just two days until the blessed event, Medusa, Priestess Adelpha, and Priestess Dorothea worked diligently in the Temple alcove, excitedly anticipating the big day. Medusa's heart leapt and her mind soared as she took her place where she had long believed she belonged. Sitting on the alcove floor with the late-day sun streaming in on her gentle face, the approach of a lone rider began flashing through her mind.

Iasonnas was barely seventeen when he received his diploma from the gymnasium at Sounion. Without a moment to waste, he quickly readied his horse with provisions and set out for Athens.

Though laden with guilt and remorse for what had occurred in the Temple of Poseidon, he rode without respite throughout the night until early morning when he finally saw the beautiful and imposing Acropolis of Athens jutting out of the sea as if resting atop a God's giant hand. He knew well, why many considered it the most sacred place on earth, second only to Mount Olympus.

Gazing down from his high perch onto a golden grain-coloured hillside, his eyes filled with hope and his heart nearly burst with anticipation. With a smile and a determined glance ahead, he pressed his horse forward. The beast taking off at full gallop passed the sacred olive groves towards the still-slumbering city.

Morning had just broken and the pale, pink light was just beginning to penetrate the city. Brilliant white buildings emerged as striking black silhouettes as he trotted alone down the polished-stone causeway. Riding through the streets of Athens, with the first stirring odours of the waking city in the air, he stared in awe; it had been but a few years since he last saw the magnificent city. However, within that time, it had grown and expanded far beyond his wildest expectations.

There were glorious new temples built to honour the newly emerging multitude of gods, as well as new dedications to ancient ones. On one mound to the east, the cult of the Titan goddess Dawn had erected a new sanctuary which now shone red against the sky, casting the first warm glow before the heavens began to whiten with the sun's measured rise.

Before him, spread new stoas and courts, larger and grander, in order to accommodate the ever-expanding trade within the bustling city. The agora had blossomed into a magnificent public square and there were a dozen newly-paved roads adorned with colourful mosaics before him. Beautiful green gardens bearing fruit trees and beds of bursting flowers now lined the city's flourishing, affluent neighbourhoods. New shops, bathhouses, eateries, craftsmen quarters, and brothels now dotted every block. Despite the new buildings and convergence of avenues, Iasonnas quickly navigated his way to the Temple of Athena where Medusa now toiled and worshipped amongst those most devout. As he arrived at the foot of the Temple, he leaned back on his horse, weary but, happy that he had finally reached his destination.

As he sat gazing up at the magnificent scenes depicted above the mighty columns, a female figure emerged from within the shadows of the Temple, outlined by the morning's first light. The figure rushing down the Temple steps, became increasingly familiar to Iasonnas' road-worn eyes as she made her way to the street below.

Iasonnas stood, mute and motionless as a tall and graceful woman who he had once known as a lanky and quiet girl, fled past him. His beautiful Medusa seemed to be as deliberate in nature and bound by her duties as ever before.

Her beautiful golden locks, securely made up into a tidy bun, accentuated her long and delicate neck. Her perfect pale skin, highlighted her luscious and full lips, which were naturally pink and inviting. All of her beauty was overshadowed by one striking feature, which drew all who met her to stare in awe; Her vibrant green eyes, which people would say were "surely gifted by the gods", emitted life, love and intelligence beyond her years. It was these eyes that Iasonnas lost his heart to, for through her eyes, he saw her gentle soul, her kind heart and the very essence of her being.

Breezing straight past him, woven basket in hand, she paid no heed to the young man on the horse observing her every move. She hurried several steps onto the street before a strange feeling overcame her and a memory of a face flashed into her mind.

She stopped and turned to face the rider.

"Iasonnas! Oh, Iasonnas, it is you!" Laughing and crying, Medusa dropped the basket and ran to him. Beaming with elation, Iasonnas jumped off his horse and opened his arms wide.

"Iasonnas! You know you must not embrace a Holy Priestess of the Temple of Athens!" she teased.

"Let us pretend, then, that you are not yet a Priestess, Medusa!" he replied with a cheeky grin.

They embraced there at the foot of the Temple with the morning sun dancing in their hair. Neither one wanted to break this precious embrace. They remained still in each other's arms, as their eyes gazed at one another. They tied Iasonnas' horse to a public post and set out on the streets of Athens. He carried her basket as they walked, the broadest of smiles never leaving his lips. They strolled through the Agora where Medusa purchased charcoal and fresh fruit for the Temple. Iasonnas bought a beautiful red flower, an anemone from a vendor, which he presented and she held to her breast as they spoke of their lives over the past few years. They had much to share about what they had learned of the world and its mysterious workings.

At seventeen, Iasonnas felt adulthood had arrived and that he was as wise and knowing as an aged scholar. The speech he had long rehearsed he now recited, telling Medusa of the life he had planned. He courageously now made his intentions crystal clear, that his future not only *included* her, it was built solely *around* her.

"Medusa, look deep into my loving eyes and there you will see my eternal commitment to you. Believe my words and let the sanctuary of my love engulf your heart. I want you as my wife, for all time!"

Medusa's felt her world suddenly knocked off balance. "But, Iasonnas, I…"

"By the Gods, Medusa, I have always known that this is what the Fates had in store for us. Surely, you knew it, too!"

Her breath quickening and her heart pounding in her chest, Medusa felt as if the sky had begun to descend upon her head and would surely crush her if she stood there one moment longer. Pressing the flower to Iasonnas' chest, she turned and rushed back to the Temple. Dazed and confused, Iasonnas could only trail behind her, as he had always done. Then with one sorrowful look, she disappeared into the darkness of Temple, leaving him standing alone.

He desperately called out "I should not have just spat it out like that! *Fool* — what a *fool* I am!"

His heart aching, Iasonnas waited for Medusa on the Temple steps, hoping for a chance to explain. He re-lived every moment they had ever shared.

All that day, Medusa could not stop thinking of Iasonnas, her dearest friend, and how she had left him standing there. It tore at her heart as she tried to see to her duties. However, she could not escape the dejected look on his face as she returned his gift. It was as if… *Yes* — She had always known this day would come. She had seen it in his eyes since they were young children. However, she had always hoped that the Gods would spirit his interest away to some other girl — a girl who would eagerly love and cherish him as he so desperately needed and deserved. But there he was, just as he had promised he would be. It tortured her soul that she must now break his tender heart.

Medusa had never cared for another man so deeply. He had always been a good friend to her, more than simply a companion, Iasonnas was her soulmate. Although she knew no other man could ever know her soul as much as he did, there was but one love above Iasonnas and that was the Temple. When night fell and her duties for the day complete, she stole away from the Temple to bring food to him. She found him slumped on the dusty Temple steps, dishevelled and broken. Her heart ached for her best friend. She fought back the tears and approached him. When her shadow cast upon him, he looked up to see her standing there smiling sweetly just as she always had. He quickly got to his feet.

"Medusa... I—"

"No, no, Iasonnas. You must eat."

Taking him by the hand, Medusa led him to a private spot she had found in a fig grove below the Temple mount. Reluctantly, he opened the basket and took a few bites of bread and cheese as they sat in the shadows. He tried to speak, but, Medusa could only turn away.

"Medusa, please... "

"No, Iasonnas — you must not speak of that which is on your mind. It is not befitting a Priestess of Athena and will only complicate things for us both."

"But, why must it complicate things for you? If you are dedicated to your Gods, why should you fear being close to me?"

"Iasonnas, I am not afraid, I just..."

Iasonnas took her hands and looked into her eyes. "Medusa, I know you believe I have come at the worst possible time, but I believe I have arrived at the perfect time. Before you devote your life to this Temple and be forever bound by your word, I have come to ask that your heart, your body, and your soul be mine. That we live together in harmony for all eternity." His eyes fell upon her with the look of love that burned inside him, waiting for their eyes to meet in loving unison. The warmth from his hands made Medusa weak under his touch.

"I... I am sorry, Iasonnas — you know how much I care for you. But, I cannot allow this to happen. I am a Holy Priestess of the Temple of Athena now. I have given my vow. *This* is the life I have chosen."

His touch now tightened around her delicate arms, his passion growing as he spoke through clinched teeth, "This Temple's cold stones cannot warm your loneliness! The Sisterhood of Priestesses is no substitute for a true family!" He leaned in close, his breath entwined in hers, his voice turning to a tender whisper, "Medusa, your Gods will not run to your side when your heart is broken. They will not hold you... touch your face... kiss your lips as a woman needs." He pressed his lips to hers, and to her great surprise, she did not resist. They kissed below the Sacred Temple where the daughters of Athens, *the holy chaste*, worshiped virtue and purity.

How can she return to her lonely life now that her lips have touched mine?

Iasonnas had finally released the passion long pent up in his body, mind, and soul and it felt terrifyingly right. He looked into Medusa's bright green eyes to search for the look that said, '*Yes, Iasonnas, take me home,*' to his bitter disappointment, he saw only regretful tears streaming down. She ran her hand over his soft, young face and uttered tearfully, "Farewell, Iasonnas. In time, you will find someone else."

He took a step backwards, tears flooding from his eyes. "But, *why*? Is it... is it because of what happened in the Temple of Poseidon?! Did you see it in your visions?! Is it because I am no longer *worthy*?!"

She stood and solemnly walked away from the person she knew was her only true mortal love.

"*Please*, Medusa! I *beg* you! It was *one* mistake! *Pleeeease!*"

As she ran back inside the Temple, Iasonnas fell to the cold, hard ground. His pain and anguish pouring out of him, becoming an eternal part of the darkness of night.

CHAPTER TEN

Composed and calm, Medusa stood before her shining bronze mirror painting her face with a powdery white mask, lining her eyes with dark blue dye made from chrysocolla. Ground and mixed with ingredients known only to Priestesses and Priests of Athena, this makeup was saved for the most holy of occasions.

Donning a pure white ceremonial robe of linen, she tied her golden hair back into a chignon and stood gazing solemnly at her reflection: *Is this the face of a Priestess? Behind my pale white mask, is this who I am? Only my heart can now guide me.* With those thoughts, Medusa joined the Priestesses in the Temple where they sat in meditation of the Great Goddess Athena Nike. The silence of the Temple cocooned Medusa in tranquil stillness; keeping her heart from disturbing her mind, she cloaked her doubts in prayers. The silence was broken too soon as an elder Temple Priestess clapped her hands twice to signify that it was time. The sun had just broken the sky and crowds were already forming to take part in the Panathenaea celebration.

As the elder Priestesses enacted the ancient ritual of blessing and thanksgiving for the year's harvest, ushering in the commencement of the much anticipated procession, the streets were quickly filling with pilgrims and Athenians cheering and shouting praises. Leading the procession were fifty young maidens from Athens' most affluent families. Dressed in white pleated knee-high robes and eyes lined with black coal, they danced and pranced joyously, spreading white and purple flower petals along the path as the ceremonial tympana drums pulsed as the heart of the procession. Then came twenty battle-hardened warriors of Athena dressed in red leather armour and white tunics marching in formation with long spears of bronze that reflected in the morning sun. Behind the roar of the warriors' measured steps came the sweet smell of frankincense, signalling the approach of the Temple's newly-consecrated Priestesses.

Spectators rushed to find high vantage points so they could get a better look; the women emerged through the haze as white idols in motion, their painted dark blue eyes piecing the holy smoke. It was said that those fortunate enough to witness the new daughters of the Temple would be blessed for the coming year. Elegant and statuesque, their footfalls light and silent, they strode forward, hedged by the Athenian Guards. Medusa passed by the crowd like a holy ghost, her thoughts fleeting, as people stared at her sad and melancholy eyes that shone bright. Behind her, twenty more warriors followed as the Priestesses continued on towards the Temple where Athena's likeness stood awaiting her Holy Rites.

Leaving the throng of spectators outside the walls where the parade would continue through the streets of Athens, the Priestesses now entered the holy sanctuary to enact the Adorning of the Goddess. As Medusa passed the towering white marble columns, she thought her eyes caught a glimpse of a dark, shrouded man running between the shadows. The guards filed left and right of the great wooden doors, surrounding the Temple as the Priestesses entered the alcove of Athena's Sacred Alter.

I can feel someone watching. Someone, who should not be here.

Standing beside her, was her loyal friend Xenophoni, her old adversary Melissa and three other newly-consecrated Priestess. Medusa peered down the line of women and scanned the Temple in search of the lone individual who had entered her consciousness.

As all sound was hushed, High Priestess Soteria began the sacred ceremony by passing a golden censor over each Priestesses head. Each bowed and closed her eyes to receive her blessing as Soteria passed the bowl around their heads from left to right. When it came to Medusa, who bowed deeper than most as she was much taller than Soteria, she gazed into the High Priestess eyes to signal her concerns about the presence: *Do you feel it too, High Priestess? Someone is here who does not belong… please be warned.* Soteria instantly heard Medusa's thoughts and turned her consciousness to her surroundings.

Passing the censor to a younger Priestess who returned it on its stand, Soteria turned to face the likeness of Athena, now wrapped in the sacred amethyst and saffron-hued peplos like the one she had worn during her victory over the *giganta* Enceladus. Soteria raised her arms to the icon and began to sing a hymn; her powerful voice piercing the tall stone walls and carrying itself on through the air to the celebrating masses far outside the holy enclosure. The vibration of her voice echoed throughout the Temple, magnifying her song to the Goddess. But, as the echoes resounded, a male voice could be heard calling from above.

Puzzled and alarmed, the Priestesses looked around to see who dared interrupt Soteria's song and their most holy ceremony. The sound of his voice travelled like a lightning bolt to Soteria's ears and struck harshly on her nerves as she swung around in anger and pointed upwards towards a beam across the entrance of the inner sanctum.

"*You*!!! *Guards, guards*!" she called out.

All looked up to see a cloaked man balanced across the narrow wooden ledge that ran around the Temple's interior. Instantly, twenty Athenian warriors filed into the Temple and readied their spears at the intruder. One launched his spear with great strength, but missed his target; the spear bounced off the stone, landing at Medusa's feet. Another, sent his spear flying causing the man to lose his footing and fall to a lower beam. As he scrambled to reach a window to escape, Medusa caught a glimpse of the man's face. "*No…* tell me it is not *you*!" she whispered. Seeing the concern in Medusa's eyes, Soteria signalled the guards to climb the columns and capture the man alive. Medusa's eyes opened wide as she prayed for the man to escape as five of the guards climbed the columns and pinned him in. Grabbing for his legs, he kicked back at them again and again. Finally having had enough, one of the guards grabbed the man's leg and roughly pulled him from the ledge.

"*Medusa*!" was all the intruder could shout as he fell backwards to the hard stone floor, the sound of crushing bones echoing through the Temple. The group held silent, stepping back from where the man lay bleeding. Medusa tried to rush to him, only to be stopped by Soteria grabbing her arm firmly. Shaking her head *no,* the High Priestess gently pushed Medusa back into position.

Encircling the intruder, one of the guards lifted the cloak still covering his face. "He is just a *boy*! Not more than eighteen years!" said one, clearly surprised. As the High Priestess approached to see who this impudent man was, a guard viciously threw him onto his back so she could get a clear look at his face. Soteria peered over him sternly, now fully aware of why he was there. She knelt down.

"Boy… Open your eyes," she said firmly as she lifted his head. "Open your eyes." Slowly the boy focused on the honey-brown eyes gazing down on him.

"I… where is Medusa?" His voice was barely audible as he felt the world spinning around him and pain shooting through his body.

"I know why you are here, boy, but your purpose is misguided. Be silent and we will take you to have your wounds treated."

"Wait, no… I must *speak* to her! *Medusa!*" He tried to find the strength to stand but was too weak and dizzy. Soteria nodded to the guards to take him away. A guard took each limb as they carried him off while he struggled.

"No, *wait!*" shouted Medusa, "*Don't hurt him!*"

Everyone turned in dismay while Xenophoni tried to hold Medusa back before she said or did something she would later regret. Medusa pushed through the wall of guards and took his hand, "Iasonnas, *why* did you do this?"

Why did you not just go home! Now, you are injured! *Why?*" She tried to remain strong but soon blue tinted tears began to stream down her beautiful face. The guards lowered him to the ground.

"*Medusa…*" Iasonnas could not help but smile at the sight of the one he thought he may never see again.

"Just lie still, Iasonnas. They will take you to the physician to mend your wounds."

"No, Medusa *wait…* Please understand me — I *beg* you — do not refuse me again!" Iasonnas said, sitting up and taking Medusa's hand.

Outraged, Soteria commanded the guards to push him down and then signalled two of her acolytes to hold Medusa back.

"Medusa, resume your place immediately, lest this unfortunate incident tarnish your reputation!" the High Priestess warned.

"I just want the physician to tend to his wounds, Priestess. He is my friend and he is lying here injured because of me."

"We will discuss this later! Now, take your place and I will see that he is properly taken care of!" Medusa gave a lingering glance to Soteria and then peered once more at the broken, bleeding Iasonnas.

"Of course, High Priestess. As you command."

Iasonnas attempted to get up, however, the guards kept him at bay with the butt of their spears.

"Medusa, please do not *leave*! If you turn me away today, tomorrow dawn will arrive without me, for my soul will be at the western gates of Hades!!"

Pushing away their weapons, Iasonnas struggled with his captors.

Medusa calmly replied, "You must leave me, Iasonnas. *Please*! I do not want to see you hurt, but I cannot love you. My place is here." Medusa turned away, as one of the guards delivered a sadistically bone crunching blow to Iasonnas' ribs. The pain from the strike paled in comparison to the agony of Medusa's hurtful words. No longer struggling, he allowed the soldiers to carry him away. His heart bursting, his dreams shattered, he had been betrayed by his one true friend; the woman he deeply and devotedly loved for so long.

Medusa fought back the tears as High Priestess Soteria took her into her private chamber to question her about her unacceptable behaviour. Medusa explained that she and Iasonnas were just childhood friends, denying any present involvement. Soteria said it was beyond her province to decide her Fate, having chosen to convene the Peleiades of Thesmoi. These four Gerontise Elders, were once High Priestesses of Athens who now served as arbiters of Holy Temple Law. They would decide if Medusa would remain or be banished from the Priestesshood.

Led into a small, dark room lit only by a portal in the ceiling, Medusa was instructed to sit directly in the beam of incoming light. Medusa felt her body go numb as one of the four lifted her white robe and closely examined her body to assure she had not been violated. Satisfied that Medusa was undamaged by any man, the procedure continued.

"This boy who pursues you. Who is he to you?" asked one.

"Just a childhood friend, Priestess. A boy I knew while growing up." She tried to defend herself while remaining vague; she feared they might read her thoughts or set out to prove exactly who he was.

"And, you did nothing to encourage this boy? To... lure his attention?" asked another.

"No, my Priestess. Nothing."

"So, this was not the boy you were seen conversing with on the Temple steps?" asked the third.

"Yes, Priestess, However, I was only greeting a childhood friend who had come to see me after a long journey away."

The three whispered amongst themselves.

"In our experience, a boy such as this, does not make such a nuisance of himself without encouragement."

"I swear, Priestesses, I offered no encouragement. Perhaps it was the fatigue of the long journey... days spent under the burning sun."

"Perhaps..." said one of the priestesses, unconvinced. "You may go."

Medusa slowly left the chamber, questioning her place in the Priestesshood. *Had she made a mistake which could never be forgiven?* Having missed the grand proceedings, Medusa now stood outside the Temple as the hot dry morning turned into a humid and windy afternoon. The sky now dark, the sea winds sent thick, black clouds roaring in. Medusa stood pale and grim as she braved the coming storm, the rains now washing away her makeup as the cool, refreshing drops caressed her anguished face. As she looked to the skies in prayer, her beautiful green eyes intensified and brightened, tears beginning to fall once more. With her Fate now lying in the hands of four Peleiades of Thesmoi, the arbiters of Holy Temple Law, she felt her place slipping away from her. While not long ago, all she had wanted was to become a Holy Priestess of the Temple of Athena — to devote herself to the spiritual life dedicated to the Gods — she now wondered at what price she had attained it. How many hearts would be broken, how many lives altered, even ruined.

Far across the city, Iasonnas too, had been caught in the storm. Instructed to leave Athens and never return under penalty of death, he reached the city limits without looking back. His lips silent, his heart empty, and his body broken, he slowly guided his horse west, stopping at the sea's edge where he stood and faced the great wide waters that were just as gray and cruel as the angry skies above. His body aching with every movement, he swayed in the wind's pitiless power, feeling himself about to fall with each gust. He gazed into the churning waters as the waves spoke to him.

He could hear them singing a sweet melody from their dark and stormy depths. Sirens began calling him with their alluring, ethereal song. A symphony of voices now echoed as their beautiful faces began to emerge, smiling invitingly from within the waters rage. They raised their waiting arms to him, beckoning him closer with their beautiful naked bodies, "Come join us, Iasonnas. We will forever love you. We are dedicated to you and only you."

Then, as a mighty bolt of lightning struck the sea's surface, it suddenly turned bright blue and the beautiful images turned into the malevolent scorn of an angry Poseidon who appeared to re-mind Iasonnas that his feeble attempts to win his love were foolish.

"I warned you, **boy**! She will **never** have you, now!" Poseidon gloated. "She will **never** have you, now!"

He now knew Poseidon was right. Medusa had made it clear that she would never leave the Priestesshood for him. Now that he had betrayed her and made a fool of himself, all hope was gone. Looking west, Iasonnas spotted Mount Hymettus on the horizon and set course for it. Reaching the foot of the ancient peak, he tied his horse to a felled tree and looked up at the top. As the sea wind whipped through in his long, black locks, and ominous storm clouds mounted their assault from above, he set his sights on the summit. Bruised and battered he struggled to reach the top of this towering precipice that reached high into the heavens, losing his footing several times. Approaching the precipice, he stood at the edge and looked down at the crashing waves below. With nothing but misery in his heart and soul, he commended his spirit to the Gods.

CHAPTER ELEVEN

Athena Nike: Patron Goddess of the city of Athens, protector and keeper of the city's sons and daughters. Ruler of Justice and the guiding conscience of all those loyal to her infinite wisdom and moral judgment. This deity, is to whom Medusa had dedicated her mortal life, her chastity, her industry and her heart's desire. In honour of the Goddess Most Holy, Medusa had many times reached deep into her soul, enduring unthinkable personal tribulations, that she might bring enlightenment to her people through her mysterious gifts of prophecy and visions.

Unbeknownst to her however, she had been under the Great Goddess' ever-watchful eye even before her fateful arrival in the Holy City. Knowing from the beginning, the Fate of this immortal creature turned fragile earthling, Athena had been keeping a jaundiced eye on this exception to the rules. Never before had an immortal child conceived of darker forces, been granted such an amazing gift; an opportunity to live amongst the humans in a life that could hold a brand new Fate and redeem humankind's mortal souls. This alone was enough to give Athena pause, reason to follow Medusa through the events of her mortal life.

Were the children of Gaia deceiving their mother? Did they, by false pretence, use the Great Mother's kindness to form an alliance that would ultimately turn the tables between the Gods of light and the Gods of darkness? For what other reason would Ceto wish this mortal life upon her last child? The decision and dedication to her plan, seemed more than suspect to the Goddess of Wisdom. Thus, she had been watching Medusa intensely. From the moment she had been presented to the earthly couple, Athena had witnessed her grow. For if Medusa's human existence was the key to unlocking the secret, then Athena, the Goddess of Wisdom, would be the ever-vigilant guardian of that lock. A lock she intended to guard just as the High Priestesses of the Temple of Athena guarded her sacred purity.

Athena was not the only one watching from high above.

As she had long known, the Great God Most High, Poseidon, had also been following Medusa with an ardent eye, though his thoughts were far from apprehensible of Athena. Drawn to Medusa's enchanting beauty and ocean-green eyes, a net had been cast over the God of the Sea's cold heart, as nothing and no one ever had done before.

Poseidon knew Medusa quite well, thanks to Iasonnas and his frequent visits to his Temple. And from the boy's first impassioned utterance about this ethereal creature most divine, the Great God's curiosity had been piqued; curious as to what had inspired the young mortal boy to act so foolishly — so *recklessly* in his very sight. So, as Medusa bathed in a fresh water pond outside Athens, Poseidon paid her a visit. There he discovered for himself her pure and flawless white skin, with neither a scar nor blemish. He saw with his own fiery eyes her hair that flowed in golden waves — indeed worthy of a Goddess — that had so captured Iasonnas' heart. So Poseidon too fell beneath her mortal spell. Gazing upon her undeniable beauty, he saw a face so lovely that neither human nor immortal beings could resist. There and then, he decided that no mere mortal was deserving of one so fair. She must be the consort of a God! Never had mortal or God captured his heart as she had.

Her very essence drew him closer; invited him to come near to behold the wondrous beauty with which Gaia had blessed her. Never a patient God, Poseidon was not content to worship Medusa from afar. His heart and lust urged him to venture closer. So as she stood in the cool and refreshing water, he struck his trident to the ground and caused the earth to shake violently, opening by his command and causing Medusa to be drawn down into its murky depths. So quickly was she pulled down into the pool of water that she had no time to react; just as he had planned.

Transforming himself into a powerful, dark stallion, the cunning Poseidon galloped by the sinking torrent of water, bending his neck low so that Medusa could reach out and grab his long, dark mane. Pulling herself atop the great beast, he carried her safely to a hilltop where gentle, pale grass rustled in the peaceful breeze. As the earth quieted, her heart raced as she held tightly onto the animal, wondering from where this dark saviour had appeared.

With only her long, wet hair to protect her naked body, Medusa crouched low and led the horse back to the water's edge where her clothing lay. Quickly dismounting, she donned her virginal robes and cinched herself. Seeing that her mysterious saviour appeared to stare at her nakedness, she approached the horse and looked closer into his eyes. Algae green in colour, wild and bright as the sea, they were a hue she had never before seen a horse possess.

"You have such beautiful eyes, my brave hero! I do not know from where you came or how you knew to save me. I thank the Gods that you are a brave and considerate creature! Thank you, my friend!"

Stroking his face in appreciation, she turned and headed for Athens.

This brief encounter with Medusa only impassioned Poseidon's longing for her more. The touch of her soft skin against him had set afire the embers of his smouldering desire; his reasoning now lost amongst the drunken passion that consumed him more with each passing moment. His Godly duties forgotten, his sacred responsibilities ignored, Medusa became Poseidon's sole obsession.

Thus, he planned their next meeting meticulously. He would be patient and wait for the best possible time to reveal his true form to her. After watching her from afar for weeks, he knew well her every move.

Medusa devoted every spare moment of her time to the Great Goddess. She chanted and prayed, gave offerings and voiced devotion beyond any other Priestess the Temple had ever had. Medusa's solitary goal was to please the Goddess and keep her honourable name sacred as it always had been. To offer her talents and gifts to help the loyal followers of the Temple find peace in their souls and understanding in their lives. Each day, when the sun set and her Temple duties were complete, Medusa could be found in the small, circular garden in the centre of the Temple where trees, herbs and shrubs were always in bloom and a spring fed a small reflection pond. Reserved solely for the Temple Priestesses, this garden of tranquillity, with its stone statues and depictions of Athena in her many glorious exploits, had become Medusa's sanctuary; her place of contemplation.

It would be here, Poseidon decided, that he would make himself known to Medusa. Here, where the object of his burning desire would arrive at sundown, to offer her undying devotion to the Goddess.

Choosing a warm, late summer evening when the moon would rise early and the sultry warm breeze would help entice her desires,

Poseidon planned his seduction. He would appear within the garden as Medusa was deep in meditation, and then seal out the rest of the world in a dome of silence so as not to be disturbed while he wooed the fair and chaste Medusa. Watching as she entered the garden alone, he gazed longingly upon her as she placed a blackened clay censor filled with dried olive leaves and myrrh upon the altar and set them alight. She then raised her arms skyward and began her heartfelt chants. Her song, was the sweetest Poseidon had ever heard; strengthening his resolve and spurring him on to act. Emboldened, that no female (human nor immortal) had ever resisted his charms, he would wait no longer to reveal his desire.

His passion brimming, he materialized amongst the fig trees, instantly cloaking the garden from all sight and sound. His approach, he decided, would be slow and gentle so as not to frighten his new love. Medusa sensed a change in the air, the distinct presence of a more powerful force. Turning slowly, she saw a man standing amongst the greenery. It took only a moment for her to realize that he was no ordinary man, but an immortal. She saw the distinctive glow inherent of the Gods and knew by his royal blue robe, this was the Great God of the Seas, Poseidon. His large and imposing figure, stood tall over all mortals. His full beard and wild long locks gave him a beastly appearance; yet his calm eyes told the story of his knowledgeable mind.

Dropping to her knees, she prostrated herself. "Oh, Mighty Poseidon, you have blessed me with your presence, how may I serve you, Lord?"

Poseidon smiled at her display of reverence and replied, "No, Medusa, it is you who have blessed me with your presence! Get up now and approach me!" Taken aback by the God's kind assent,

Medusa did as Poseidon asked and nervously walked towards him.

"Medusa, you see, I have been touched by your presence. And this is not the first time I have been drawn to you... I have desired for a long time, to feel your touch upon my face..." Poseidon took a step toward her and became lost in Medusa's stunning bright eyes. Never on earth or in the sea had he encountered such enthralling eyes. Growing more captivated, Medusa opened her mouth to speak as the God gently took her hand in his and held it tenderly to his chest, "Look into my eyes, Medusa. You have not seen this gaze before?"

Medusa looked deep into Poseidon's eyes and suddenly remembered. Trembling, she felt an overwhelming feeling of dread that crept through her spine. Medusa had realized the tale unfolding before her. Poseidon, the Mighty Lord of the Seas had not appeared before her to confer an import task, but to confess his desire to take as his own this Priestess of the Temple of Athena! The great sense of honour she had felt turned to panic as she saw the lustful look in Poseidon's eyes.

"Please, my Lord Poseidon! You must not go on! I am a Holy Priestess of the Temple of Athena! A pure and chaste servant to glorious Athena *the wise and just*!"

Poseidon let out a boisterous laugh. He knew well, no mortal woman could ever escape a God.

"My child, what I offer you is what you have been seeking all along! I know who you really are, Medusa, Daughter of the Sea! We are one, you and I. You belong with me in the vastness and greatness of my world!" He boisterously declared.

Medusa's breath quickened as her countless visions and dreams began to blend into reality. "No, no, I belong *here*! *This* is my world...

This Temple; this Holy sacrifice is my world! You cannot make me see what has never been!"

Poseidon pulled her close and gazed into her eyes once more. Suddenly, visions of stormy nights and darkened caves, the past and future all dissolved into one cruel and unforgiving vision with terrifying clarity. Her eyes fixed, as if in a trance, her tone became resolutely somber: "The strange woman who taunted me in my dreams all these years, she is no stranger at all! *No*... I feel her now! I see her staring at me... right before me! She mimics my movements! Her *face*! There is something wrong with her *face*! It is pale and grey and her eyes are so *sad*..." Medusa's voice got stronger as she grew panic-stricken, screaming, "**She mirrors my movements! She mirrors my movements!**"

Poseidon looked soberly into Medusa's eyes as he held her wrists tight, aiming to calm her. "Medusa, nothing could ever change your spirit! You have the sun in your heart and the stars in your shining, beautiful eyes! There is no power in creation that could ever change that! But, you are not of this world and your place in this universe is greater than you could ever imagine!"

Medusa saw beyond the insincere deigning Poseidon offered, but could not ignore that he had just confirmed what she had long feared and could not admit to herself. "**This other being inside me!**" She turned and peered into the water flowing from the spring, her eyes swelling with tears as her thoughts rushed through her mind at lightning speed. Slowly, an image emerged from the gentle ripples that radiated across the surface of the water. It was Medusa's own tearful face, peering down grieved and sombre, her hopes for the future destroyed.

Now, Poseidon's quest to conquer Medusa began. His shocking revelations resounded in her troubled mind, her attention was all his. He began:

"Medusa, my beautiful child, do not despair, for there are those of our true world who love you and who you will learn to love as well!" He turned her around and took her anguished face in his powerful hands. His eyes filled with mounting desire, he said, "*I am one of those who love you, Medusa.* I have watched you from afar for such a long time. Desired you so strongly that my passion fuelled the ocean waves to rise higher than temples and smash into the shores with the force of a thousand hurricanes! Medusa, if I do not have you now, my passion could turn to rage — such a rage as never before seen on this mortal world! The oceans will turn dark and furious! The land will shake mercilessly and every mortal man will feel the wrath of Poseidon! This is how strong my desire is for you, Medusa!"

Backing away, Medusa pressed her quaking body against the cold, stone wall as Poseidon inched nearer. No match for a God, she pleaded: "Poseidon, I beg you to stop now! You say that you love me, then you must understand that this act you are about to force upon me will kill my soul! I am a Priestess! A Holy Priestess of the Temple of Athena! If you take that away from me then I will die inside, becoming nothing more than an empty shell!"

Medusa's eyes bled streams of tears down her delicate face. A look of utter terror came across her as her entire body shook and trembled. His desire set, Poseidon took Medusa in his powerful arms and held her to his naked chest, caressing her tender, white neck. "I can show you wonders your heart has never even dreamed!"

"*Please stop, please... **I beg you**!*" she screamed.

Struggling as he wrapped her body around his, he took her to a bed dressed in white satin that suddenly appeared on the garden floor. Though screaming inside, not a single word would come from her paralyzed lips. She looked up at Athena's the stone white face, begging her for help, but the statue's cold visage stared outward, silent to her pleas. In horror, Medusa watched from outside herself as two bodies struggled in an eternity of pain. There she stood watching Poseidon thrust into her body, her arms pinned to the bed, with no thought of the damage he wreaked. And there Medusa lay unmoving, tears rolling down her cheeks as she pleaded with Athena to intervene. A moment later, it was done. His lust satisfied, Poseidon released her. But she could not move. Mouthing silent prayers, she believed the Great Goddess would come to her even now. Her prayers, however had fallen on deaf ears as the Goddess Medusa had cherished, had witnessed with glee and satisfaction, the whole degrading violation.

Long had Athena suspected Medusa's guise to be more than it seemed. Though a Priestess for a short time, stories of Medusa's beauty matching or even besting Athena's immortal beauty, were already spreading throughout Greece. Comparing Godly beauty with that of a mortal was more than an insult, it was blasphemy! Sacrilege! An attack on her authority! And not one Athena would tolerate, especially from the daughter of Ceto!

Athena had come to believe that Ceto and Phorcys had devised a plan to overthrow the Gods. By placing this child amongst the mortals with an outer mask of unmatched beauty and charm, ready to beguile all men to her cult while possessing secret powers of a Goddess, a new form of deity could be created! One stronger than any seen in heaven or on earth before! And so, this… *this* was the moment Athena had long waited for! The chance to expose Medusa for who she really was and allow the Fates to take action upon her! For surely, if the people knew the truth, that Medusa was nothing more than a hideous, blood-thirsty monster, they would hunt her down like the foul demon she truly is!

Unveiling herself from behind her shield of invisibility, Athena gracefully floated down from above, a look of satisfaction on her lovely face. Just as depicted on every bust, in hundreds of temples across the Greek lands, Athena Polias, was an ethereal beauty, a just and virtuous deity whom all could visibly see wisdom and fairness through piercing blue eyes that judged the misgivers of the land.

Upon seeing this holy vision before her, a look of hope came over Medusa, believing her saviour had come to her side at last. For if Athena failed to prevent Poseidon's crime, then at least now, she was here to heal the wounds and amend what was woefully stolen from Medusa.

Covering her bare breasts with her torn robe, she bowed dutifully before the Goddess; shaken by Athena's almighty presence, she never dared look up at her illuminated face. Unmoved by the sight of Athena, who he had always considered a pretentious bore, Poseidon stepped back from Medusa and conjured up his Godly armour and trident. He looked down at Athena with a self-satisfied gaze. Although he burned inside for Medusa's heartache, he knew that now that the deed was done, she could take her rightful place at his side as the Goddess of the Seas. In time she would forget the silly mortal games, and learn to play and use her powers as they were intended.

Silence befell the Temple; even the sound of Medusa's weeping ceased as Athena stood before them with a condemning scowl.

Poseidon spoke: "So nice of you to make yourself visible at last, Athena! Did you enjoy the… *performance*?! I thought you would never dare make your presence known before such beauty, knowing that all men will judge in favour of the fairest!" Poseidon nodded towards Medusa.

Medusa's eyes opened wide as she repeated Poseidon's words in her mind, '*Make yourself seen at last?' Could it be? Did Athena witness this horrible sacrilege and do nothing to save her most devoted follower?*

Athena's anger could be contained no longer. She raised her arm and commanded, "***Silence!***" The Temple shook and trembled as her malice towards them grew. Poseidon smiled and allowed Athena to speak.

"Rise to your feet, Medusa, child of Ceto and Phorcys!"

Medusa did as she was told and stood silently staring at the Goddess with a look of hurt and disillusion; her heart pounding, her breath deep and hard. Athena continued, "I have watched you most warily since your arrival upon this earth, Medusa. Waiting for the time of judgment when I would learn with certainty where you stand: in the light of *righteousness*, or in the shadows of **darkness**! There is now no doubt in my mind that you belong in the darkest of places as you have committed the utter most sinful atrocity in my sacred temple!" Athena stepped forward, majestically towering over the cowering Medusa. "Prepare for your verdict and judgment!"

Lost for words, feeling pain and panic as never before, Medusa stared wide-eyed at the Deity, who she had long believed was her unflinching protector and guardian, now a judge and holder of her Fate. Medusa fell to her knees and held one hand high towards Athena as the other clutched her torn robe. "I beg you, Athena, *please*, do not bring punishment and more shame upon me! I implore you! I should not be held to blame for this malicious attack! I am true to *you*, Athena! I will always be your humble servant!"

Medusa's impassioned plea meant nothing to Athena who was not about to squander this long-awaited opportunity to remove from the world, this extraordinary beauty. Should Medusa keep hold of her pure state of beauty and grace, then her standing as a High Priestess would grow amongst the people of Athens, becoming a much greater threat to Athena and all the Gods Most High. As one with such extraordinary power, Medusa's words could become law, her teachings dictating belief — *for* the Gods or *against* them. As Athena knew well, word of Medusa's gift of prophesy was already spreading insidiously across Greece and soon followers would come, seeking guidance and spiritual teachings. Soon, she would assume the title of the wisest in Athens, a title Athena — the greatest goddess in the universe — would never share with a mere mortal.

"I decree that on this day, the High Priestesses of the Temple of Athena Nike will bear witness to your indiscretion and will pass judgment upon you accordingly, here upon this once sacred ground, which you wilfully desecrated!"

With those words, Athena tore open the veil Poseidon had created and summoned the High Priestesses to enter the garden sanctuary. Selected for their loyalty, purity of thought and action, many were the trials they had faced together. Years were spent in the Temple, praising, praying; serving both God and humankind in the name of Athena, the group of women now included Xenophoni and Melissa, (whose change of attitude had garnered her, great respect and position). Indeed, many were Medusa's closest friends who cared for her deeply; sisters bound in holy mission for all eternally. Others, however, were not so sad to see Medusa facing this punishment. Be it jealousy or ecclesiastic contempt, some were competing for a chance at glory. For a woman to hold such power in the most holy city on earth held glory untold. However, whatever their personal feelings, their loyalty and duty to Athena was absolute. Their destiny declared by the Oracle, they dared not fail the Fates' decree. They now stood inside the dome in formal ritual attire to observe the trial of Medusa.

Athena in her most glorious corporeal form was an overwhelming sight to all. Some could not take their eyes away from the Great Goddess, others dared not look for fear their eyes were not worthy. Poseidon, growing ever tired by Athena's arrogant and grandiose demeanour, broke the reverent silence:

"Stop this farce here and now, Athena, and allow the girl leave with me! She can do you no harm while under my care!"

Unmoved, Athena replied, "Quiet! You have no authority in my city, Poseidon! It is *my* city, *remember*! You lost your power over this land eons ago!" Gripping his trident firmly he growled back, "They call you Athena *Parthenos*, Athena *the Pure*. However, there is nothing *pure* about you, vile reptile of a woman!"

Athena gasped, her persona of serenity and prudence would not be undermined by Poseidon's wounding words. She countered, "You have gone too far, Poseidon, son of *Cronus the Imprisoned*! I hereby **banish** you from my city, never to return. So it shall be done!" Her voice boomed throughout the Temple and echoed down its pristine columns of cold, white stone, shaking the ground beneath their feet.

"You cannot hold me back, Athena! You are no match for **me**! I will shake the earth beneath your feet and topple your precious Temple with a blink of my eye! Let me have the girl now and I will forgive your impudence! Release her to me this instant and I will vow never to enter your city of kowtowing sycophants ever again!"

Athena scoffed, she had had enough of his grandiose insolence. Waving her arms, she cast a veil of her own, bounding Poseidon in a net of golden cords where he would remain until the proceedings were completed and her judgment decreed. Poseidon (though a God whose physical strength rivalled Zeus) could not break free, for even the Gods had rules and restrictions and as Athena knew well, he had already broken more than a few laws of the universe that night. She then turned her gaze upon Medusa who had remained still, silently praying that everything would return to the way it had been. But putting things back to the way they were was far from what Athena had in mind.

Finally after the annoying disruption, Athena spoke to her subordinates:

"Priestesses, behold the one who once vowed to honour and keep eternally pure, this Holiest of sanctuaries!" She pointed contemptuously at Medusa, her eyes a ring of fire. "Now the Fates have unravelled their web and shown us the true face of Medusa!" Athena faced Medusa, her majestic grey eyes meeting Medusa's piecing green glare; full of fear, Medusa knew that Athena held the power of life and death in her capricious hands. Tension mounted as Athena declared:

"Medusa, you have desecrated my Sacred Temple! You have become impure! You have offended this sacred ground which has remained unspoiled for millennia. I find you guilty of this defilement most unholy and of the following crimes: Conspiracy to overthrow the Gods of Olympus… *Guilty*! Entering the Sacred Temple of Nike under a false identity… G*uilty*! Plotting to become the supreme patron deity of my Sacred City, Athens… *Guilty*! And your punishment, Medusa, shall be just and fitting: I pronounce before this convening of the Priestesses of Nike that you shall spend eternity as that which you despise most! Your inner demons shall compliment your outer appearance! The monster that you truly are will be known by all, far and wide, across all the lands! No mortal or God will ever love you again!"

Medusa's eyes filled with tears, her heart beat out of her chest as Athena's decree fell on the ears of all present. Her eyes now glowing a green so bright, that both mortals and Gods would be blinded by their brilliance. She stood alone, broken, in shock and disbelief as she felt her utter powerlessness so acutely. She understood now, the feeling of bitter helplessness that confounded humanity. As her tears poured down, Medusa's body began to shake. She now knew that her life as a human mortal was about to come to an end.

She mustered up the last ounce of dignity she possessed, the only thing that was still under her control and declared:

"Please, Goddess *Most Gracious*, take my life *now* and send my languished soul to the deepest bowels of Hades for all eternity if that will satisfy your judgment! But know this, and know well, all who witness this injustice. I am the sole victim of the horrible act of violence that took place here tonight! I neither desired nor invited it!"

The Priestesses looked on in silence, shaken by Athena's revelations; questions began to fill their thoughts. Soteria, Athena's High Priestess of the Temple stepped forward, wishing to make her thoughts known. Athena turned an authoritative glance: "If you wish to speak, I will grant you a moment; but only one." All the Priestesses watched on in amazement as Soteria spoke openly on Medusa's behalf.

"*Great and Powerful* Athena, my Goddess. As you know well, I have been steadfastly loyal and faithful to you, my entire life. I have never doubted your infinite wisdom, nor will I ever. And for that, I have never asked nor expected anything in return. If I could ask but one consideration, I would ask that you be lenient in judging Medusa. I have come to know this servant of the Temple of Athena well. She is among the most loyal and dedicated disciples ever to grace this Scared Sanctuary and has been of immense service to both the people of Athens and to your most Holy Temple. Her great gift of prophesy has served well, our undertaking to maintain the holy sanctity of Athens and preserve the order of your design within this universe."

Though well-intended, Soteria had unwittingly confirmed what Athena had already assumed, that Medusa was gaining popularity and power among the masses. Unmoved, Athena replied, "And what do you believe would be a fitting punishment?" Cautiously, Soteria replied, "My Goddess, I would humbly suggest banishment from your magnificent city. This alone would punish her as no other pronouncement could."

Athena gave no reply, making her way to a weeping Medusa

who stood trembling. Poseidon, unable to move, stood helplessly witnessing the dispensing of punishment that even he knew was unjust. Standing before her, Athena gave Medusa one last glare as she prepared to pass sentence. Seeing not a drop of compassion in Athena's eyes, Medusa prostrated herself on the cold, stone floor, pressing her lips to Athena's feet. Disgusted by Medusa's impure touch, she shoved her back viciously with her shield; the strike so great, that it sent Medusa reeling through the air, crashing into the fountain and smashing it to pieces. Then, in a movement as quick and decisive as lighting, Athena swung her arms towards Medusa and grabbed her face, sending a surge of white-hot electricity through her fingertips.

Medusa held on tightly so as not to scream as the unbearable pain of transformation began; much to Medusa's terror, the ordeal was just beginning, as Athena's almost limitless power lifted Medusa off the floor and into the air where her half-naked body began to glow with a brilliant blue-green light as electric power coursed all around her body. Expressionless, Athena then placed her thumbs on Medusa's eyes and pressed with all the force at her command. No longer able to endure the pain, Medusa let out a piercing scream that echoed hauntingly through the dome as bolts of lightning turned her flesh transparent. So horrifying was the ordeal that many of the women turned away in shock.

Soon, nothing but Medusa's bones and a transparent outline of her glowing body, remained visible. Building and building in intensity, the energy entering Medusa's body became so powerful, that the light she emanated expanded and filled the dome. Everyone present felt the warmth of the light surrounding their bodies; the warmth of *love* now being drained from her tortured being. Weeping at the sight, High Priestess Paraskevi drew it into her own heart as it surged through the air lest it be forever lost.

Then, within the blink of an eye, the energy disbursed, withdrawing into itself with such force that it sucked all light inwards towards the centre of the garden, pulling with it the veil put in place by Poseidon, until only pitch black darkness prevailed. Fearing they had been blinded, two Priestesses cried out in terror. "*Silence!*" Soteria yelled out in a powerful voice, "Fear not! Your sight has not left you! Face towards the centre of the garden, there is light!" Turning, there, they saw two glowing, green orbs low to the floor that shone with such a powerful glow that they captivated all who set eyes upon them. Then, as all went silent, fixated on this beautiful sight, it vanished just as swiftly as it came. Eventually, under Athena's command, the darkness was illuminated by the appearance of twelve brightly flaming torches. Now all could see Athena standing ominously over Medusa who lay motionless at her feet, face down on the ground in the pool of water, completely covered in a black, satin shroud.

"She is *dead!*" shouted one Priestess with a trembling voice as they all stood looking down at Medusa's unmoving body. "Medusa is *dead!*"

Athena turned and faced Poseidon, smiling haughtily. Some Priestesses wept while others watched curiously as Melissa moved closer to Medusa's lifeless body. However, she had not taken more than a few steps when a moan was heard coming from where Medusa lay. Then, there was a gasping sound as Medusa's head jerked up from the ground.

"Medusa!" Melissa announced.

Slowly placing her hands to the polished stone floor, Medusa raised herself up on her knees, still covered by the satin shroud Athena had draped over her so that her nude, tainted body could no longer desecrate her sacred Temple. She gasped for air and emitted raspy sounds as her hand slid out from beneath the cloth.

"Medusa! Your *hand*... look at your *hand*!" Melissa cried out.

Medusa sat back with her legs folded beneath her, her face still shrouded. Beneath the cloth, she brought her hands to her eyes and saw for the first time what the others could see. Through her fingers she caught a glimpse of her reflection in the pool of water. Incomprehensible sounds rose from Medusa as she rocked child-like back and forth beneath the veil, the sound of whimpering turning to a terrified scream that reverberated throughout the Temple and travelled down into the silent city; her mournful wail was the most horrific sound the people of Athens had ever heard. So piercing to their ears, it filled them with sudden dread and sorrow, that it shook them to the very core of their souls.

Medusa wrapped herself in the long black cloth and fought to gain control of her breathing as she rose to face Athena, inching forward in slow, deliberate steps. Athena stood cold and resolute.

"*Why?! Why*, Athena, would you do this?" Medusa's voice had become all but unrecognizable. It deepened and crackled as her emotions turned darker and filled with mounting rage. "*This* is not *justice*! I have done you no *wrong*! You know well that I have committed no *crime*! No *sin*! And that which you see before you now is merely your *creation*! Your perverse *invention*! First Poseidon savagely *violates* me... and then you viciously *punish* me! This form I now hold and the darkness I now feel inside were all forced upon me by *you*, Athena! And by the Gods, it will become your worst *mistake*!"

Athena remained unimpressed, replying as always with supreme and unwavering authority:

"The *mistake* will be *yours*, Medusa, if you do not leave my sacred city *immediately*! By my good graces, I permitted you to *live*! Do not make me regret that decision for then the *mistake* may fall to others foolish enough to hold you dear! Do not challenge *me* you impudent *child*!"

Medusa held her tongue, knowing that Athena was certainly capable of such a malicious act of violence. She was living proof of it; moving a single step closer, she faced the Goddess and uncovered her head. The Goddesses' eyes widened as Athena saw the depths of Medusa's soul and the source of her new powers: two penetrating eyes that glowed of emerald coloured light so brilliant and penetrating that only a God Most High could set eyes upon them without instantly turning to stone. Masking her eyes with her new black shroud, Medusa turned to leave the Temple now painfully aware of the devastating powers her eyes held over mortals. She had seen it many times in her ghastly visions. And now, the path the Oracle had set her upon, became crystal clear.

Alone and frightened, Medusa followed the path leading from Athens, tears pouring down her ravaged cheeks, her mind a disheartened muddle as she scuffled along. Her bow and quiver and the gold ring given to her by her mother, were all the possessions she had in the world. Snapping it from its chain, she slipped it on her third finger where she now knew it belonged. Reaching the top of the final crest, she paused to take one last look back at the city she loved so dearly and had promised to spend her life protecting. Closing her eyes as she turned away, a single tear rolled down her cheek and fell upon the ground.

Watching from the clouds high above, for the first time in his existence, Poseidon felt shame; deeply regretting his actions and the consequences he had set in motion. His rage uncontrollable, he took Medusa's single tear and rolled it down the path back to Athens. As it rolled, it grew in size and gained such speed that it turned into a raging river that soon rushed ferociously down the hillside, taking with it a swath of trees and every other living thing in its path. Rushing towards the city, a tidal wave rose taller than the tallest trees, widening until it overshadowed the sleepy city. As

Athenians woke to the sun's first faint pink light, they saw the light suddenly blotted out of the sky as a wall of towering black water swept in and devoured the city in the blink of an eye. Catastrophic in destruction, most of the city submerged beneath Medusa's tragic tear.

CHAPTER TWELVE

Aimlessly wandering the valleys and hills, Medusa walked on, lurking in the shadows; hiding from the mortals whose path she crossed. Her mind a tangled web of confusion, she questioned everything she had ever known and believed.

Where do I go now? Home? But, where is my home? Who am I now? Do I still exist beneath this hideous shell?

Her rambling thoughts and answerless questions persisted for days untold. Medusa no longer felt the need for sleep nor rest nor food. At times she questioned if she were still alive and at these times she would hold her pale grey hands to her chest and feel the beating of a broken heart.

There... There is proof that I still live, I still breathe and feel and want; but why? Why live and breathe and want, in a world that is not my own? In an existence that betrays me with every breath and crushes my every want?

Despairingly she trod barefoot, on the cold mossy grounds of a fog laden lagoon. Her mind a flutter, her heart heavy, like a hazy dream her eyes saw only shadows and blurs of reality.

However, what is want? A selfish and childish emotion, an urge, a pull that blinds you from the truth… I WANT we proclaim! And if we want then we MUST have and if we do not receive then we curse the gods for ignoring our pleas. Adversely if we receive, then we praise and spread the word that the gods are good and the gods have mercy…Are the gods really so fickle? Or can it be, that we speak only to ourselves? Is it really we, who control the fates?

Coming out of the marshes, she walked long across a cool stone path. Smooth and red, she followed the path up until she reached upon a cold and damp cavern set atop a tall mountain overlooking a sprawling meadow. She took refuge in the darkness, staring at the vast emptiness of her surroundings. Days passed, yet she remained motionless; sitting still, the events of her life crossed again and again before her mind's eye. All that she had ever accomplished now seemed insignificant; pointless.

Is there a point to anything we do? Can there be a reason that the fates favour some and abandon all others in hopelessness? There is no logic to this world!

Setting out again across the vast countryside, her feet seemed to choose their own path. Seemingly fixed on leading her home, they pulled her onward, sometimes against her will. Allowing the fickle Fates to light her path, she fought the urge to see her family once more. She knew it was best to stay away for their sake. Finding respite and peace of mind only in the darkness, she spent many days in the caves she came upon, traveling only in the darkness when she could pass unnoticed.

One such day as the sun rose high in the sky, she heard the scrambling of footsteps approaching the grotto she had been holed-up in. Remaining still and silent in the shadows, she watched as a small herder boy of perhaps eight or nine years entered carrying food wrapped in a cloth. Planning to eat his meal in the coolness of the shade, the boy began humming a happy little tune as he sat on the cold stone floor; he unwrapped his meal while keeping a watchful eye on his charges below. Medusa watched curiously as the boy sat unaware of the monstrous observer lurking in the darkness behind him. He ate his bread and olives as he kicked his legs playfully at the hardened soil of the cliff's edge. With each olive he consumed, he threw the pit over his shoulder and into the dark recesses of the cave, some barely missing Medusa or landing at her feet. Amused at his innocence yet weary of being discovered, Medusa just looked on in silence.

Once the boy had finished his meagre meal, he lied back on the dusty stone and closed his eyes; taking a small rest before going back to his herd. Almost asleep, he felt something hit him on the cheek. Startled, he swung his head around to see what it was. Though he saw nothing, he felt a presence within the cave and so decided to call out.

"Hello?! Is somebody there?"

Though his curiosity had been met with silence, his inquisitiveness led him quite dangerously to explore the cave further to find who or what was lurking in the shadows. Mountain goats and sheep often wandered from the flocks and found their way to places such as this, so he thought it likely one of the flock was there; perhaps injured. With no exit for Medusa, she quickly scuffled behind a rock as the boy drew near. He heard movement.

"Why are you hiding from me? I will not hurt you," he said innocently.

"Go away, little boy. Let me be!"

Taking no exception to her unusually raspy voice, he caught sight of the bow lying close by in the stream of light.

"You are an archer! I would *love* to be an archer! I would be a good one too, maybe a great soldier of Athens. But my father has me watching these dumb, smelly sheep all day!" He ventured closer to get a better look at her bow and Medusa quickly reached out and snatched the weapon before the boy could lay hands on it.

"This is not a toy. You should go back to your sheep now."

Curious to get a closer look, the boy leaned in and said, "Could I have an arrow then? Just *one*… one to take home? I promise I will not tell a soul where I got it from."

"No! Little boy, please go away!"

"But… you do not have any food or water in here… you must be hungry! Wait here and I will be back later!" With that the boy rushed off down the hill leaving Medusa unnervingly rattled by their brief encounter. It had been her first encounter with a human mortal since her transformation and she had been frightened for both the boy and herself. A few hours had passed and Medusa decided it was time to leave as darkness began to fall upon the land. If one human had found her hiding place, perhaps others would, too. When the boy saw his new mysterious friend taking the eastbound path in the distance, he ran after her calling, "Wait! I have brought you some food! Please, do not leave. I have told no one!"

Bothered by this small boy's unrelenting presence, she raised her bow when he approached as if to strike him. The boy did not move or even cringe. He just gazed at her with a trusting innocence that only a child could have. Looking at her face hidden behind the black shroud, he asked, "Are you hurt? I… I can go and bring back medicine if you want me to. Or… anything else you need!"

Suddenly, Medusa broke down in tears and the boy sat down beside her.

"It is alright to be sad. When I am sad, I just go to my sister. My mom is not with us anymore, but as long as I have someone who loves me, pretty soon I am not sad anymore. I know my sister will love me no matter what." He laid his hand gently on her arm. "Who loves *you*? Maybe you should go to see them?"

Who *did* love Medusa now? She did not know. Her sisters were now married and raising families of their own. Her loving grandmother had surely passed on, and her mother and father were now quite old and weak; she dare not risk seeing them. *Iasonnas?* He had loved her once, but what of him, now? Did he hate her as he had reason to? After some thought, she knew where her path had to lie.

"I think it is time for me to go home, boy. I am going home."

Reaching into her quiver, she pulled out an arrow and handed it to him. "Perhaps one day you will become a great archer, as you desire!" Medusa took the fastest route across the land that she knew. Over the hills and through the open expanses of the barren wilderness she ran through the darkness, hiding in the shadows when the sun rose, setting out again when the sun set. Across the land she ran without rest, still feeling neither thirst nor hunger. Finally, she found herself once again on the outskirts of her childhood home, Avernae. As she looked out over the countryside excitedly, it was exactly as she remembered it. Looking down from the hill above, she saw no one on the road to Iasonnas' family home, so through the darkness she crept to take a closer look.

Her heart racing as she neared the house, she peered in through the window and found a cosy fire in the hearth and oil lamps lighting the rooms. A warmth emanated that she had not felt for many years; not the warmth of flickering flames, but from the memories now flooding back into her mind. Uncertain of what she might find inside, she crouched beneath a sprawling old olive tree, praying that Iasonnas would be there. And moments later, her spirit soared as she heard a familiar voice inside.

Though deeper and time worn, his voice lit lightly upon her ears like a sweet, long-forgotten melody. From her hiding place, she watched as a beautiful, golden-haired woman walked by and lovingly embraced a robust and handsome Iasonnas in her arms.

As she had prayed, Iasonnas had indeed abandoned thoughts of ending his life that terrible day in Athens and had gone on to build a wonderful new life for himself. He now seemed to have what he needed most, a glorious farm and a beautiful, loving wife. As Medusa peered deeper into the rooms, she caught sight of several small, bouncing faces. Yes, Iasonnas had a family.

Tears of joy and relief swelled in Medusa's anguished eyes as her blessings and prayers for a better life for Iasonnas, had proven true. Now, confusion set in, as Medusa began to contemplate if her plan to meet Iasonnas, had really been such a good idea after all. The thought that her re-appearance could disrupt Iasonnas' blissful existence, troubled Medusa deeply. Re-living a broken heart that could lead to a broken family, she now realized, was not a risk she was prepared to take. Distressed by the mistake almost made, Medusa turned to leave this happy home. She vowed never to be weak or selfish and succumb to seeing Iasonnas again. But, as she quietly made her way through the orchard, she suddenly heard a shout from within the home. One of the children had caught sight of the strange green glow emanating from Medusa's deadly eyes and had alerted Iasonnas of an outsider.

Hiding her face beneath the black shroud that had now become her protective mask, she ran off into the night, her heart beating as loudly as the drums of an approaching army. It was too late. Seeing movement through the trees, Iasonnas picked up a scythe from the porch and closed the door behind him, telling his boys to stay in and keep their mother safe. Like a shot, he tore off into the shadows of the night.

Shouting, "*Stop!*" at the top of his lungs, Iasonnas attempted to overtake the figure that moved with almost superhuman speed. Now, more than ever, Medusa knew she had to get away. As the intruder headed up into the hills and quickly reached the orchard beyond the boundaries of his land, Iasonnas wondered if he should continue to give chase as it seemed he had already succeeded in protecting his home. After all, he thought, maybe it was just a harmless traveller passing through; a wanderer, or pilgrim on their way to Athens who just needed a resting place. Still, his curiosity of this extraordinarily swift figure drew him to follow it into the hills. The way it moved was unlike any man nor beast Iasonnas had ever seen.

Reaching the crest of the first rise, Iasonnas paused by a eucalyptus tree to catch his breath. Looking down at the stream flowing below and then back up into the hills, he spotted the figure moving swiftly to higher ground. Unable to let it go, he took a deep breath and resumed the chase, trying ever harder to keep an eye fixed on the figure as he sped through the jagged rocks and slippery slopes, the gap between them seeming too close. With just a pous between them, he watched in astonishment as the dark figure leapt into the air and landed some distance away. Iasonnas realized it had hurdled an open ravine! Coming to the chasm edge, he stopped, backed up a few steps and determined now to catch up, took a giant leap. Knowing that no human could possibly span such a great distance, Medusa stopped in fear for her old friend's life. In the blink of an eye, she watch as Iasonnas fell into the darkness below.

Without thought, she leaped out to catch him but it was too late. At the bottom, Medusa leaned over him and put her ear to his chest. She heard a heartbeat. Thankfully, though Iasonnas lay unconscious, he had only had the wind knocked out of him. The soft, moist moss of the stream bank had cushioned his fall. Quickly picking him up in her arms which she discovered was incredibly easy, she carried Iasonnas to a spot beneath a rock ledge illuminated by the Moon. Carefully laying him down, she caressed his handsome face while studying every perfect feature of her old, beloved friend. She had not realized just how badly she had missed Iasonnas until this very moment, now feeling the beating of his warm heart against her cold chest. The urge to look into his magnificent eyes of heliopora coral had never been so strong. Yet Medusa knew the horrible fate that Iasonnas would face if she did.

Pain surged deep into her lonely heart as she slowly released him from her embrace. She looked upon his face one last time as she prepared to leave, before putting him in further danger. As she stood, Iasonnas reached out and latched onto her wrist tightly. Quickly closing her eyes, she faced away as she felt herself lose all strength and the will to escape his grip. As his eyes slowly focused, he looked up at his captive and saw a sight even more unexpected than his own near death.

"Medusa?" He whispered, thinking he may be seeing a vision.

Medusa did not speak but tears began to pour profusely from her eyes; for the first time in a very long while, she felt truly and horribly human again as tears of joy filled Iasonnas' eyes when they fell upon a sight dreadfully wrong. Though the creature that stood before him was clearly his long lost love, the alarming greyness of her skin was not from shadows cast by the pale Moon light nor tricks played by his eyes. His mind spinning, his thumb glided lightly over her arm as he held her tightly. His heart pained as he gasped and his throat caught. Her once soft and supple skin was now rough and cold to the touch. Pulling her arm into the moon-light, he saw not the gentle, white hands of the Medusa he knew, but the disfigured claws of a horrible, terrifying monster. Though his first thought was to recoil in horror, his curiosity compelled him to pull her closer instead. With her eyes closed tightly, he stared at her turned face, unbelieving of what his eyes told him. He lifted his hand to her face and gently touched it. Medusa shuddered and began to weep as the gentle warmth of his touch on her harsh and cold grey skin moved her heart in a way she had thought she would never feel again.

Trembling, Iasonnas carefully guided Medusa's head in his direction, quickly releasing her when it came into view. He held his hand over his mouth as tears streamed down his cheeks. What was once a living image of a pure goddess, had now been masked by the dark vision of a demon. Emotions pouring out from within his tears, he tried to find his voice. Quivering, he managed to say, "*Medusa*... what, by the Gods, has *happened* to you?"

Medusa shook her head and turned away, pulling her veil over her face. Looking her up and down, Iasonnas tried to fathom what he was seeing. His mouth opened again and again, trying to find words to speak. "Why... *why* will you not open your eyes?" he said as tears poured out as hard as did hers. Though Medusa tried to explain, the unbearable truth, kept her silent. Keeping a firm, tight grip on her arm, Iasonnas slowly began to pull the shroud from her head. With a frightful hiss and a rattle, he felt something move beneath the cloth and quickly loosened his grip. Medusa pulled free and stood up, turning her back to him.

"*Look* at me Medusa! *Please!*" he said, getting to his feet.

"Look into my eyes and tell me what has happened to you! No matter what it is, I promise I will not judge you nor turn away! I am your friend!" Iasonnas gently placed his hands on Medusa's quivering shoulders. "Turn and look at me, Medusa," he said, attempting to force her to turn around. Stepping away, she spoke with a controlled whisper so as not to frighten him with the cruel harshness of her voice.

"I can never look into your eyes again, Iasonnas. *Never!*"

His confusion growing, Iasonnas thought of the only possible reason she would say such words. "Is it because of our last meeting? Is it *shame*, Medusa?" Medusa stood silent. "Please forget the past, Medusa. We are both much older and wiser now! Much has happened in both our lives! I feel no hurt or disappointment, now! Just, look at me and explain the sight I see."

"I can never look into any mortal's eyes again, Iasonnas, for Athena has commanded that my eyes be the sight of death. The very last sight any man would see before turning to a pillar of stone!"

"Athena? *She* has done this to you? But… *why*? *Why* would she do such a thing?! You have spent a lifetime devoted to her, giving up your own life in her honour! What do you mean by this?"

Resolved to show her old friend the creature she had now become, Medusa said, "Follow me, Iasonnas and I will show you." Medusa led him back down to the stream and stood in the flowing water, her robe and shroud gently moving with the motion of the ripples. Iasonnas followed and stood beside her on the stream's bank. "Stop there. Now, look into the water, Iasonnas, for your answer. Look into my reflection. But I warn you, no matter what you see, do not turn your gaze upon me!" Trusting his friend, he did as she asked. Gazing curiously into the moonlit stream at Medusa's distorted reflection, he waited for her to reveal her great secret. As she removed her veil and opened her eyes, the over-powerful glow within her, reflected brilliantly upon the water's surface, her sombre expression showing her, as she was now. She was a *Gorgon*! A frightful creature known to all of Greece! Her silken fair hair was no longer; it was replaced with a mysterious mist of dark water that moved gently, as the sea did at night. Within this dark mist, vicious black snakes hissed and curled across her head. Her once luscious lips were turned pale and cold as stone with sharp fangs that rested on each side of her bottom lip. From all that Iasonnas could see, nothing drew his attention more than her luminous emerald eyes whose reflexion was broken by the ripples of the stream.

Iasonnas understood that no further words needed to be spoken as he saw the pain and terror in his friend's eyes, even through this monstrous reflection. He reached out and held her hand tenderly in the babbling silence.

CHAPTER THIRTEEN

The next morning Iasonnas rose early to meet Medusa in her hiding place. Not a moment did he sleep as the thrill of the night before, kept him awake. Stories of Gods and of Medusa's true beginning, her transformation, old feelings of love and hate resurfaced; all of these events, kept his mind astir. The image of her ravaged face was now burned in his mind; the beauty that once was, now hidden somewhere beneath the monstrous mask Athena had so unjustly created.

Seldom was he untruthful to his wife; however, that night, he had promised to keep Medusa's presence a secret for everyone's safety. He explained away his lengthy absence during the night, as watchful vigilance. After all, the intruder could have returned in the night and he needed to be there to catch them. Never did he think he would find himself in such a thorny situation; his love for Medusa had resurfaced as strong as ever, but so had his deep disdain. Hatred, that had taken root years before when she stood by and allowed the Athenian guards to forcefully remove him, had grown and festered in his heart and mind. The anger that had seeded deeply inside him now had many layers. His reaction surprised him because he began to realise that hurt changes over time; unresolved anger grows and burns a silent smouldering fire that can arise without warning and consume you at any time... All of these thoughts, feelings and more, circled around Iasonnas' mind as he made the pre-dawn hike into the hills where Medusa was lying in wait under cover.

He prepared a large white sack of food, carefully wrapped and tied, to present to Medusa. As he approached the densely wooded area, he stopped and turned his eyes to the ground. Medusa had told him to stand in that very spot and look nowhere but downward, lest he risk being turned to stone. Medusa had been watching, even as he approached. As she sat high up on the hillside, she thought about her reunion with Iasonnas the night before, still with a mixture of feelings, doubt and concern. She questioned her selfishness for risking Iasonnas' life this way. All she knew for certain was that now, she was not alone and a friend was what she needed most. Though he stood calling out her name softly, she did not want to respond just yet; content with just watching him from afar. She watched and let her troubled mind reminisce a little longer about more innocent times in their lives. Her memories were interrupted as Iasonnas impatiently turned his gaze in her direction. So she quickly covered her face just as he looked back down towards the ground. Approaching him from behind, he heard her footfalls and spoke:

"Did you sleep well, Medusa?"

"I... Do not sleep anymore Iasonnas. You?"

"I do not think I slept at all."

"Do you think your wife suspects?"

"I do not think so. She is a very trusting woman and she has no reason to doubt me... but... Medusa, what happens now? What will you do? Where will you go?"

Medusa shook her head. "I do not know, Iasonnas. I thought coming here might give me perspective. But, where in this world is there a place for a hideous monster? A *Gorgon?*"

Bothered by her harsh self-reproach, Iasonnas closed his eyes and swiftly turned towards her. "Medusa you are *not* a monster. It pains me to hear you speak of yourself that way!"

Medusa quickly lowered her veil. "Iasonnas, I believe you saw enough to know I am not the woman I once was. I… "

Iasonnas interrupted, "But, you *are* beautiful, Medusa! I do not believe some *spell* cast by an angry goddess could ever *really* change you!"

Medusa smiled as her tears began to flow once more.

"Iasonnas, you do not understand. The monster is not what you see before you now, hidden behind this veil. It is on the *inside* of me. There is a rage and darkness no human could ever imagine. My soul, if I still have one, is black and hollow, I fear. Sometimes I can hardly control the fury within me and day by day it only worsens! I no longer feel like myself, Iasonnas. I am *changed… damaged… unsettled.* Sometimes I feel it is not safe for others to be around me."

"But… you would not hurt *me,* would you, Medusa?" Iasonnas said, hiding a sudden twinge brought on by the mere thought, of further betrayal.

Medusa paused then reluctantly replied, "I do not know, Iasonnas. I have hurt you before. I do not know what I am capable of. I am not always in control of my thoughts… my emotions."

Iasonnas' smile faded as his thoughts were taken back to the dark past. "Medusa, you cannot hurt me anymore. Nothing could wound me greater than the knife you set into my heart that night in Athens. I… too, am changed."

Medusa took a step back and looked at Iasonnas as if she could see into his ocean blue eyes at the pain they held, even through her shroud. "Iasonnas…"

"I know, Medusa, I should not speak of the past. That is behind us now. But for many years, that hurt, burned inside me, silently, it smouldered. There was so much I needed to say, so many heartfelt questions to ask. But you would not hear me, Medusa. You were not there for me and I could not go back to Athens; not after that terrible day; being shamed that way. Even now, there is one question above all, that I *must* have answered and I need you to answer it with complete honesty. I ask only the *truth*."

Medusa knew she owed him answers and so much more. "If that is what you need, Iasonnas, I will surely give that to you."

Iasonnas spoke quickly before his chance was lost. "Medusa, did you wonder of my Fate that night? When I was taken to the city limits broken and beaten, humiliated beyond all reason, was it of any concern to you that I might end my life there and then? It *is* what I had planned."

Medusa replied self-assuredly, "No, I did not wonder… as I knew my prayers and blessings would guide your judgment and protect you from harm."

Stunned and deeply wounded, he said, "Was there no *doubt*? No *guilt*?"

"I had faith in the Gods, Iasonnas. I had faith that… *look*, here you are! Prosperous, healthy, with a fine family! Athens is now just a distant memory of your youth, I am sure!"

Not wanting to believe it was true, Iasonnas gave her one more chance: "Medusa, are you hiding your true feelings from me? Please, answer me honestly! I beg you! How could your feelings for me have been so cold after so many years together?"

"Iasonnas, *doubt* is what breaks *hope* and… if I had let doubt enter my life, my hope would have been lost and my prayers futile."

Tears streaming from his eyes, his broken heart revealed itself. Grabbing her arms, Iasonnas shook her. "*Medusa…*" he said, drawing her closer, "I need you to say that night broke your heart, too!

Crushed your soul! I could not have been the only one tortured by what happened between us! I will not accept that!"

Medusa fell silent, unsure of what to say. *Should she confess to something she did not really feel to lessen his pain? Should she admit that she had never felt the love he had?* Before either soul could say anything more, they heard the sound of rocks sliding down the hillside behind them. Alarmed, they both turned and looked up; Iasonnas caught a glimpse of someone running away in haste.

"Medusa, you must hide!" Iasonnas grabbed Medusa's hand and her belongings and they ran and did not stop until they reached his farm; the moment Medusa saw the humble abode she began to pull back.

"Iasonnas, you cannot take me into your home! I will not put your family at greater risk than I have!"

"It is the only place you will be safe, Medusa! No man dare look for you here! I have the perfect hiding place!"

"But, why would any man wish to look for me in the first place?" she said, suddenly confused.

"Come!" Quietly ducking inside a grain storage shed near his house, they sat down on a sack of flax to catch their breath. "Stay here, Medusa," Iasonnas said, panting. "I will go and look into this."

"But… "

"*Shh…* Stay here and do not move until I discover what is happening!"

Medusa reached out and put her hand on his shoulder. "Iasonnas, promise me you will keep your family safe from all of this. You must do whatever is necessary to protect them. When night falls,

I can easily head off to the cliffs and far away from your family."

"You can decide that later, Medusa. For now, please wait for me to return."

Hidden in the dry and quiet storage shed, Medusa felt safe from the world for the moment. Enjoying the comfort of a loving friend and knowing that she was not alone, had been the kindest relief she could have found at this time. The very sound of Iasonnas' reassuring voice had calmed the torment within her. Still, her presence posed great danger for him and his family. Iasonnas was no longer that carefree boy of twelve, with nothing more on his mind than trailing along behind her into the woods to watch her shoot arrows into fruit. So reluctantly, she planned her departure. Waiting for nightfall, she vowed to leave before things went terribly wrong.

That night with a black, moonless sky above, Medusa took her bow and few possessions and crept out of the shed. As she did, she suddenly came upon a small figure standing in the darkness before her. Iasonnas' youngest son had caught the light of her eyes moving about the shed, as he had that first night and had been drawn to investigate. Though Medusa had covered her face as quickly as she could, it was too late; he had looked into her eyes. Peering sidelong, she had expected to turn and see a pillar of stone before her, but instead to her relief, the child was still very much alive; not frightened, but obviously curious. He continued to approach; Trembling, Medusa stumbled backwards into the shed, falling back into a stack of grain sacks as she tried to keep her deathly gaze under cover. Seeing the shed door standing open, Iasonnas rushed in to see what had happened. He found his boy standing over a cowering Medusa, her black shroud hiding her face. He ran to pick up the child.

"What are you doing?! He could have been *killed*!"

"The boy approached me as I was leaving… I…"

"*Leaving?* Did he look into your eyes, Medusa?"

"Yes, I think so, but… "

"He turned the boy to examine his face.

"I must go, Iasonnas. My presence here is posing much danger. The boy looked at me but…"

"Please wait here, Medusa. There is something you must know, first!"

Iasonnas had never been so frightened. Cradling the boy in his arms, he quickly rushed him inside the safety of his home. Medusa began to cry; she had almost taken the life of Iasonnas' child! But for some reason unbeknownst to her, though she was certain he had looked into her eyes, there he was, alive and seemingly unchanged. When Iasonnas returned, he told her what he had learned.

"Medusa, somehow the villagers know of your presence here, but do not know who you are. For now, your family is safe."

"Thank you, Iasonnas, but your son…?"

"It seems, Medusa, that no harm has come to him thanks to the Gods."

"And has he spoken of…"

"Yes, I am afraid he has. I have promised to explain the whole story to my wife, Elissa, when I return. I owe her that… especially now." Medusa turned away, realizing the damage was done.

"But, that does not mean you must leave! We can find you another hiding place and…"

Medusa knew that staying a moment longer would be foolish. She had come dangerously close to taking a life and the risk she posed by her very presence, hit her like an urgent bolt as it never had before.

"Iasonnas, I will be in the caverns by the ocean for a few days. Do you remember the place?"

"Yes Medusa. Of course."

"I will be there until I can decide what course I must take, if you want to say good-bye." Touching his face with the back of her hand, she set out under cover of darkness.

Safely nestled in the caverns by sunrise, Medusa sat in quiet contemplation as rumours of her presence spread throughout the countryside. She prayed to the Goddess Artemis for divine guidance as she had many years before because she reasoned- if there was anyone still listening, it would be Artemis. By now, most of the surrounding villages had heard that a Gorgon had been seen lurking in the shadows and were alerted of the horrible danger she posed. Her legend quickly grew; for the next several days she passed the time composing prayers, writing them on the cavern walls. Always hidden from the light, she came out only at night when the darkness cloaked her hideous appearance and deadly eyes. She had no desire to hurt anyone needlessly. Now, with the dead of Night as her domain, she walked the shore in the moonlight as the wild seas pounded at her feet. However, the mighty sea no longer brought comfort to Medusa as it once had done. Somehow, the ocean had become almost a stranger to her. Staring out into the boundless darkness, she would call out to her family — *Mother, Father... Dorkas... Elpis... dear Hagne... have you forgotten me? Am I dead to you?* Never did she receive a reply, but she knew somehow they could hear her mournful lament.

Late one night, as Medusa sat desperately beseeching the Goddess for a sign, she heard the sound of footsteps at the entrance of the cave. She quickly hid in the shadows and armed her bow as the faint glow of a small torch appeared at the cavern's mouth.

"Iasonnas?" she whispered. "Is that you?"

A hesitant, quivering voice called back, "No, Medusa, my child. It is Agathi, your mother." Medusa slowly approached and found a frail, old woman, her head wrapped in a grey shawl. Though at first suspecting trickery, she looked closer and realized that it truly was her mother. Breaking down in tears, Medusa called out, "Mother...*no*... *please*... do not come closer! You must not lay eyes upon me!" she exclaimed, dropping to the floor and covering her head with her arms.

Agathi's face was wrought with worry and her eyes had never looked so sad. She spoke tenderly and reassuringly "I *know* my daughter... I know *everything*. I received a vision from your protectoress Artemis." She slowly stepped forward and placed her hand lovingly on Medusa's shoulders. "Oh, my child, why did you not come to me?"

With tears streaming down her face Medusa said, "Mother, I could not. I did not want to endanger you. And I did not want you to see me this way."

"Medusa, you are my daughter and I will always love you no matter what happens. Your father... your father wanted to come but is feeling too weak to leave his bed. Forgive him, he wanted so desperately to see you, but... your sister Dorkas is watching over him until my return. Your grandmother, may the Gods bless and keep her eternal soul, passed two winters ago."

Medusa reached up and took her mother's hand. "Mother, I love you more than anything in this world. That is why I did not come to you. That is why you must now disown me! If the people of the village discover who I am... "

"Medusa, nothing could ever make me do that. I would give my very life for you..." said Agathi, her thoughts and words trailing off. Though calm and self-assured as ever, Medusa could hear the pain in her voice.

"I know Mother, but my family is all I now have left. If something were to happen to you or my sisters... I... I would never forgive myself," she stuttered, a lump forming in her throat. "The villagers surely know of me by now… "

"Nothing will happen, my daughter. We must trust in the Fates!"

"You say that with such certainty…. but…. "

"Nothing will happen…" her mother repeated "I am certain. Artemis has assured me of this. Is there anything you need me to bring you? Food? Clothing?"

"Thank you mother, I need nothing. I feel no hunger, no thirst… Things are so very different for me now. My needs are few."

Throughout the night and the following day, Agathi just listened and nodded thoughtfully, allowing Medusa to free her mind, offering wisdom and insight when asked. She wanted to do all she could to comfort her daughter while she decided her future.

"Now is the time to make your choice, Medusa," she stated with determination as the sun rose on the second morning. Taking Medusa's cold claws in her aged hands she asked, "Medusa, will you return to Athens for a chance at redemption? Or will you let me take you home to your family? Your father, Hagne, as well as Dorkas await you there. Both have sons and daughters who look up to you. Or, will you choose another path?" Medusa remained silent, knowing the answer might mean never seeing her family again. "The choice is yours as always, Medusa. Please know that we will support whatever decision you choose. But please, do not waste away your life here, hiding from the world. Choose your own path — do not allow *it* to choose *you*."

Medusa closed her eyes and hugged her frail, old mother, the person who held more patience and wisdom than any of the great scholars she had ever met and more love and compassion than any mother could. As Agathi set out on the path home, she stopped and called back to Medusa, "Love will be victorious my child, let it guide you to your true destiny."

Medusa now knew she must risk all and face Athena; whether in battle or with reason, she had to attempt to reclaim her previous life. Now decided on a course of action, she hoped before she left, to see Iasonnas one final time. So Medusa waited; certain he would come to say good-bye. The next morning he found her sitting just inside the cavern entrance, deep in thought. Relieved and happy at the sight of her friend she exclaimed:

"Iasonnas, I began to think I would never see you again."

"I had to come and see you Medusa… I made sure I was not followed. I…. "

"I am not afraid of them, Iasonnas. I just want you to be safe."

"I am fine Medusa…." Iasonnas' eyes were full of sorrow, "however, my youngest boy seems to have the black sleeping sickness… since that night in the shed. Each night as the sun sets, he suddenly falls into a deep sleep that he cannot be wakened from. He loses consciousness with no warning. Then at sunrise, he awakens and remembers nothing. Each night, we fear he will fall under this sickness and not wake."

"Iasonnas, I am so sorry… I… "

"He will be alright, Medusa… by the Gods, I am certain. I have sent for the best physician in all of Athens to come and watch over him. He will find a cure… he *must*."

"And, your wife? Elissa?"

"I have told her everything. She has no desire to bring harm to your family, so she has promised to tell no one of what she knows. She has graciously allowed me to come and say good-bye despite… all that has occurred…"

The two sat together and talked throughout the day and night. Knowing the pain and fear he felt, Medusa said nothing to further disturb him. She tried to send him reassuring energy, but, that was not enough. His heart was nearly broken. She sat close to him and held him in her arms as he cried and held onto her as if life itself depended on it. Then at first light, Iasonnas prepared to leave.

"Medusa, you must know that your life is in danger here. Fear is mounting in the village and the village wives are insisting that the men hunt you down and end this. You must be on guard and find a new place as soon as possible."

"Yes, it is time that I leave this place, Iasonnas. I must find someone who can put this injustice right."

"Do you know where you will go?"

"It is probably better that you do not know. But one thing is certain, this is not my home anymore." Holding each other close one last time, they said good-bye. Down the path, he disappeared.

That night as she stood at the cave entrance with her possessions slung over her shoulder; she looked resolutely in the direction of Athens. No matter where her path would lead, she knew the journey ahead would be long and arduous. Now, as she thought back to that horrendous day, she wondered why she had left the Holy City without first trying to right the injustice done to her. As her mind took her ahead to what might await, she saw a line of torches approaching. A band of men, fifteen, maybe twenty in number. Readying herself for the worst, she declared, "It has begun".

Quickly hiding in a thicket of overgrowth a short distance away, she watched as a few of the men went inside the cavern and then came back out a few seconds later.

"Nothing in here!" one announced. "But, there are signs that someone — or some*thing* — was here not long ago! Where is that damned monster? Iasonnas said she would be here!"

These words almost knocked Medusa off her feet.

Iasonnas? He betrayed me?! That cannot be so!

"Well, maybe she headed back towards Iasonnas' house! He said that is where he first spotted her!"

At this moment, she felt as if the world had fallen, crashing with force on top of her as anger, betrayal and abandonment consumed her fragile mind. As she watched the line of torches trail back down the path, she crept furtively down the hillside behind them. Readying an arrow, she pulled back on the bow string and through weeping eyes prepared to fire a deadly bolt into the leader's head. She clinched her teeth as her fangs protruded, now looking like the ravenous killer that the townspeople believed she was. However, her heart said otherwise. As she lowered her bow, her angered expression became a sad and solemn grimace. Over and over she heard the words in her mind, *Where is that damned monster? Iasonnas said she would be here! Why? Why would he want me killed?! Is that what he really thinks of me — a damned monster?!* With her mind more confused than ever, she returned to her cave hideaway to collect her thoughts and reassure herself that returning to Athens was the correct choice.

"This is *impossible... insane!*" she announced out loud, pacing back and forth, feeling more and more like a caged animal. "It must have been a *ruse* to get me to show myself! One they use at *every* cave!"

Throughout the night, her tortured mind kept asking the same questions over and over again until finally just as the sun peeked over the horizon, her anger exploded: "**This must end!**" Just as she screamed out, an arrow grazed her upper left arm.

Quickly spinning around, her expression turned from anger to disbelief as she saw the archer's face. "*Iasonnas!*" Staring in shock as if she had never seen him before, his eyes were red and swollen, his beard rough, his curly hair unruly and his body shook as he held the deadly weapon in his hands. She had so many questions to ask but no words would form. Growling and lunging forward, she effortlessly snatched the bow from his unskilled hands, snapping it in two. He then desperately reached for a hunting dagger which Medusa quickly knocked from his hand into the meadow below. "Why, Iasonnas?! Why are you doing this?!"

He did not answer, but instead, with his eyes full of rage, he charged at her, forcing her to pick him up off the ground and throw him to the back of the cave. Screaming incoherently, Iasonnas ran back at her as fast as his weakened legs could carry him, lunging at Medusa with a rage so fierce that it contorted his face. Grabbing him, she threw him to the ground and pushed his face into the dirty, stone floor screaming into his ear, "Why?!! "Why, by the Gods, did you turn on me?!! Plot to have me killed?!!"

Sobbing hysterically, he screamed, "Because you killed my son, you disgusting monster!! You killed my son!!"

Medusa froze in shock. Her skin tightened and pulled from her flesh and all she could say was, "How, Iasonnas? What happened? The sickness?"

"Your **eyes**! Your horrible **eyes** killed him!" he screamed. "The physicians told me so! It was the work of **dark magic**! Evil forces entered his body and made him shake and foam at the mouth until his life was robbed from him! He was just an innocent **little boy**! **Just a little boy**!!"

Medusa stood up, letting Iasonnas pick himself up from the ground. He stood there gasping, inconsolable. "This began the night you cursed him with your poisonous presence, Medusa!!" Medusa shook her head resolutely "No, Iasonnas I am not to blame! It could not have been by my eyes or he would have been turned to stone on the very spot where he stood!"

Iasonnas grew ever more enraged at her attempt to deny what she had done. "There is no other explanation, **Medusa**! It was **you** and I will **kill** you for destroying my family!!" Grabbing her arms, Iasonnas tried to shove Medusa backwards toward the edge of the cliff within the cavern. As they struggled, Medusa tried to not hurt him as he repeatedly assaulted her; his arms flailing wildly, made contact with her face again and again. Wrestling him to the ground again, she held him by the shoulders as his tears streamed down and he weakened beneath her superior strength. When Iasonnas became exhausted and limp, she let lose her grasp. In a quieted voice she stood before him, "Iasonnas I am truly, truly sorry for the loss of your child! Nothing would pain me more than to think I had taken the life of a child, especially *your* child. However, I swear, it was not by my doing! Death from my eyes is quick and exact. There must be another force at play here!"

Catching his breath, he got to his knees. "Medusa, you have brought me nothing but misery and pain my entire life! I curse the day I pulled you from that well! I cannot live like this a moment longer! I want to end this **now**!"

As he spoke, Medusa saw a change come to Iasonnas' eyes; she could no longer see the sweet and thoughtful boy she once knew within their bottomless deep blue colour. Jumping to his feet, Iasonnas lunged at her, pulling Medusa towards him, pressing his lips to hers as he held her tightly. Reaching up, he tore the shroud from her head and looked directly into her eyes. Too late to turn away, she watched as his suffering melted away. All of his pain, worries, thoughts and memories were pulled out in a smoky mist from his eyes and at the speed of light, had entered her own. Her vision fused with Iasonnas' and his life, in all its entirety, was now her own. At peace at last, there he stood. Not a tear in his eye, not one glimmer of pain upon his rigid face.

Medusa backed away, shaking her head in disbelief. *Had she just killed her only friend? Or, had he only wanted to make her eternally responsible for his death? Joining his soul with hers for all eternity?* A drum within her core began to beat faster and faster, beating louder and louder until it beat straight through her chest. His life flashing across her sorrowed eyes, she held still, her mind racing a million light-years a second. She did not have time to process this ephemeral experience though, as the silence was suddenly broken by the sound of marching men growing ever nearer. Reaching for her bow and quiver, she stood before Iasonnas and placed her hand to his cold, stone cheek. Gazing at the perfectly sculpted beauty Iasonnas exhibited, even in death, she moved in closer so that their lips almost touched.

She whispered, "You used me Iasonnas. You wanted to burden me as you believed I had burdened you! A reflection of what lies beneath, my dear, old friend; a cold heart you had, a cold death you met." Her words ending in a sinister and angry tone, Medusa set her jaw as she moved her hands from a gentle caress to a violent push to his perfectly sculpted face and chest. Crashing to the cavern floor, his lifeless body shattered into a thousand pieces. Gazing down upon his remains, her face showed no expression at all. A moment later, the townsmen entered the seemingly empty cavern only to discover the serene face of Iasonnas, gazing back at them from the unknown. Angry cries were heard from deep within the cave as Medusa once again had eluded them.

"Iasonnas! The monster has murdered Iasonnas!"

Unmoved, she covered her head and headed deeper into the woods, staying well away from the beaten trails. Taking a path unknown to her, she fled the town and all things familiar to her. Taking to the far reaches of the mountains, she became the beast all men feared.

CHAPTER FOURTEEN

Medusa was now infamously known as a monstrous murderer; an evil incarnate; a malevolent beast to be hunted down and destroyed like a rabid animal. Many villages across Attica had organized hunting parties, with many offering handsome rewards for the one who would present her hideous, severed head. Athena had made it known, that the beast Medusa was an enemy to all Greece and even the meekest of earthlings would not risk ignoring Athena's decree: Medusa was to be hunted down and killed without hesitation.

Having now given herself to the darkness, Medusa continued without rest, staying one step ahead of the ever-growing hordes of huntsmen who sought her out for fame and a sack of gold. Her legend grew quickly as exaggerated tales of her superhuman powers and monstrous abilities spread across the lands of Greece and beyond. A price on her head and a taint on her soul, she would never have a moment's rest as long as she was still alive. So she ran, fleeing from one part of the countryside to another, always staying on the fringe of life, in the wilderness, in the caves, in any quiet and secluded hideaway where the angry multitudes might not think to look for her. Invariably however, she would always eventually be discovered and would once more have to flee for her life.

Most times she could make a clean getaway, simply disappearing like a shadow, making her pursuers question if she had really been there at all. Sometimes she would be trapped and would have to do whatever was necessary to escape, even if it meant taking a life. It was not her will to kill, but like Iasonnas, these men had brought it upon themselves. Relentlessly hunted down like a wild animal by glory-seeking mortals, it was her constant will to live that spurred her on and kept her alive.

Among the many who came to challenge her, was a man named Theron of Salamis. A mortal with the aspirations of a God. Known far and wide as ruggedly handsome with strength as mighty as a god, he was the bravest hunter in the land. Theron decided, one late summer night while drinking cool wine by a fire made of broken boats with the local townsmen who held him in highest esteem, to talk about the tale of Medusa.

With the sound of the gentle ocean rolling onto the rocky shore in the near distance, the group of men sat around the glow of a low smouldering hearth, half-drunkenly singing bawdy sailing songs off-key, while alcohol spurred boasting both great and small. Theron downed his skyphos of cheap, red wine as he began his intoxicated, self-serving rant:

"Nothing is she but, a woman with an ugly temper!"

"But, Theron, she is a *monster*! A merciless creature of the night! A mare of dark destruction!" said one, nodding his head authoritatively.

"Have you not heard the legends told?!" said another. "One hundred men did she kill! Ripped out their entrails as she turned them to pillars of stone! An effortless task for such a powerful, black force!"

"*Monster* you say?" Theron countered. "*Ha*! She is a *female* is she not?! Like any female, I could woo her to my liking with *ease*! All she needs is a firm hand to her fat rump and a good slap to the mouth and she will soon bow down to her master!" Laughing out loud, his deep bass voice boomed, "Or have *you* not heard?! *Theron* is master of *all* women, monstrous, Goddess, and mortal alike!"

A few of the men chuckled and tapped their cups raucously on the rocks; one of them shamelessly passing gas. Then Acteon spoke up. "You do not know of what you speak, Theron!" he said, wiping wine from his dirty chin onto his hairy arm. "She is not of this earth! A woman's form she might hold and a beautiful form at that! But the savagery of a beast, she conceals in her bosom. Only when the time is right, when you are in her seductive hold, only then will you see the monster hidden beneath and then — it is too late! One gaze into those cold, fiery eyes will turn your blood cold and your heart to stone!"

Bemused by the colourful depiction, Theron smiled and continued. "Yes, yes, Acteon, the tales are told, the stories are there, but was there not such a tale of a powerful nymph of the wood? A creature so fair that many a man hunted her down to gain control of her only to fall under her deadly spell?"

"Indeed, Theron only… "

"Only *nothing*, Acteon! Did I not accept that challenge?"

"Yes, Theron, that, you did, but… "

"And did I meet with a horrific and untimely death, Acteon?!" he said, shaking his head arrogantly, pursing his wine-soaked lips.

"No, *indeed*! I met with a shrew of a woman who had taken it upon herself to call herself *Mistress of the Wood*! Who spread wild rumors of her imagined exploits until she enlivened herself a legend! A killer nymph? *Ha*! No, indeed, my good men! More likely a woman who had to be put in her place by a man — a *real* man! The likes of *me*!"

"That you did, Theron… that you did!"

"And a fine *place* I provided her!" Theron said, slapping both hands on his bare thighs suggestively. All the men in the group let out a loud roar as Theron continued. "Yes, Acteon, I did what I do best! I hunted my prey and I *savaged* the beast! Although… I might say she really did not put up much of a fight!" The men laughed once more at the boastful insinuation.

"Well, then that settles it, Theron!" came a voice from the corner.

Everyone turned to the slight, shadowy figure sitting unnoticed in the darkness. His voice old and shaky, something in his demeanour interested Theron. "Settles what, old man?" said Theron, as he picked up a flaming ember from the fire and lifted it towards the voice. There, they saw the mysterious old man reclining casually on the large rocks behind them, drinking wine from a shining smooth, silver cup. His clothes almost as ragged as those of beggars, they were somewhat perplexed by his appearance. He laughed, knowing the young and hot-headed Theron would not be able to deny the challenge. He leaned into the light and glared at Theron with his one good eye.

"You, *Theron the great hunter*, the man with no fear will be the very man who will take on the vicious vixen and gain all of the glory and worship that will come with that victory!"

Theron's eyes opened wide, for the old man knew exactly what to say to evoke the greed and lust in his heart and loins.

"Lead me to her old man and I will show you what the great Theron can do!"

The old man smiled as a great wave rose up and smashed into the rocks behind him with great rage, the ocean spray covering him like a silver halo in the fires dim light.

Setting out, the five men travelled north along the shore on foot. Taking most of the night to arrive at their destination, they were astonished at how the old man had led the way without need of rest. As the Moon climbed highest in the sky, two dolphins caught Theron's eye in the murky waters, their echoing calls serving as beacons as they travelled. They followed the men as if escorting them safely to their destination.

Light had not yet broken over the land as Theron stood in the wet sand by the foot of the cliff; standing with his shoulders back and his fists clinched on either side of his broad hips, he gazed up at the caves above him, fearless and strong.

"Now, you can still change your mind young man, if you are having second thoughts. No one here would fault you."

"*Second thoughts!*" Theron quipped. "Theron has never denied nor had second thoughts about *any* challenge! Just stand back and watch as I woo this monstrous whore into submission!"

The group of drunken men cheered him on and shouted his name with glee as he confidently began to climb the cliffs to Medusa's lair. There, as he had stated resoundingly, he would confront and conquer the Medusa, having his way with her as no other man ever had. Reaching the dizzying heights of the cave within minutes, Theron took a moment to look down at his fellow villagers as they clapped their hands and toasted his resolve with more sweet wine. He could not help but notice though that the mysterious old man now leaning on a tall walking stick, was gazing up at him with a sly smile. Ignoring the small, nagging doubt that flashed through his mind, he waved self-confidently to the men below.

"Save some for me boys!" Then, Theron turned and ventured alone into the dark entrance where the now mythical Medusa was said to dwell in the dark recesses.

Slowly and cautiously, Theron made his way through the many narrow and low passages that made the cave a nightmare of sharp, blackened tunnels and bottomless pits that echoed with mysterious and unrecognizable sounds; echoes that enveloped and vibrated through the hazy mind of anyone making the mistake of stepping foot in this devil's playground. Theron had come prepared with all that he needed to defeat Medusa: a torch to light the way, a thick dark cloth to tie across his eyes to avoid her deadly stare, and a long leather whip to wrap around her neck and twist if she did not concede to his wishes. Once subdued under his masculine power, he would then have his way with her and leave her whimpering on the cave floor like a tamed kitten.

Being the skilled hunter that he was, Theron treated this endeavour as any of the countless pursuits he had performed and succeeded in. He stood calm and poised, focused and confident, discerning all he could about his prey; ready to exert full power over it with lightning speed. Focusing his keen though somewhat dulled senses, he was able to distinguish from the cacophony of muddled sounds that surrounded him, which were echo and which was the point of origin. Then he skilfully maneuvered his way through the narrowest of pathways to find himself at the very core of the stone maze. It was an enormous cavern sparsely lit with torches that enlivened strange shadows across its craggy walls.

Here! This is where the elusive beast lies! Theron thought excitedly.

His smirk quickly turning into a look of intense resolve, he unravelled the cloth from his arm and blindfolded himself. Unlike other hunters who relied upon all their senses, especially sight, in the heat of the pursuit, it meant little to Theron. A hunter since the age of four when he killed his first mountain lion, he had learned to hone his senses, never relying on just one, when tracking and taking down his prey. With his eyes shielded from danger, he unfurled the leather whip wrapped around his waist and curled it artfully around his right arm, ready to strike at the first sign of his adversary. Hunkered down, he crept through the cavern, waiting for a sign; even a change in the air or the whisper of her breath would be enough to give Theron her exact location. Only a few moments had passed before the first signal was felt; the sound of rocks tumbling into water somewhere. *She is just ahead in this passage* Theron thought readying himself.

In swift pursuit, he silently made his way through the winding tunnels, following the sporadic clues coming from her direction. He had heard the last echo sound, which meant a wall was straight ahead and then a second echo… and then a third. "A dead-end! She is trapped!" he said, his excitement building in both his heart and loins. He quickly unravelled his whip, slung it back, and prepared to put it to work.

At first there was silence, then a slow scrapping sound just to his right. Knowing that the match had begun, he lifted the whip over his head and swung it fiercely towards the sound, a wide smile crossing his grimy face. It cracked in mid-air and recoiled against the moist and mould-covered black wall; rocks crumbled from the force of contact. Quickly drawing his whip back over his head, Theron prepared to make a second strike. Hearing a scuffle of bare feet, he felt something quickly rush past his right side. Pulling his whip from his shoulder, he sends it out with deadly force. It cracked and the sound of crumbling rocks was heard again signifying, to his disbelief, that he had somehow missed his target again. Coiling the whip around his shoulder, he set out in pursuit of Medusa, crouching low and using the sound reflecting off the walls as his guide. "She *fears* me! That is why she flees!" Theron whispered confidently.

Following the sounds of distant footfalls, a pause was heard and then a distant *thud*. Stopping in his tracks, he had to feel the ground ahead of him. Not wanting to be tricked into taking off his protective cloth, he knelt down and as he had suspected, discovered an open chasm in the ground before him. Tossing a pebble to discern its breadth, he discerned that it was much wider than a man could leap. If he wished to continue his pursuit, he would have to climb along the edge of slippery walls and find where the path continued on the other side. "She has leapt ahead, but she will not lose me that easily!" he whispered

Without forethought, he began to climb the wall and skilfully make his way across to the safety of the other side. Clinging to the walls as they became smoother and slippery, he lost his footing once on the slick surface, causing him to lose his balance and cling on only by his fingertips.

The sound of gruff, female laughter could be heard echoing in the distance. Undeterred, he maintained his composure and carefully regained his footing, finally making his way to the other side. *If she had wanted to send me to Hades, she could have done it there and then,* he realized. *She is only toying with me! That foolish move will cost her!* Somewhere ahead, the sound of running water could be heard trickling and splashing into a pool. Testing the ground with his foot, he unwrapped his whip and held it between both hands. "If this beast can leap such a distance, this might be a little more of a challenge than I had first anticipated," he uttered beneath his breath. "Which will make the capture even more rewarding!"

Following the path, the echo of dripping water drew him on. In the distance, the sound of harsh, sadistic cackling rang loudly in his ears. Startled, Theron's reflexes kicked in; he swung his whip around in circles over his head, ready for battle. The echoes of the laugher seemed to split into a hundred directions masking her location. He poised himself for an attack. Then he felt something hit him on the back of his head, a rock no doubt, but the hit was not hard enough to knock him off balance. "Resorting to throwing stones, beast?!" were the first words he spoke directly to Medusa as he swung his whip tauntingly. "Come and get it, Bitch from Hades!"

Playing games with Theron, Medusa began dodging side to side, testing his speed, accuracy and nerve. With each near miss, Theron was becoming more agitated. The more agitated he became, the less he calculated her movements. Now she began to sing a disturbing song to ridicule Theron and further prick his rage. Her voice, raspy and rough, sang out an eerie, ominous tune that reached into Theron's mortal soul, sending shivers to the core of his being. Slow and menacing, each verse ended with sarcastic, jeering laugher.

> "The great hunter came to kill his pray,
> So weak and small a mere woman to tame.
> The great man of strength took out his whip
> But little did he know he fell into the monster's grip.
> Run little man, hide while you can.
> For you have made a grave mistake
> Beg for forgiveness and I will forgive
> Continue to be foolish and you shall not live."

Theron started to sweat as his nerves gave way to Medusa's unrelenting torment, even moments of silence now made him anxious and tense. Swinging his whip wilding over his head, he repeatedly released attacks where he believed the elusive Medusa was perched, yet time and again he chose wrong. With doubt now lain deep in his heart, it was time for Medusa to stop toying with her prey and set herself to finish him off. From the tense silence, she suddenly leapt towards her target. The sound of her black, leathery wings cutting through the air, alerted Theron of the attack. He had no time to react; he felt Medusa's claws rip savagely through the back of the leather doublet he wore under his white, linen tunic. With the leather came his pink flesh; his back was now laid open like a gutted sheep. Theron let out a mighty howl of pain, wildly swinging his whip in circles around him, trying desperately to hit his target or at least drive her away. Medusa laughed at his clumsy attempts to protect himself. His desperation grew as Medusa teased, taunted, sang and hissed at him. These sounds seemingly coming from every direction at once. Desperately, he kept swiping his weapon wildly in all directions.

Finally, the torment was more than Theron could stand; he thought he had surely lost his mind as every second spent in this monster's lair now seemed like an eternity; every failed attempt at landing a decisive blow left a devastating wound on Theron's confidence that began to tear at him from inside, as if eating through his chest. No one and no *thing* had ever been able to do this to the mighty Theron before! His spirit almost shattered, he kept swinging wildly, knowing he could never hit his target. Then, to his surprise, his whip connected with something other than the stone cold walls of the cavern. Poised and panting, he waited for a sign.

The whip became taut. Something began to tug at him; slowly at first, but then more forcefully.

Medusa had grabbed the whip and now stood just the length of the whip away, smiling as she drew the whip ever closer. Refusing to surrender to her, Theron pulled back with all his might, certain he was stronger. Medusa casually held on, waiting for his nerves and will to snap. He cried out, "To **Hades** with you, you rabid demon!" just as she jerked one final time, sending him flying through the air and into the deep pit he had crossed with such care just moments before.

Hanging by the whip coiled around his arm, the enormous weight of his muscular body made the whip cut deep into Theron's flesh; his own blood trickled down his body. Dangling him with one hand, Medusa bent down to watch Theron struggling to hold on, like a worm on a hook.

"Why do you not remove that which blinds you, foolish human!" Medusa called down to him. Theron yelled out as loud as he could while trying to pull himself up out of the pit, "To Hades with you, she-bitch! By the Gods of Olympus, you will surrender to me or burn at the Gates of Hades!"

"Then, release your hold, Theron, and fall to your death if you are not willing to follow my advice."

"My blindfold is my shield. You will not trick me that easily!"

Medusa laughed loudly as the hissing and rattling of a chorus snakes could be heard. She angrily spat, "What blinds you is not the cloth around your eyes but your pointless, human arrogance, you pitiful mortal! The utter audacity to presume that strength lies only in brawn and your self-righteous virtues and that the accused are always guilty; *that* is your ultimate weakness! And that will be your downfall! I am no more a monster than you!"

"That you are an evil and vicious monster is clear to all, *Gorgon*!"

"Then perhaps, I should just let you go!" Medusa leaned in closer to get a better look at the foolish mortal who had come to subdue her. "No, I think you deserve what I was never offered, a chance at redemption."

Infuriated by having been overpowered by this inferior creature — a *female*! — Theron shouted back, "Drop me down this infernal pit if you so choose, for I shall survive! You shall not dictate my Fate, you pitiful monster! And, you *are* a monster, no elegant words can hide that truth! I am your master in every way and if I cannot tame you, then I shall have your hideous head to hang on my wall!"

Feeling a moment of pity for his mindless and misguided rant, Medusa drew up the whip, allowing him to crawl out of the pit and stand as straight as his battered body would allow. She stood before him, holding the whip taut, waiting for his reaction. Unable to contain his anger, he swung his left arm wildly to strike her down, but this was no match for Medusa's reflexes; she caught his fist in mid-air, grabbed his throat, and picked him up off the ground. Pushing the tip of her claw into his throat she stated calmly, "*Pity* you wasted your chance! But in the end, you will see the beauty of my design!" Twisting his arm until it nearly snapped, Theron tried to scream out in pain but her claw was pressed so deeply into his throat that he could barely breathe. "Do you not feel sorry now? Do you not wish you were a different man? A *better* man?" Releasing her grip, he dropped to the ground like a sack of grain, clutching his throat and gasping for air. Smacking him then with the back of her hand, she swung around and clawed at his face, slicing his mask to shreds. "Come, Theron, look into my eyes and see who I really am and I will let you live!" Coming within inches of his face, he raised his good arm over his eyes and shuddered as she stroked his long, black hair. She whispered softly, "You came here to tame *me*. However, now I offer you *this*! Give in to *me* and I may let you live!" On his knees with his hands over his eyes, Theron cowered for the first time in his life. As he heard her moving away, he felt compelled to follow.

Though rough and beastly, her voice had an irresistible allure; a sweet trap that he felt himself falling into. Getting to his feet, he followed behind her. Stumbling along the path just steps behind, wiping blood from his face, he kept his eyes fixed on Medusa's strangely seductive body. The rise and fall of her hips. The bounce of her ample breasts. Somehow, it seemed that there had been a change in her presence; the cold and frightening essence she held moments before was turning into something enthralling. *Desirable*. He watched her long legs stride through the passageways, and found himself desiring her as he had desired no other. He followed as she disappeared into the shadows, then down a set of ancient stone steps leading to a path thick with vapour and heat that quickly rose to envelope him as they descended.

The heavy air in the lower cavern made him sweat; he wiped his brow, then absently glided his fingertips over his thick brown belt, remembering the knife he kept there. He passed through the mist and as his vision cleared, he could make out a beautiful, inviting pool of steaming water fed by an underground springs flowing around the smooth black rocks. Shining light beaming in from high above through openings in the cavern roof lit upon the gentle water, forming glistening spots that danced over the water like new pearls. This calming sight caught Theron off guard as all he knew thus far, were dark and gloomy recesses filled with trickery; trickery that could have been playing on his mind at that very instance. His guard raised, he pulled out a few inches of the short square pommel of his blade, hiding it between his index finger and his thumb, readying to strike.

With light from the climbing sun streaming down, Theron now saw a shapely figure standing in the pool. Stepping nearer, he found Medusa standing nude with her beautifully sculpted back towards him; pouring water over her shoulders that streamed seductively down the contours of her back, across her hips, and between the cheeks of her bottom. She tenderly caressed her arms and breasts as the light accentuated her seductive movements. In awe of the statuesque beauty that Medusa was, Theron stood motionless, forgetting for a moment the monstrous strength she had demonstrated. He tried to keep his mind focused, now knowing that she could never be tamed. His passion growing, he lowered his tunic over his shoulders, revealing his fine, muscular chest, all the while keeping his eyes fixed on Medusa. Wading into the pool, he studied Medusa's beautiful body, his desire building. As he drew near, he could now see that her hair had movement. "The legends have truth! Her hair lives!" Theron whispered to himself. Swaying as if alive with waves and ripples like anemone of the sea, he became transfixed by their movement. He was compelled to move in closer to touch her; the sound of serpents could be heard hissing and rattling; all whispering to come closer. Closer still.

Taking his hand from his belt, he reached out to touch Medusa's hair. As he attempted this, a Black Whip snake suddenly leapt out and snapped at his hand. Medusa laughed as Theron fell back into the water, startled. Still unable to resist, he crawled back on hands and knees saying, "Medusa! Your hair… it is… *beautiful!*" Medusa smiled and took a step away. Luxuriating in the warm, bubbling water, she knelt to pour water over her shoulders, over her ample breasts, touching herself in places Theron desired to touch. The steam growing denser, Theron pulled himself up, not wanting to waste a single moment with this mysterious creature that stood naked before him. His mind now unsure of his true intentions, he did not know what to do next. He did know with certainty however, that the next move was his to make. Stepping closer, he pressed his muscular body against Medusa's back. To his delight, she reached behind and grabbed his buttocks, pulling him closer. Digging her claws deeply into his ravaged flesh, she turned her head towards him, revealing a glimpse of the source of her fatal power. Like a moth to flame, Theron's gaze was drawn ever closer to the ominous but powerful energy that flowed from Medusa's eyes. Resting her head on his powerful chest, he opened his mouth and glided his lips over the pale grey skin of her neck. Medusa moaned with delight, "Do you now see? I am only trying to *help* you? By breaking the rogue I see before me, I am bringing out a better man!" Taking her full and generous breasts in his two hands, he planned his move. Whispering into his ear, she welcomed him, "Take me, Theron! Take your prize!"

Smirking as he threw her down into the shallow, steaming waters, he quickly closed his eyes. Positioning his perfectly formed body over hers, he began to rub his hands over her pale, grey skin. As he lied on top of her, spreading her legs with his muscular thighs, Medusa dug her claws into his muscular buttocks, drawing him nearer, the pain excruciatingly delightful. Reeling at his empowerment over Medusa, Theron's senses soared, his thoughts turning to the townspeople who would be holding him high over their shoulders chanting, *Theron the great!* Long live *Theron the great! Slayer of beasts!* — the merriment of the people rocking him back and forth as the men slapped him on his back and gazed upon him with admiration.

His daydream was suddenly broken as Medusa flipped him onto his back and climbed atop of him, pressing down on his body. "It is time a woman had the upper hand!" she said, wrapping her thighs tightly around him. Theron did not care. He had already reached the point of no return. Gliding his hands over her breasts and across her stomach, he made his way to his belt where the knife was hidden. Plunging his manhood inside her, he reached up and pushed her head back to expose her neck. Opening his eyes, he pulled out the blade and with one fluent motion took a long hard stab towards her throat as he rammed inside her. In the blink of an eye, she caught the blade in her hand and with a steely gaze directed at him, tossed it aside. Holding him down, this time, her legs felt like steel cages around his waist, she viciously rode him until she was satisfied and he was spent. Then gliding her hands over his face and chest, she said, "There! That was *pleasurable*, was it not, Theron?! You are a very attractive beast after all!"

Suddenly repulsed by what he was doing, Theron tried to throw her off, but, she squeezed her thighs together around him, tighter and tighter still, until tears began to run from his eyes. "Stop this!" he cried out. "Release me... release me and I will leave and promise never to come here again!" Medusa only smiled wickedly and clenched tighter. "Please! I *beg* you! *Release* me! You are crushing me!" he shouted desperately, feeling as if the stone walls themselves were closing in on him.

"You have *used* up your chances, Theron! Now you will lose what you prize most — your **manhood**!"

Theron grabbed her throat but it was to no avail. Feeling his strength withering and his back breaking, he grasped at her face, again and again, thinking to tear out her eyes. Then, Medusa grabbed his hand and leaned in close to his face. The impulse to turn away now a distant memory, the irresistible glow of her eyes drew him ever nearer.

"Your *eyes*! They are so... *beautiful*! In your eyes I see... *everything*!" Spoken with such astonishment, his fears, his lusts, his longings and all his wishes had all suddenly vanished from his heart as he turned cold. For the very first time in his life, he had found peace; complete and utter peace. Medusa got up and put on her robe and then turned to look at Theron lying there with one arm reaching out; his eyes fixed in an eternal look of love, his lips slightly apart. He made a perfect sculpture of male perfection in every way.

The pursuit now over, Medusa wanted to be left alone with her solitude once more. Walking to the cave entrance high above the ocean waves where the men sat in wait for their hero, their drunken merriment had withered. With aching heads they sat in the sand waiting for Theron's return, with sleep almost overtaking them as they heard the sound of rocks falling from above. Rousting themselves, they looked up towards the entrance of the cave high above and saw an imposing figure standing beside another draped in black. Believing Theron had completed his quest, they began to cheer and shout for joy, their champion, *Theron the Great* had done it again! Appearing to be holding something in his hand, the men all stared, trying to make out what it was. Then, before their very eyes, the figure seemed to leap off the precipice, landing at their feet. As it broke into pieces, they saw the disembodied stone member of their hero lying in the sand. Dropping their jugs of wine, they ran as fast as their intoxicated bodies would take them. Theron's broken, peaceful face lay in the sand, his emotions frozen in stone as a lesson for all through eternity.

The old man stood below, looking up at Medusa with glaring ocean blue eyes, smiling. Seeing through the Poseidon's disguise, Medusa turned away from the light, her eyes ever sadder as she knew she continued to be a pawn for the amusement of the Gods. Returning to the shadows of her lair, she vanished into the darkness, alone once more with her regret and despair. It was time once again for her to vanish; to slip into the night and never return to this place.

CHAPTER FIFTEEN

Leaving the familiar for the unknown was no longer difficult. Everyone Medusa had ever known and loved had left her one by one. People she loved and lost, places she longed to be but could never return to, her own image, her own voice, not even the daylight seemed familiar anymore. The bright colours of a sunlit day now scorched her sensitive eyes and made her sometimes wonder if those idyllic days of her youth in Avernae were just a dream; like so many other visions that now passed in and out of her consciousness at will.

It was once again time to leave, so she picked up her only remaining possessions, her bow and quiver, slung them over her back and covered her head with her dark cloak. Although it had not been Poseidon's intention to send Medusa into further sorrow, he again without clear thought pushed her deeper into despair.

The killing was now taking its toll on Medusa.

Her conscience had begun fading in and out of reality; at times not sure of what was fact, what was fantasy, as shadows played over the army of stone corpses she left in her wake. Howling screams emitting from stone shut mouths, tears dripping from granite tear ducts; *why do some men appear at rest while others seem entombed in a body of stone for all eternity?* She needed direction. Though she prayed to Artemis for guidance, she received none. "Give me a sign my Goddess! Why have you forsaken me?! I use the bow you had given me; I dedicate my prayers so devotedly, as I did in Brauron.

Why do you remain silent? Are you even there?" Medusa spoke to the cloudless night sky as the countless stars shined so brightly, in hope that someone was listening, that she was not alone. Unbeknownst to her, she was not truly alone, for her mother, Ceto, had prepared for this occasion with great foresight.

In her most grievous moments of desperation, calls from afar began. Her Gorgon sisters Euryale, *She of the Bellowing Cries*, and Stheno, *the Forceful*, who had been keeping a watchful eye on their little sister's progression into darkness, had become quite pleased with the number of souls she had so efficiently accumulated in recent months. From an island at the edge of the world, the reigning Queens of the Underworld now stood at the precipice of the highest cliff and beckoned their sibling: "We will find you, Sister! You are not alone!"

Screeching cries that shrieked across the waves and boomed over the lands of Greece like heat lightening, Stheno and Euryale were prepared to finally bring Medusa home to her rightful place.

Caught in a mortal siege and drenched in human blood, Medusa had on this day, destroyed an army of villagers who had cornered and ambushed her in the narrow canyons of the Tymfi Mountains just before dusk. Bodies of the slain, now lay strewn across the once green marshland, silently dripping oceans of blood into the unsuspecting river, turning it sickening red. Stepping over the mutilated corpses, she knelt at the river's edge to wash the stain of death from her hands, pausing for a moment to look at her horrid, blood-covered reflection in the water's stillness. Like every time now that she met her tragic reflection; tears flowed from her tormented eyes as the sight of herself sickened her. Pulling herself up, she stared hopelessly in the bloody waters once more.

Over her shoulder, the sun had begun to rise behind the jagged mountain peaks, a single stream of dim light now illuminating the stone army that stood beyond a field of scattered, mutilated bodies. These were the soldiers who were not afforded the chance to fight. Frozen in place by her deadly glare, they stood perfectly preserved as testament to her awesome and treacherous powers. Placing her hand once more in the cool waters, she began to feel a strange vibration from beneath the surface.

Without further warning, and at a speed faster than the lightning reflexes of the Gorgon, a gigantic red tentacle emerged from the waters and wrapped itself around Medusa in a fatal stranglehold. Before she could break loose of its grip, it vanished into the depths of the murky waters, pulling Medusa down with it. Struggling to be released, she tried with all her great strength to tear the monster's tentacles from her body, but her efforts proved futile, its strength proving far beyond any ordinary creature of the deep. Pulling her deeper still, the gigantic creature dragged her to the bottom of the river and then out to sea, her quiver of arrows lost in the struggle. Succumbing to its grip, she ceased clawing at its tough, armoured skin and waited for the chance to escape.

Her radiant, green eyes served as torches in the shadowy depths, acting as beacons through the black abyss where coral reefs illuminated in bright shining colours and the sands glimmered golden like the ring on her finger. Though submerged in deepening water, her lungs did not long for air; now calmly, she scanned her surroundings in anticipation of an escape. Through the shadowy waters ahead, she saw a cave entrance encrusted with coral and teaming with sea creatures of every kind. As the beast took her nearer the entrance, she felt herself being drawn to something within the cave. And there within the green and black, shell-encrusted limestone formations, two faces began to emerge. Two ghastly female visages seemingly trapped within the rock, their fangs slipped fittingly over their full luscious lips. Then from the silence of the water's depths, four mesmerizing globes came like a clap of lightening, hitting Medusa's eyes; two globes of crimson red and two of macabre violet that pierced her vision with blinding ferocity.

The animated faces swayed like great serpents of the deep, their lolling tongues protruding — hissing at Medusa from within their living tombs. Curiously, she watched as the monstrous beings detached themselves from the rocks and reached out to her as the tentacled creature brought her near, pieces of coral and stone dropping from their long arms and shining, bronze claws. As she struggled to break free of the red beast's grip, the monstrous pair caught Medusa by the arms, pulling her into the dark cave they had been guarding. Again finding herself overpowered, the two pulled her through the water with great speed, leaving her no time to escape. The journey through the dark passage ended as she was hurled out of the black waters and onto a dry cavern floor far below the ocean surface.

Quickly leaping to her feet, Medusa looked out towards the bobbing surface for a sign of the two; her heart thumping as if trying to escape her chest. Dripping wet, she stood with her misty black, serpentine hair wild with rage, writhing like seaweed in an ocean storm. Ready to pounce at anything that moved, she saw something slowly begin to emerge from the water. Like two great living winged pillars from the Temple of Zeus, two hideous female beings gracefully rose from the water and approached Medusa. Their eyes burning brightly through the darkness, Medusa felt an awareness of these beastly creatures she had never experienced before. Both taller than her, their black wings fluttered in the air, the golden tips of their feathers clanked like swords crossing in battle. Medusa watched as they stood before her, their long, draping gowns matching the colour of their eyes — one of blood red and one of striking violet.

One of them reached out her shining bronze hands to Medusa and forced a serene and low tone: "Do not fear us, Medusa. We are not here to harm you." Medusa remained silent as the creature with violet eyes shrieked, "Medusa, I am Euryale. It is good to see you, sister..." The red-eyed figure stepped forward and put her hands on the other's shoulders as she spoke. "Medusa we, like you, are daughters of Ceto!"

Medusa stared into their faces, long enough to turn them into silent pillars of stone. Looking closer, she saw that Euryale's deep, violet eyes swirled like two universes flowing with stars that sparkled and shone so captivatingly that surely once a mortal man caught their beauty, he would forever be trapped in fascination. Cautiously reaching out to Euryale, she placed her hand in hers, feeling the bronze move with life as if it were flesh and blood. She saw that she wore the same golden ring set with a large, flat, green stone that Medusa wore. She felt the immediate, familial connection.

Stepping closer, the red-eyed female said, "I am Stheno. And as you will soon discover, we are one and the same." Stheno's eyes were different from Euryale's; fiery and explosive. No hypnotic placidity could be found within them. Instead, the power of a thousand volcanoes erupting could be seen at a glance, for a human mortal to look into these eyes, would surely mean being burned alive from the core outwards; her eyes were like windows into Hades' fiery depths. Stheno placed her hands on Medusa's arms and embraced her lovingly. There was no need for words as each sister, united at last, felt each other's spirit and heard each other's thoughts.

The healing energy brought by this union reminded Medusa of her childhood and her earthly sisters who had loved her so; something she missed and needed dearly; unconditional love was offered to her once again. Here, she felt a place of belonging she thought she would never share. With her newly-found sisters who understood what it meant to be in-between worlds, she could finally calm the pain. They led Medusa up through the underground caverns to the top of the mountain where they pointed towards the climbing sun. Stheno spoke proudly with a loud, commanding voice, "*There*, Medusa...*there* is where we must take you, to the caverns deep below Mount Olympus where we will teach you to use the full extent your powers."

Medusa looked at the sun and all the magnificent colours her new eyes showed her. Staring outward towards a future she was not yet certain she wanted, her sisters took her by the arms and leapt off the cliff's edge... spreading their giant bronze wings as they descended and swooped off towards their home.

Reaching the bright and magnificent Mount Olympus, home of the Gods Most High, the sisters hid their true appearance by turning themselves into large, black crows that could slip by unnoticed. Flying through a shielded stone entrance at the very base of the mountain, the view changed quickly as the beautiful majesty of the mount above revealed its terrifying deep and dark underbelly. Caverns worthy of the torture chambers of Hades were found; each deeper than the one before; each robbing further, the breath and pressing the mind to primal thoughts of terror and panic. No human had ever survived entry here; Medusa still being mortal, felt her mind begin to stray. However, once inside, she felt a sense of belonging she had never felt in her life.

Learning now what it truly meant to be a Gorgon, Medusa found herself once again a student; an apprentice under the guidance of Stheno and Euryale. The lessons, were many and the preparation difficult and gruelling. However, time had no measure in this middle place between the worlds. Euryale directed Medusa to a shallow running stream.

As you now see, Medusa, our eyes are our windows into our victims' Psyche. They are our most precious gift, giving us vision no other being possesses, and letting us draw close, our victims, until their mortal lives become ours.

Believing that her humanity had left her long ago, every kill having further numbed her mind, the beast within Medusa began to take greater command. She listened intently to the teachings of her sisters, their thoughts conveying purpose and method without the need of a single spoken word. Finally, the day arrived for Medusa to be unleashed upon the people of the earth.

As a fierce and relentless enemy of mankind, she was now conditioned to kill without remorse; to cause grief and suffering to those who, in her mind, were deserving of her wrath. Standing naked in the darkness of the cavern, Stheno anointed Medusa's body with sacred herbs mixed with myrrh as Euryale emerged with a black dress to clothe Medusa's well-conditioned body. Euryale replaced Medusa's lost quiver with a thin, black quiver, stocked with three ebony arrows saying: *Take this quiver. It was crafted by Hephaestus himself. The arrows will fire with unequalled force and pierce any armour. The quiver will never run empty as long as you are the archer, Medusa.*

Medusa ran her fingers along one smooth shaft to the dark, razor-sharp tip. Presenting her hand, she was thrilled at the sight of black blood dripping from her finger. Her sisters smiled at one other, now certain their little sister was truly ready for the bloody rampage she was made for. Medusa took wing.

During the bloodiest attacks in the region of Epirus, Chaos and slaughter ran rampant. Through the silence after the battles, only the eerie swirling of the wind could be heard as Medusa scornfully marched through the decimated streets, stepping over the butchered bodies of the warriors sent to destroy her and her sisters. The banners of the fallen army hung ragged and torn over the white marble archway that stood, still intact, as a testament to the magnificent architecture of the acropolis. So pleased was she with the carnage she had created that she almost did not notice the hand that meekly grasped at her ankle.

Swinging her claw in rage, she turned to find a severely wounded man at her feet; not a warrior, but a young, unarmed boy who had been caught up in the massacre. No more than seventeen years of age, his eyes were glazed white, his chest torn open; his precious life was draining from his adolescent chest in a river of red. With his final breath quickly approaching, Medusa betrayed her convictions, finding sorrow in her cold heart. Kneeling down, she took him into her blood-stained arms. The world around her fell dark and silent as she realized the boy she had torn to pieces was blind. As time stopped and the seconds passed, she looked into his face as he faded further away from life.

With mere seconds left, Medusa made her choice. Digging one of her black arrows into the palm of her right hand, she let her cold, black blood run freely. Bringing her hand to the boy's white lips, she felt his heart's final beat. She watched silently as his pale face froze in place, the blood on his lips dripping down his rigid lips, to his neck. Believing that her brief moment of mercy had been given in vain, she held the boy's lifeless body to her bosom and turned to face the sun's blinding light. Silently she rocked him in her arms as she could hear her sister's screeches in the distance, calling her back to resume the butchery.

Suddenly, her thoughts and grief were broken by a groan. She looked down to see the boy's lips moving. Tearing open his tunic, she saw the gruesome wounds she had inflicted to the boys chest were starting to heal themselves, her sister's words ringing true. As Euryale had told her, a single drop of blood from her left hand would kill even Colossus. However, a drop from her right could resurrect the dead. She watched his chest mend as he began to take shallow breaths. Her brief moment of serenity was once again disturbed however, by the familiar sound of arrows whizzing through the air.

With lightning-quick reflexes, she shot off into a nearby abandoned home with the boy still safe in her arms. Placing him against the battered stone wall, she watched for approaching enemies. Feeling a tug on her robe, she turned to see that not only had the boy's wounds healed, the rosy colour of the living had returned to his boyish face. As she looked down upon him, she watched as his eyes began to regenerate. His very first hazy vision was of Medusa pulling back and averting her gaze. Smiling, he whispered a simple, "Thank you."

Conflicted by her monstrous thirst for revenge and her inner human compassion that still tugged at her heart, she quickly left the building, taking one last glance back at the boy whose life she had returned. Combating a rain of arrows, she fled the city through the rough and dry mountains that lined Epirus, knowing she had had her fill of carnage and death. Sickened by the life of hunt and be hunted, kill or be killed, she now knew she must somehow break free of it all. Listening to the terrified screams of men being massacred and the ferocious sounds of her sisters' bloodthirsty attacks, she quietly made her way up into the mountains. Climbing with great speed, she leaped and clawed her way up until she could no longer hear the sounds of death. Reaching a bare, stone plateau where only a single lifeless tree stood, she sat down, feeling the whistling wind on her skin. Her eyes half open, her face and body splattered with dried, human blood, she sat perfectly still for the first time in a very long time. As night fell, there she remained, motionless and deep in mournful thought.

What have I done? What have I become?! Whose word to follow? Am I cursed to be between worlds forever?

Through the night's silence, her senses caught the distinctive acrid odour of a torch burning. Pulling her bow from her shoulder, she prepared an arrow. Scanning her surroundings, she stood poised, ready to launch a volley to warn off any aggressors as she made her escape. Then, as she slowly turned, she saw the faint glowing of light coming from a cavern a short distance away. Cautiously making her way down, she expected to find another band of heavily armed soldiers tending to their wounded or preparing to mount an attack. What she found instead was a most unexpected sight.

There, a beautiful temple lit with bright torches illuminated walls vibrant with painted stories. Venturing inside, she realized she had stumbled upon the fabled Necromanteion of Acheron, a mystical place long rumoured to have been skilfully carved into the mountain. Here, it was said, pilgrims from all across the lands of Greece entered to contact their deceased ancestors. The walls depicted stories of souls leaving this mortal realm and entering the underworld through the ancient fountain of Lake Akherousia, a lake so serene that not even the wind moved it. And if anyone was to ever see a ripple in the crystal clear waters, it was surely a soul passing through to its final resting place.

Medusa cautiously made her way through the maze of narrow, well-worn corridors, descended into a great hall. The angular turns of the path were so precise and smooth, it seemed almost impossible that human hands could have created such a place. Rounding a turn, she sensed many mortal souls and found huddled there, on the floor, dozens of pilgrims covered in blankets of white wool, shielding their eyes from Medusa. As she cautiously walked past the trembling assemblage, one dared raise her hand to Medusa, holding a small gold coin.

"T-Take this below for my husband... *please.*"

Medusa looked at the coin. "I am not a messenger."

"Please, Gorgon, forgive me! My husband died in the sea. The coin is for you, protectress."

"Protectress?" She repeated bewildered. A loud crash thundered throughout the temple halls and shook everyone into terrified silence. Medusa gently took the coin from the woman's trembling hand, seeing the chance to escape her monstrous role in the half-life she had been living. "I will take this for his soul's peace," she said.

"Thank you, protectress. May the Gods bless and keep you."

Medusa cringed at the woman's words and walked on, her mind a clutter, for this was the first conversation she had had with a human being in such a very long time. A few paces along, she found a large, open entrance leading into the temple of the dead. Dividing the corridors and upper chambers from the temple below was an opening in the floor, no wider than a step through which flowed a pale blue curtain of steam and smoke. Not taking heed, she crossed the step, inhaling the sweet cerulean steam cleared her mind as she stood in awe of the sight before her.

There, a massive, pristine white temple carved in the shape of a perfect dome with perfectly formed deep flowing lines sat, crafted in a great swirling vortex that circled around the dome walls which met at the very top where an open, round shaft invited in the sun's celestial light. She touched the walls, intrigued by what she saw; not at all certain it was not all an illusion. Her dark form emerged in the brilliant light; she saw her skin shine as bright as her eyes.

For the first time, she felt so very small and humbled within this world. The serenity was broken as she heard a female voice softly calling out her name. "*Medusa...*" the echo resonating all around. Reaching for her bow, she quickly turned towards the voice. There, standing behind a simple alter that was carved within the room's rock, she saw a sight most unexpected. Emerging from behind the alter, stood Soteria, the High Priestess of the Temple of Athena, dressed in a dark green peplos that flowed to the ground, she wore a magnificent golden mask that averted her eyes. Medusa held tight to her bow. The last time she had seen the High Priestess was that fateful night when Athena had exacted her cruel revenge. Now, calculating Soteria's presence, with the mask, this was not a chance meeting.

"What is all this?" Medusa authoritatively enquired.

Calmly and with the same clear and powerful voice Medusa had always trusted, Soteria moved forward as she spoke. "Medusa, the day Athena came down from Mount Olympus and manifested before me was the most glorious moment of my life. Absolution for the many years I had devoted to her Sacred Temple."

"High Priestess! I mean, Soteria, if you are here to praise her name you can..."

"That day, Medusa, I saw for the first time the true colours of the Gods; or sadly, what they have now become. There was no justice, Medusa, in afflicting such torture upon you and this from the Goddess said to be of the wise and just. That is why I am here now. To serve *you*."

"Serve *me*?! I am no *God*!"

"You, Medusa, are the future. I believe that your dreams, yours visions, the purpose of your very existence is to expose the Gods for what they have now have become. It is within your power to free us from the Olympian tyrants who have dominated our lives for so long and restore purity of heart and spirit, as the universe intended. You can give us a new dawn where people can rely on a truer form of belief."

Medusa scoffed bitterly, "You are mistaken, Soteria. There is nothing *I* can do! Nothing but run and hide in secret places, within the shadows far from mortal sight. I am constantly hunted as a vicious demon! Why would you... why would *anyone* want to follow me?"

"Because, Medusa, a change is on the near horizon and many believe that you will be the one to usher it in. Long has the great Oracle of Dodoni spoken about a shift of power... a *Liberation*, Medusa! For all humanity"

"I will not listen to this, Soteria! I have been toyed with enough by Gods and mortals alike. I just want *peace*. I just want to be left alone with my Fate!"

"That is the very reason you have been chosen, Medusa. For eons, the Gods have played with our lives and left us as helpless as children at their mercy. We pray, we beg, we whimper under their mercy. You... *You*, Medusa, who is neither of this world nor another, *you,* are the one who can tip the balance of the scales in favour of those who deserve to be liberated! The people of Athens! The people of all Greece!"

Medusa turned in contemplation. "I have no chance at redemption, Soteria. There is nothing left for me now. Do you not see that I am an outcast to both mortals and Gods?!"

Soteria approached, lowering her powerful voice to a tender tenor, "Listen to me, Medusa. I am not alone in this quest. Not the only one who believes you are the chosen one. There are others... *many* others in *all* the temples of Greece; in *all* places of worship! They are waiting to join us, to lead us! Please! Sit, Medusa! Take your rightful place on your throne and accept the glory that is yours and yours alone! Think about it! Have all the events of your life not led up to this very moment?"

Medusa turned to see a throng of women emerging from behind the stone white altar, each wearing the same long green robes, flowing elegantly, as they moved across the room. Each wearing golden masks that allowed them to see only the ground before them. As Medusa looked closer, she saw her dear friend Xenophoni and Adelpha and Dorothea among them. Xenophoni stepped forward and put her arms around Medusa. "Medusa, I love you with all my heart, as do all these women who now stand here before you. Neither God nor demon could ever deter our devotion to you. You were born for this moment, Medusa. Please. Hear the words Nephthys has come here to say."

Nephthys, a young woman of no more than twenty years, stepped forward. Ghostly pale and thin, she had always been *"different,"* as if she were of two worlds at once. She came forward without a mask to shield her eyes, eyes black as night against her ivory white skin. She bore the appearance of an apparition; an ethereal being nearly translucent in the almost blinding light of the dome temple. Her words, slow and deliberate, Nephthys' soft voice was barely audible, as if every word took her breath away and left her completely exhausted.

"Me-du-sa, it has been shown to me many times… your path is not a dissent into dark obscurity but, a quiet rise to power. Just as the God Asclepius was unjustly killed by Zeus only to be resurrected, you too shall take your place amongst the stars of the heavens. "You, Me-du-sa, will leave this body behind… very soon. However, it is for the rebirth of an undying spirit, one that will forever be the protector of the innocent."

"Do you mean I must soon *die*? Is that what you are trying to say?"

"Me-du-sa, you must be released from these earthly, mortal shackles and all they represent by a man who is himself but a puppet of the Gods. He will have no choice but to come for you... and you will sacrifice yourself one final time for eternal glory."

"Dying does not frighten me, Nephthys. I welcome an end to this misery. However, my new-found instinct does not allow me to surrender. I am only able to fight to the death to survive."

"And you know, Me-du-sa, just as I do, what that is inside you. But fear not, the true essence of you will survive. It is eternal, unbreakable..."

Soteria stepped forward, "Stay among us, Medusa. Fulfill the prophecies and I swear to you on my mortal soul that you will find peace of mind, body and spirit in the end. And we will all be here waiting for your return. Go down the path to Hades and see what the souls have to say about the Gods."

The High Priestesses turned and revealed a hidden doorway within the dome's white, walls. Parting it, Medusa saw a dark, foreboding passageway with jagged, black stone barriers roughly hewn, steep and narrow. The heat emitting from the darkness burned and smouldered against the cool white dome. The smell of sulfur sickened the priestesses who turned away. A mysterious, harsh green fume emitted through cracks that swirled out of the dark passage, evaporating as it reached the upper reaches of the dome. Medusa drew closer to the opening and peered in, listening to the eerie echoes that sounded like the wails and screams of tortured souls. Soteria stood behind her urging, "Complete your journey and find your answer, Medusa. We will all be waiting for you on the other side." Medusa glanced back over her shoulder at Xenophoni, who held in her hand a small wooden votive of a Gorgon. Xenophoni smiled at her and bowed "go forth and seek justice for yourself... and for all my friend... my savior". Medusa then fearlessly stepped through the archway into the cramped, black passageway.

The door closed behind her as she took the crooked, descending path through the intoxicating mist and into the bowels of the earth. Disorientating sounds played around her as the pitch black corridor dropping rapidly like a hypnotizing vortex that swirled and plunged downward as quickly as Medusa's thoughts.

Could they be right? Could this be the purpose I was created for? Ceto, you may have sealed your own fate with your actions. Maybe you wanted an end to this as I do?

As her mind spiralled, her thoughts flew off into fantasy as through her illuminating eyes she saw images emerge from the walls' ominously dark surface. Countless faces of fallen men swirled around the walls; their expressions frozen still, their eyes could only follow the Gorgon. Hearing their silenced screams from within their stone tombs they begged her for salvation as she descended further into the oppressing heat.

The ravaged, screaming eyes of the dead followed her down the sloping path as she heard bellowing cries for help that penetrated her weakening consciousness like daggers. Finally reaching the entrance to the great underground Temple of Hades, she grasped the polished basalt walls of the temple entrance. Through the green vapour she could see the ancient and destitute shrine of the dead. The shrine, a simple hole cut out of the dark stone, lead to an endless pit of hopelessness and despair. This was guarded by a giant skeletal figure, holding a razor sharp blade as tall as itself, with four great horns on his skull, two large white horns on top and two smaller black horns protruded from its jaw. Medusa stared at the stationed giant, questioning whether it was sentient. "He cannot see you Medusa…"

Persephone, daughter to Demeter, Queen of the underworld, dressed in a fine red chiton and regal black robe, approached Medusa with an unearthly smile. "Although this is his original form, his mind had left him long ago. Now he stands and guards, only capable of attacking whomever disturbs the shrine."

Medusa needed no introduction to this pale beauty, whose luscious red lips where the only colour on her almost translucent white skin. Her eyes, the colour of snow, her hair white mist of a water fall, Persephone's story flashed before Medusa's eyes.

Persephone in a great field of green and yellow, a tall shadowy figure approached; her fearful look dissipated as he caressed her face. A black chariot, carrying them into the darkness.

"Persephone, do you know why I am here?"

Persephone smiled "Of course, Medusa, and I would like to aid you in your quest."

Medusa curiously looked on as Persephone continued.

"Your quest is no threat to the underworld. In fact we welcome your challenge. You are a part of us after all..."

"How can you help me?"

"There is someone you should meet... He has been with you a very long time, and now that you are here, he would be delighted to speak with you directly." Persephone walked past the dormant giant and nodded to Medusa to follow.

Cautiously, Medusa followed. As they walked, their feet began to tread on ground soft and dark as marsh. The atmosphere cooled and the smell of sulphur was replaced with the sweet scent of lotus flowers. As Medusa trod the moist path, she entered the largest and most vast canyon she had ever seen, with thick patches of red poppies and a single slumbering lamb safely dreaming away under the serenity of this enclosed canyon beneath the earth. Looking up, she saw a false night's sky, complete with stars and a waning moon.

As the path came to an end, she saw that Persephone kept walking.

"Wait! Where are you going? There is no path ahead!"

"Trust me Medusa…"

Persephone walked on, and through the air she continued to tread forth towards a floating island in the very centre of the canyon. Medusa followed, and felt the invisible path beneath her feet hold steady, as she approached a dark, smooth onyx slab. Reaching the island, Persephone looked up and by raising her arms revealed two great gates that floated in the air at either side of the onyx bed which sat on what appeared as solid ground.

"Medusa, these are the gates of Ivory and Horn. The gates of Ivory represent empty dreams, false meanings and deception. The gates of Horn represent the true meaning of dreams, fulfilment of destiny and clear visions. You have always been true to your destiny Medusa. Now it is time to choose if you want to continue on this path. A path that will bring you the burden of enlightenment, with sorrow and strain but one, that will also liberate the innocent and bring greater good on a greater scale. Or… you have the choice to revert back and be as the skeletal Giant now is, free of worry, sorrow and understanding, but peaceful in his ignorance. Follow the path of Ivory if you wish to take this fate; or… head up to the gate of Horn if you want answers to your most hidden thoughts. Once you are awakened, there is no turning back Medusa."

Medusa had a choice to make, a chance to relieve her soul of this heavy burden, to become free of any guilt, thought or curiosity; a chance to live forever in a dream of serenity.

"If I choose serenity, I will not ever change, nothing will ever matter again, it will all be over… An eternity will pass and I would never know it… but if I choose to be awakened and follow the path Soteria believes I have been created for, I might never find true peace.

I will be constantly burdened by my own guilt and regrets."

Medusa stepped back…

Persephone waited silently for Medusa to choose her path.

Medusa whispered to herself: *Resting forever in ignorance is a death I would not wish on anyone.*

"I will take my burden in the faith that I will make it through and fulfil my role in this game."

Persephone exhaled with relief and stated "Then… Medusa, I will see you very soon."

Medusa looked up and walked the invisible path to the gates of Horn.

"Thank you Persephone" were her parting words as Medusa vanished through the gates.

Medusa now found herself in a world of illusion; where night and day simultaneously shared the skies, where waterfalls rained diamonds and where the ground was made of soft white cloud. A shadow came over her as she looked up to see a man flying overhead with golden brown wings for arms. As the figure flew from the day into the night, a feather floated down and landed on her shoulder. Picking it up, she felt it stick to her hands as the wax dried. Intrigued, she stepped forward in this dreamy existence to see a male figure emerging from a Cyan forest.

Handsome and tall, this dark stranger arrived with a friendly smile on his full, beautiful lips. Medusa found herself stirred and staring at this enchanting man, whose inviting beauty kept her breaths short and heartbeats fast. Scanning from the ground to his head, she marvelled at his well-conditioned body that was only partially covered under a cape of blended colours that moved within the cloths' black surface.

With an everlasting smile he spoke tenderly to her "Medusa, I have not seen you in such a very long time."

He leaned gently forward, embracing Medusa fully and lovingly in his strong arms. Medusa's eyes opened wide at the unexpected familiarity between herself and this beautiful stranger that held her so tenderly.

Pulling back, he continued:

"It must bring you great sorrow, to not dream anymore… Other Immortals would not understand, but you, who have lived as a human, surely you must long for a dream?"

Medusa thought a moment before her reply, "I have not slept since the transformation… Yes, I do miss the respite of sleep and especially of dreams, even the darker ones that unnerved me. Given my choice of eternal slumber or eternal consciousness, I know I entered the correct gate. I… I know you… not by face, but by presence. Please, tell me your name?"

Medusa looked into his bright eyes which were multi-coloured with a base of black as his cape; they danced and swirled with colours and the sparkle of polished diamonds.

"Medusa, I am Morpheus, son of Hypnos. Thus far, I have lived only in your dreams which I shape and form to give you rest, pleasure and calm. But most importantly, I help you see the path ahead, your future, and your destiny. I caution you and inspire you. I am the shaper of your dreams…"

Medusa reached out, her pale clawed hand and caressed Morpheus' short black hair. Bringing herself closer she closed her eyes and passionately kissed Morpheus; held in a warm embrace, she saw his soul and true form emerge in her mind. A dark void with majestic black wings, his entire being was made of the night sky, with stars and planets that shone and flickered from within its darkness. His eyes kind and dreamy, his aura gentle and calm, Medusa felt safe in his arms.

"Morpheus, in this awakened state, where am I to find all answers to my questions? Will I ever dream again?"

Morpheus kissed Medusa sweetly as they reclined on a bed of black onyx.

As their eyes met once more a surge of energy released between them. As the green and black sparks merged, Medusa's sight fell black. Through this blindness, flashes of colourful smoke exploded and vanished; growing ever closer to her. Through each flash of smoke, an image of a male could be seen approaching. Green, purple, red, blue, gold, grey, every flash, left, then right, she saw a man with wild golden hair; his athletic stature catching Medusa's mind's eye.

From a golden haze of smoke, he emerged directly before Medusa. Resembling Morpheus, this fairer man had golden wings in his hair and golden sandy eyes; clothed only with a black cloth skirt. He smiled provocatively at Medusa while bringing to his lips a golden bowl of which he drank a dark fluid. Coming closer, he passionately kissed Medusa, the fluid from his lips tasted sweet and smelled like flowers. Releasing his embrace, he slowly distanced himself.

"Sleep well my dear friend."

Medusa's vision became smoky and hazed, her eyes fell heavy, her head lightened as she found herself drifting off to a sweet slumber; the first in a very long time. Through the peaceful respite of sleep, her subconscious awakened in the form of a beautiful dream. In this dream, her body felt light and graceful, her surroundings were bright and welcoming. Soft golden sand caressed her bare feet as a bright sun that shone against the tender blades of grass, that lined her path warmed her. She was surrounded by a beautifully rich foliage made of dark green shrubs and tall silver birch trees, whose trunks glistened in the sunlight.

She heard the sound of the living ocean calling her from the far end of the path. The sound of rolling waves from the gentle tide a foaming shore, filled Medusa's heart with unprecedented joy. She began racing down the path, the soft sand sparkling like diamonds as it flew in the air by her furious footsteps.

The invigorating smell of the salty seas filled her lungs as her heart pounded at the excitement of seeing the ocean once more. There it was — the vast, open body of water that Medusa called home. Approaching the water's edge, she closed her eyes and bathed in the sun's warm glow; with all the ocean's essence surrounding her senses.

Opening her eyes once more, she saw that the colours were real and her sight was normal, her soul felt light and she saw her long golden locks being swayed by the gentle ocean breeze. With the pleasant realization that she was human once more, she looked down to see her soft white skin beneath a thin white peplos she was clothed in. Tears began to roll down her gentle face as she saw her reflection in the water: *I'm back…*

In this wondrous dream she happily sat, following her human urges, to pick and eat fresh fruit from the bountiful trees which like the garden of the Hesperides, flourished endlessly as far as the eye could see. She drank from the cool waterfalls that fountained down to crystal lakes.

The sweetest fluid to ever touch my lips.

Soon forgetting her plights, her fears and her guilt, she became lost in the Elysian Fields that were mercifully created by the master of all dreams, Morpheus. He sat contently and watched on, as her memories faded and her spirit freed.

"A gift unparalleled by any other, Medusa; I give you peace of mind, body and soul. Something I know you have longed for now for a very long time. Enjoy your sweet freedom, as soon, I must come to awaken you…"

His words true, this shaper of dreams had to awaken Medusa before her memories had slipped away completely. Gently he caressed her shoulder as she stood watching the magnificent sight of sun setting silently over the now crimson waters of the evening.

Turning with a placid smile, her calm eyes glittering with happiness. She looked at this perfectly handsome stranger. "Do I know you from some place? Perhaps we met once in town?"

Morpheus' eyes ever calm and smiling replied "Perhaps…"

Medusa's expression became curious, her mind trying to place her memories of this gentle stranger's kind eyes. Following her inner instinct, she placed her hands over his beardless face; her fiercely green eyes bonding with his serene dark gaze. She leaned in and kissed him sweetly.

The sun had silently slipped away behind the water's edge. As she released her embrace she felt a shroud of darkness fall over her. Suddenly the sky felt empty, the ocean barren, the once Elysian Fields now grew dry and dead. Lost in his gaze, her vision tunnelled down the darkness and passed all of the sparkling stars and galaxies that lived in Morpheus' eyes. In its entirety, Medusa became a Gorgon once more.

Morpheus smiled as he kissed her forehead, "Come Medusa, it is time to see what the future will bring…"

Taking her hand he led her through the panicle points of all her future events. Rushing scenes changed before them as they walked calmly forward. Seeing as the years progressed and the lands changed, Medusa saw the entire evolution of society before her; stopping inexplicably with a flash of light. Fading back to black, her eyes adjusted to the sight of Persephone before her. Rising up from the onyx bed, she found herself back at the island deep below the necromanteion.

"Did you find him?"

"Yes, I found what I was looking for…"

This one and only peaceful respite was to be her only rest, before falling back into the harshness of the living world. Thanking Persephone, she left through a secret veil from the underworld back to the necromanteions exterior. As she emerged from the black stone, gasps and chatter could be heard from below. One female pilgrim shouted, "The Gorgon has emerged! Avert your eyes!" to the crowd that grew by the hundreds to see the Gorgon.

Medusa looked down in utter disbelief as the number of followers were far greater than she had seen in her vision. An indication that not everything in her dreams was to become in reality absolutely accurate. She saw Soteria and the priestesses at the forefront, waiting for her to announce her decision.

Having seen enough, Medusa looked around and she spoke loudly so that all could hear:

"Your gods! Your gods were once my gods. Your fears were once mine. Your desires, your needs and wants, once enslaved me as they still enslave you. Your gods have given me this fate, and now your gods will prepare to fade from your existence as they have now faded from mine."

Hearing the words that they had long for, the crowd kneeled before Medusa in respect and adoration. Soteria bowed and raised her left hand in the symbol of a snake; using her index and middle finger as fangs and crossing her other fingers with her thumb, the symbol shared both the characteristics of a snake and an oath known as an "Orkismos". This was to be the new secret symbol for the followers of Medusa.

CHAPTER SIXTEEN

On the idyllic island of Seriphos, far from mainland Greece, Athens and the legend of Medusa, a vigilant King named Polydectes looked down from his magnificent stone fortress built atop the highest mountain of his small, rocky isle. He peered down with fox-like eyes into his private fig orchards where his heart's desire, the fair Danaë, sat with a golden harp perched in her porcelain arms playing an enchanting melody sweetly. His emotions possessed and overwhelmed him as his eyes followed her elegant fingers gently strumming the lyre he had gifted her. It was as if she was playing with the very strings of his aging, love-struck heart. His bosom bursting with desire, he knew he could not wait much longer to have her as his own.

"There… there she sits, Kleon, so near to my sight yet so far from my touch."

"Yes, my Lord."

"For years she has been under my protection and for years I have I watched her flutter around my heart's broken gates! As time passes, I grow evermore distant from her affections no thanks to that bastard child whom she claims is the son of Zeus — the *King of the Gods*, no less! No wonder her father, Acrisius, cast them both into the wild seas. With such *extraordinary* tales, who could blame him? Is the King of Seriphos not good enough to be her suitor?" The King paused and stroked his long white beard in a moment of apprehensive reflection. "He cast her out — to my good fortune! To be caught in my little brother Dictys' nets. The sea had provided me an unparalleled gift! However, to my very *bad* fortune, the seas also returned the *boy*, alive and well, to grow here coddled and protected by my dear naïve little brother who treats him as if he were spawn of his own loins!"

The King scoffed bitterly and shook his head. "Indeed, my Lord," Kleon said, shaking his head in concern. "He has raised the boy considerably well, *considering…* Given him all that he ever wanted or needed, to reach a strong manhood. Taught him to fight like a warrior of Sparta and fuelled his spirit with praise and ideas of becoming unstoppable in achieving greatness!"

"Bah!" said the King, batting his eyes scornfully. "It is that very *boy* that distances me from taking Danaë as my bride! Why would my brother nurture him so? One would think Dictys had no love for his dear older brother… *something must be done*!" The King sat on his imposing throne of heavy dark mahogany and dyed red leather and raised his hand to his pale and furrowed brow in contemplation.

"Well, my Lord, there is *something* that can be done…" Kleon leaned in close, so as not to be overheard. "Send the boy away, *permanently.*"

"You know we have tried *everything* conceivable to eradicate that pest! But, nothing seems to take him from her side where he continues to suckle at her bosom like a puerile milksop! The boy is definitely favoured by the Gods! Although only the *Gods* know *why*!"

King Polydectes felt a deep and evermore demanding anger welling up inside him; anger fuelled by his longing that was reaching its limit. Kleon was right. A clever and perhaps *devious* plan had to be devised. One that would tactfully separate son from mother at least long enough for the king to charm and wed the object of his aging desire.

Taking his thoughts to his bedchamber to contemplate a solution, the King sat in the darkness alone; or so he thought. Unbeknown to him, the answer to his prayers was already close at hand. Athena, who had known of Zeus' bastard child of the mortal Queen Danaë from the very moment he had been conceived, had been gleefully listening to the King's desperate pleas. She had watched Danaë's young boy grow, seeing in him a savage fighting prowess surface early in his gifted life. She also saw in him, an openness to persuasion; a weakness that was created from his desperate willingness to please those who praised his gallantry. This was a situation Athena could utilize for her own dark motives. A perfect setting where she would pit desire against desire, leaving herself as the only true victor.

Athena sat and watched the lonely, agonizing hours pass for King Polydectes. The Sun God Phoebus traversed the open sky in his golden chariot, pulling the Sun from the eastern shores across the land's shining face, then resting majestically beyond Seriphos' great mountains. Just as the sun's glimmering golden light gave way to the darkness of Night, the King drifted off into a deep slumber, taking with him, his fervent desires, into this other realm.

In his world of dreams, the King was free to release his deepest longings. To his utter delight, he found himself in the bedchamber of his beloved Danaë. He watched as she sat on the edge of her luxurious bed with the gentle light of the Moon streaking through her open window, illuminating her soft, white breasts for his admiration. He ran to her and got down upon his knees, taking her lovely, soft hands in his. He smiled adoringly and with a look of pure love in her eyes, she slowly brought his mouth to her young and tender bosom. Pressing his time-ravaged face to her supple breast which had the scent of exotic sandalwood, he suckled anxiously, his long bony fingers drawing her breasts near:

"Oh, Danaë, if you only knew how I love you…! All my greatest treasures… all the *world* could be yours, if only you would say yes to me!" Awakened by the heat of his own desires, the King opened his eyes to find himself lying alone in his bed, seeing before him, only particles of golden dust fading from the form of a beautiful woman now dissolving in the soft breeze. He quickly reached out his hand, but the shimmering particles that played in the Moon's faint light, simply slipped through his knurled fingers. His heart sank once more, his despair evident even in his dreams.

As a desperate tear began to roll down his stern, anguished face, he heard the cackle of an old woman's laughter coming from the room next to his. Wiping his eyes with the sleeve of his bed shirt, he wandered curiously out of his room to an arched entrance where colourful silk and satin cloths hung over the opening. Gently pushing aside the drapes, he entered the room, quickly realizing it was a room he had never seen before. "Who is here?" he called out. "I heard peculiar sounds." No answer came. Moving further inside, the room darkened with each step and by his fifth, he found himself submerged in total darkness. Standing alone in the stillness, he heard the voice of an old woman say: "King or pauper… love makes slaves of us all, does it not, Polydectes?"

Unnerved by this crackling, old voice from the darkness, the King replied, "Indeed." His curiosity piqued, King Polydectes decided to see who offered such acumen. Proceeding a few more steps inside he said, "Truer words have never been spoken. I am eager to hear more of your precious wisdom, Oracle."

The old woman laughed, "Oracle, am I? How did you arrive at that conclusion, Oh, wise King?"

"The intuition of a King seldom goes awry, wise Oracle. I have hosted thousands in my fortress and know the nature of people well. But, I must confess, your powerful energy draws me like no other. From the darkness you have manifested with inexplicable knowledge of my soul. My private thoughts. It would seem you have entered my consciousness to offer, perhaps, a solution to my troubled heartache? Is that so, wise Oracle?"

"And if that were so, Oh, King?"

"Then I would wonder at what price you offer such a solution? Nothing is truly free and without its cost, is that not so, Oracle?"

"A man of clear thought and vision, I see. Practical and to the point. Please, step closer that we may discuss the troubled heartache you speak of, Oh, King."

As the King approached the voice still hidden in the darkness, oil lamps suddenly lit around him and an old woman, wrapped in dark blue indigo cloth, appeared. Small and fragile, her wrinkled hands were neatly crossed, resting on a low, black marble table held up with four fine legs of gilded gold. She looked up to reveal to the King, piercing blue eyes whose stern stare drew the King's failing sight to her, like a moth to the flame. She invited Polydectes to sit down before her. Smiling, he pulled to one side his long, regal red robe and knelt down across from her, watching as her eyes of sapphire traced his every move.

"Hidden within the table's four chambers you see before you four gold coins." She pointed to four small openings, one set into each corner. "Each contains a different solution to your troubles."

"And I am to choose one?" the King said anxiously.

"Indeed. But, the one you choose must be the path you will follow."

Always ready for games and delights, the King eagerly shook his head. "It seems a simple enough task. Do I begin?"

"Then we are in agreement?"

"We are." The King nodded and smiled haughtily, raising his aged hand over the table.

"Very well. But, *first* you must place your trust in me," the old woman said, keeping her eyes fixed on the King. The King looked puzzled. "Reach out your hands, Polydectes and place them within the two black pockets at the centre of the table." Arching his eyebrows suspiciously, the King only smiled.

"All I can say is *trust* me, Polydectes, and you will have the solution to your problems at your disposal."

The King now stared precariously at the old woman. However, he reasoned that given that this was just a game and he was willing to do almost anything to rid himself of the thorn in his bottom that stood between him and his love, he decided this simple task did not seem so daunting. Looking into the old woman's hypnotic glare, he placed his hands in the black pockets and waited. Suddenly, the King began to feel something tightening around his hands. He began to struggle as the old woman's jagged voice grew uncompromising. "*No*! *Do not remove your hands yet*!"

The King began to panic as the grip tightened even more. He looked down at his hands and then back at the old woman's intense stare. "*What are you doing to me, old woman?!*" he shouted. The woman turned her eyes to the King's hands, her gaze never blinking. The King began to moan as what felt like thorns, pressed into all his fingertips. He tried instinctively to get on his feet but, the old woman wrapped her hands around his wrists and held him down, exerting remarkable strength. "Patience, King! Endure the pain!" His eyes bursting in agony, he was just about to scream for the guards, when the old woman released him. Quickly bringing his hands to his eyes, he found that they were flushed red and dripping blood. Tempted to strike the wretched old woman with the back of his bleeding hands, his instincts told him to wait; to remain silent a moment longer. He could live with a little pain if it meant getting rid of his young rival.

Pleased to see that he was wiser than most men, the old woman smiled and opened her palms upon the table. "Excellent. Now you may choose your path to serenity, Polydectes, and seal it with your blood!"

Now the king understood. Peering down at the table where the four squares were faintly outlined, one at each corner of the table top, he brought his bloody hands over the table. "I have but one chance," he said aloud. "I must choose wisely or this will all have been in vain and I will be saddled with that interloping bastard until my dying breath, never to have known the sweet caress of my beloved!" His old hands shaking and his eyes fixed on the table, the old woman's glare willed him to make a choice. Throwing both hands into the top left corner, he pushed the square open. With only the sound of his heart thumping from within his hollow, bony chest, the King reached in and pulled out the coin with his bloody hands. Raising the large shining coin to his eyes, he saw the face of Athena Nike pressed on one side. He studied the image for a moment, his senescent, old eye glaring and his lips slyly ajar. Flipping it, he realized that the real message was on the other side of the coin. Slowly turning it in his fingers, he saw the face of a Gorgon staring back, the blood from his fingers making it appear ever more horrifying. The King dropped the coin to the table and got up quickly to his feet, exclaiming, "A curse?! This is what you offer me?! Why would you present such a hideous beast before my eyes?"

The old woman smirked and calmly said, "The beast is your solution, Lord." The old woman's powerful gaze focused on the

King's beady eyes as if implanting the knowledge, to see the wisdom of her words. But, the King's anger only grew as he watched her sit there silently staring at him as if she knew something he did not. He grabbed the old woman's wrist as if to snap it.

"*Trickery*! How could this hideous creature rid me of the pest that has invaded my kingdom? Give me some *true* answers, sorceress, or I will *force* them out of you!"

In his grip, the old woman spoke no words; she simply closed her eyes for the first time. Within the blink of her eyes, they were both transported to the very peak of a cold and stormy mountain, far away from his kingdom. An ill-omened place where the skies were red and black clouds thundered by with raging fury. Now, the old woman stood straight and tall as a young maiden, her robes were the majestic raiment of a queen. She led the King through the enveloping ether, over the barren and grey mountain peaks by his reedy wrist. Tempestuous squalls caused him to flutter like a rag in the wind as he saw before him the bottomless pit of Hades below. Crying out in fear, the King kicked his legs wildly, the pain of his pricked fingertips now long forgotten. The woman looked at him sternly and said in a commanding voice: "The face of the coin is a portent within your grasp, Polydectes. It is up to you to use it to your own gain."

The King listened closely to her words but could not find the voice to speak as he clutched tightly her hand, desperately trying not to fall into the abyss below.

"*Hummm…* perhaps it will take a fall to awaken your mind!" she said, looking down into the bottomless cavity. "May the Fates smile upon you, King!" With those final words, she released her grip and watched as the terrified King plummeted to his doom, screaming, kicking, and grabbing futilely at the air. Closing his eyes in terror, he waited to crash into the fiery Lakes of Hades. But, feeling the wind no more, he opened his eyes. He found himself safely cloaked in the darkness of his own bedchamber, her wicked cackle still echoing in his ears.

Sweat pouring from his forehead, his heart pounding like processional drums, he awoke from the strangest slumber he had ever experienced in his life. Quickly checking his fingertips and wrists, he found nothing; not one tell-tale scratch on his regal hands so he sat up on the edge of his bed. "It was only a *dream*!" he sighed in relief, his pulse beating in his ears. "But… seldom does one learn a secret from their dreams… Unless it was a *vision*," he said, wiping his brow with his sleeve.

Suddenly, a small round object fell from the folds of his bed shirt. "Seldom does a vision provide such a remarkable clue!" Picking up the bloody coin, the King quickly rose from his bed and called for his royal guards who quickly came running.

"Kleon! Send these men immediately into the mainland! Find out all that you can found about this creature called a *Gorgon*! May they not return until they know all there is to know!"

CHAPTER SEVENTEEN

On the dawn of the fiftieth day, King Polydectes' men finally returned with the information he so desperately needed. The cunning and clever King then quickly devised a plan that would end his suffering once and for all and proceeded to put it into motion. He peered out the large open window of his bedchamber as his servants gathered his personal effects and prepared for his departure.

Under the ruse of going to retrieve a young woman who was to become his new queen, the King boarded a small ship with his most trusted bodyguard, General Alcon, his closest confidant, Kleon, and eight of his most trusted men, all of whom were made to take a blood oath of secrecy. Refusing his ministers' request to accompany him on this most auspicious mission, the eleven set off to a place far beyond the safety of the Grecian boundaries on a course into the setting sun, towards the edge of the earth.

The clear and shining eyes of Athena shone bright in the deep night sky, lighting the way to the threshold of oblivion. Colours of deep blues and purples swirled around their tiny ship as the boundless night sky met the churning sea, stirring the ancient sea creatures of the deep, who found the tiny boat bobbing helplessly on the surface like a piece of wayward driftwood. Charybdis, the great sea serpents who, by their inhalations could cause great whirlpools to suck ships to their watery graves; There were also the armies of Hippocampi who were angry creatures, part horse, part fish, that slapped their mighty, barbed tails into unsuspecting ships, reducing them to splinters in the blink of an eye; and most dangerous of all, the giant Kraken, a thousand times larger than any sea vessel and wily enough to silently snatch unwitting victims off the bows of ships without so much as rustling a wave. All of these mighty creatures watched with interest. However, while each made their terrifying presence known, none released their wrath, as if warned against it. Still, their mere presence brought fear and misgivings to the crew.

At long last, King Polydectes' anxious eyes caught the first glimpse of the island of the damned where the Gorgons were said to hold reign as the undisputed Queens of Darkness, ever surrounded by Chaos. Even the Ocean protested the wickedness of this island as the unbearably turbulent currents caused their small ship to be thrown back again and again into the direction it came, as if being forewarned, *Turn away from this place while you are still able*!!! Raging against the insolent sea, Polydectes screamed commands at his men, "Row faster, with all your might! Row for your lives or by the Gods I will have your **heads**!!" Seeing one man tiring from the brutal, inhuman pace, Polydectes drew his sword and swung it through the salty air, chopping off two toes from the soldier's left foot. Though screaming in agony, he dare not break the rhythm of the oarsmen as Kleon hammered a beat on a battle drum and the King raged, "You see this sword?! A gift from King Darius the Great of the Achaemenid Empire! It will have all of your skulls and

those of your families, if you do not **get me to that island!**" Over
and over the vessel was thrown out of the water and threatened to
be taken to the depths of Poseidon. But not a single man was lost to
the capricious sea. Keeping his determined eye fixed on the island,
the King held tightly to the mast with one hand, the butt of his
sword with the other as Kleon's droning drum sounded in all their
ears. *One, two, three, four! One, two, three, four!* Still Polydectes
cursed the men's laggardness as they approached the island all too
slowly for his liking.

Then, from the terror and chaos there, suddenly came a deathly
silence and stillness. Like Night giving way to the rising sun, the air
turned in a moment's breath. Suddenly, the ocean was as flat and
serene as a summer morning. No winds stirred; no currents fought
to take them back to sea. Exhausted, the men stopped to catch
their breath as the King's rolling eye scanned for a sign.

"Look behind you, my Lord!" said an astonished Kleon.

Turning, the King saw that the raging, unrelenting storm was
now behind them, behind a shimmering, translucent veil that held
back the ancient ferocity that kept all life from nearing this cursed,
desolate island of the damned. Looking ahead, his vessel came to
a stop just at the edge of the sharp and jagged rocks that made up
the shallow reef. Sending two of his men ahead into the waist-high
water, the King had six of his hand-chosen men, carry him on his
throne safely to the molten black shore of the hardened tar. Bringing with him only the golden coin and not one weapon, he left his
men on the shore and ventured onto the island alone to plant his
seeds.

The King saw ahead of him, a great towering precipice like
nothing that existed in his own land. Rising thousands of meters
straight up into the air, treacherous jagged outcroppings reached
out over the land below as massive spires reached into the heavens

above. Though one not easily impressed by structures of man or nature, he marvelled at the awe-inspiring beauty this natural wonder presented. It was so captivating, that he was not at all certain it was not a vision or what he had once heard called a *mirage*, as he knew well, much of what the eyes think they see is nothing more than clever illusion. He strode directly towards the imposing structure, his regal robes fluttering in the wind. Coming to the craggy foot, he called out: "I am King Polydectes of Seriphos, and I would like to address the Gorgon called Medusa!"

Having watched their laboured approach since his tiny ship first appeared on the far horizon, Medusa had prepared for what jeopardy its crew posed. Though relieved to see that only a single man had approached, she maintained her guard, long accustomed to wilful deception. Even as the King spoke, she questioned his appearance. Like Poseidon, many Gods and their emissaries were masters of disguise. Standing high above, she called down to him, her screeching voice a jagged assault to his cosseted and refined ears. "What is it you seek with Medusa, King Polydectes of Seriphos?"

"I bring her word… a *warning*," he called up.

"*Warning*? Warning from such an old man, so advanced in years?"

"Warning of another who will come after I. One who will come to take her life for glory and fame."

"And, who might this one be? This… one… seeking glory and fame?"

"He is called, Perseus!" the King shouted. "He is known as a great and cunning warrior, determined to slay a Gorgon so that his name might spread across all the lands."

"And how is it that you know of this scheme?"

"A King hears many things."

"Why do you bring this warning, King Polydectes of Seriphos? What do you seek in return?"

"I only seek that you do all in your power to prevent this from occurring. Flee, hide, or take his life if need be. However, do not allow his plan to succeed! And for this, you will have the gratitude of a most powerful King." Medusa pondered his words as the King stood on the ground staring up.

"You wish yourself rid of this warrior?"

"I confess, there is no love lost. Whether he lives or dies, is of no consequence to me... only... that you live!"

"Then for what reason do you travel across the great forbidding sea to deliver this grave warning?"

"You need only trust that I have my reasons — reasons a wise King does not divulge. But, trust that my warning is faithful. That is why I came here myself, tempting the angry seas and monstrous sea creatures, that you might know the certainty of my words."

Medusa gave one final glaring glance and turned away. The King quickly returned to his waiting men. With a feeling of excitement for his completed quest he was also left with a cold shiver down his spine. As his vessel disembarked, the vigilant Kleon, who knew his King better than anyone, could see a disturbance in his blatant silence.

"My Lord?"

The King remained vacant.

"My Lord, did you catch a glimpse of the beast?"

The King turned wide eyed, "I did Kleon... Though looking at her merely through reflections and shadows; I cannot begin to express the unsettling emotion, she stirs within a mortal man's soul..."

The journey continued in silence as the King became lost in his thoughts.

Back in his kingdom, the distinguished guests and dignitaries had begun to arrive from near and far. Kings, Queens, Basileis,

Pharaohs, Emperors, and other royal sovereigns flowed into the palace with their magnificent retinue of servants and attendants. Their extravagant gifts overflowed the entrance hall as each guest tried to outdo the other in their generosity and show of respect. Each, felt at home as a bountiful feast was beautifully laid out before their voracious eyes; with wines, sweet treats, roasted boars, lamb and duck meat abundant. Exotic fruits from far off lands and nectars were so sweet that the gleeful guests were heard to call out, "Ambrosia! Surely fit for the Gods themselves!"

The finest actors from Greece came to perform their latest plays as beautiful dancers and talented musicians, entertained the guests with music and verse that had never before been seen nor heard. Many had composed special works especially dedicated to the King and his mysterious new queen. The young playwright, Aeschylus, premiered the first of his tragic poems, leaving guests spellbound and envious of King Polydectes' far-reaching social standing. Anxiously, the servants waited for the King's arrival as eight vigilant watchmen, kept a lookout from four heavily guarded towers, searching through the late evening's dark purple horizon with nearly eighteen days having passed since his departure. Now seeing a cloud of golden dust kicked up by frothy horses galloping at full speed towards the palace, a tower guard called down at the top of his voice, "He has arrived! Open the gates and bring the royal carriage! The King has arrived!!"

Instantly, six brawny men who manned the palace's gargantuan bronze gates, swung open the towering metal that protected the palace, just in time for the King to come roaring up, his men only a hair's breadth behind. Stepping into his royal coach, he was brought directly to the palace doors. Wasting no time, he hurried into the banquet hall as quickly as his aching old bones could carry him. As he entered, the Royal Proclaimer announced: "His Exulted Majesty, King Polydectes the Great!"

The King smiled and greeted his friends, exuding great joy. Though known by many for his uncompromising ruthlessness, many were those, who loved and admired him. Countless were the guests the King had invited to his illustrious palace through the years and countless the banquets and feasts he had held in honour of his vast array of noble friends. Standing before his intricately-carved marble throne, he addressed the cheering crowd:

"Welcome one and all, to this gathering of most illustrious guests who have come from the far reaches of the land, to celebrate my union with the young woman who will soon become my queen!" A loud roar of applause and cheers erupted. "It does my old heart good to see the magnificent generosity and love that I am witnessing here tonight by your most gratifying attendance! As you know, I have kept the identity of my love a secret — *am I not the evil one*?!" Everyone turned to one another and giggled wickedly. "*Ha, ha, ha*! And I am afraid I must keep you all on tender hooks a bit longer my beloved friends, while we make final preparations after our long journey. However, I assure you all, you will not be disappointed in my choice! So, dear friends, I welcome you again, and as always, my home is your home so eat, drink, and be merry!"

Retiring to his bedchamber, the King was bathed in specially prepared scented soaps from the lands far to the East and massaged with sacred oils brought from Kingdom of Egypt. Then, he donned his red silk ceremonial robes and royal regalia. Known for his sense of the dramatic, the King entered the banquet hall followed by a line of royal guards eighty in number, each dressed in ivory white uniforms etched in gold. With all sound coming to a sudden halt, the King climbed upon his royal throne, held his hands in the air and declared: "Let us now parade the bountiful gifts you have brought for this most blissful occasion!"

An explosion of cheers and well-wishing applause erupted from all those in attendance, each anxious to acknowledge their token. As they formed a double queue to enjoy the spectacle, servants presented the hundreds of extraordinary wedding gifts. These included exotic gems and cloth, fruit and animals from the far reaches of the known world with the line of well-wishers, reaching to the end of the King's magnificent gardens. However, the greatest ovation erupted when the line of splendid horses the potentates had brought for the King's approval, were paraded, one by one. Indeed, the presentation of great and powerful steeds were the supreme show of respect in this land. Magnificent cinnamon-brown high-tails from Arabia, beautiful chestnut-coated, flaxen-maned draft horses from the Black Forest and stunning golden-haired Palominos from the Western Territories brought *oohs* and *aaahs* from all. The King's beady little eyes swelled with tears as he clapped his hands together and nodded in unqualified approval as each was led by; each supreme ruler stepping forward and bowing, as his gift was presented.

As the gaieties went on well into the night, only one in attendance did not have reason to smile. Perseus, the son of the fair Danaë, though known even to the Gods of Olympus as a potentially great hero, had no gift to offer King Polydectes and so had been reluctant to attend. Thus, he remained in the shadows, hoping to go unnoticed. Eventually, the parade of horses ended and all the admirers cheered as the King stood and bowed most graciously. Playing for the crowd, the King jokingly shouted "Perseus, my boy, which fine gift was yours? Surely you will want to take credit for your thoughtful efforts!" Everyone turned to stare at the young man leaning against a marble pillar with his arms crossed. As the King looked down at him with a crooked smile, Perseus stood tall and stared directly at the King.

"Well, Perseus, my boy? Is your gift so splendid that you have saved it for last?"

Perseus' voice was clear and true, his bright, pale blue eyes resolute but apologetic. "No, my King. I am but a poor and humble servant who can afford no gift as glorious as a horse, so I hesitate to offer something less befitting for fear of insulting His Majesty." Those were the words the King had longed to hear. As the smile drained from his buoyant face, he tactfully set his trap.

"Please explain, my boy." Before Perseus had time to reply, the King dramatically announced, "Everybody! This boy who my dear and kind brother Dyktes found cast away and half drowned in the sea and who he, alone, raised into manhood taking no consideration of cost nor time. This boy has also inherited my brother's strange sense of humour, it seems!" The crowd laughed as the King appeared to be in on a joke with Perseus. King Polydectes sat back on his throne and arched an eyebrow as he stroked his long white beard pensively.

Nervously, Perseus struggled for words: "You have my deepest respect, my King. Mere words cannot express my happiness at your impending union. The hundreds of adoring guests who have arrived to celebrate this auspicious event only prove further the love this land has for you!"

Someone from within the crowd shouted, "You tease, Perseus! Your gift! Show us your magnificent gift!"

The King looked down at Perseus and smiled.

"I am afraid, my King, that I have no horse to offer. However, I beg you not to take this as a sign of impertinence, my all-knowing King, You see, I am a poor man of little means."

The jeers suddenly reduced to condemning whispers. The cagey King rose from his thrown and approached Perseus, placing his old hands on Perseus' powerful, broad shoulders. "My dear boy… never you mind! There is no penalty for disappointing this most charitable King! I know one day you will afford a mighty stallion with which to honour your most charitable benefactor!"

Embarrassed by the King's mocking pity, Perseus set his proud jaw and declared, "No, my King! Name your prize and I will go to the ends of the earth to retrieve it for you! Just name it!"

Smiling slyly, the King turned and musingly stroked his beard as he walked back to his throne, pretending to be searching his mind for an appropriate treasure. His back still turned to Perseus he said, "So... anything I desire? Anything at all?" The King turned towards Perseus, waiting for his trap to spring. The hall fell silent.

"Yes, my Lord! *Anything*, you wish will be my task to provide!"

"*Hmmm...*" The King said, still stroking his beard. "Very well. There is one gift that would please me most, my good boy."

"Name it, my King! Name it and it shall be yours!"

"I have heard a tale of a beast... a great blood-thirsty beast that has been terrorizing the whole of Greece. An evil tyrant named . . *hummm... Medusa!*" The crowd pulled back in awe and began to murmur. They all looked at Perseus wide-eyed, silently waiting to see if he would accept such a challenge. "She is a Gorgon, Perseus, and I want her head as a trophy!"

Without hesitation, Perseus accepted the challenge. "I accept!" The room exploded in applause as all knew the implications of the challenge. Even the name *Medusa* brought fear to most gentle of hearts. Bowing, Perseus turned and left the palace to prepare for his journey. The King sat on his throne content that his conniving plan would soon pay off.

CHAPTER EIGHTEEN

Perseus' mother ran after him, trying to reason with the boy; begging him to reconsider. "Surely, pleasing the King is not worth your life!" Dictys soon followed, offering Perseus a great white Camarillo horse to present to the King that he might avoid the treacherous journey Polydectes had set him on. But all pleas fell on deaf ears as Perseus repeated over and over again that he had given his word. And even though he felt that this *spontaneous* request had been a plan carefully set by the conniving King, he now had no choice but to follow through with his promise. His honour was at stake.

Making Dictys swear on his life to protect Danaë while he was away, Perseus set off, taking command of a ship provided by the King. This was the first mission he had captained, and if the King had his way, it would be his last. Setting sail, he watched as his mother waded into the shallow waters alone with her tears. Dictys stood proudly from the shore, watching his son begin a quest few men would undertake.

Perseus knew he must succeed as failure not only meant shaming his name, but if the King so chose, certain death. So, with a crew of twenty men, he set off to the edge of the earth to find the island of the Gorgon Medusa.

It was the fifth night at sea and Perseus was asleep on deck, his face painted silver by the pale moonlight. The ocean silently rocked the ship to and fro, aiding the shipmates in their guarded slumber. Suddenly, Perseus felt the light grow intense upon his face, alerting him, so he thought that the sun had broken above the eastern horizon. Opening one eye, he saw a magnificent bluish glow before him; opening the other, a hauntingly beautiful but foreboding face stared down at him. Leaping to his feet, he watched as the magnificent manifestation before him spoke sternly:

"Be aware, Perseus. I, Athena, Goddess of Wisdom and Justice, am here to aid you in your noble quest. Now, listen well as time is your mortal foe." Perseus turned an eager ear towards her so as not to miss a single, vital word. "You must now turn your ship towards the rising sun, on the course I etch here upon the ship's deck." Pointing to a place in the middle of the sea she said, "Here, you will find the Graeae, three old hags joined through blood to the Gorgons. They know where Hera's sacred orchard is to be found. There, you will find the three Hesperides sisters, guardians of the treasures of the Gods. They will provide you the tools needed to defeat the Gorgon Medusa. I warn you, do not attempt to slay Medusa without the tools they will provide! She is a most vicious, formidable foe... of that, have no doubt!" Perseus gazed intently at the map laid out on the deck before him. Emblazoned with golden fire, the course was clearly laid for him. "Follow these directions precisely, Perseus, or you will meet a gruesome end!" with that haunting message, Athena vanished.

Quickly running to rouse his crew, Perseus found one unconscious sailor hugging a small jug of wine. Grabbing the jug, he smashed it at the slumbering man's feet, waking him and the crew in the process.

"Rise! Man your stations! Come on… let us make way without delay! I now know the exact path to our reward!" Quickly, the men scurried around him with half-open eyes and stinking breath, preparing the ship as he and his pilot set a course to the lair of the Graeae.

At the entrance of the cold and windswept lair of the Graeae, Perseus stood with sword unsheathed. As he peered cautiously into their foul-smelling den, he saw a most revolting sight: One hag with long, snow-white hair and two with silver grey. All three, were hideous and more repulsive than any woman the young Perseus had ever seen. Their gruesome faces were hidden within the sickening vapour of the concoction brewing in a large bronze cauldron beside them. Perseus tapped his sword to the stone floor to make his presence known. Startled, the white-haired hag held up her decrepit old hand to block the incoming light, to see who had invaded their retched sett. With a crackly, old voice she called out, "Come forward, boy! No need to fear us, we will not harm you!"

Suspecting a deceptive ruse, Perseus said, "You made a mistake, old hag, for it is *you* who must fear *me*!" He raised his sword above his head threateningly. "I have come for the location of Queen Hera's sacred orchard! You will give me the correct answer or I will show you no mercy and end your wretched lives here and now!"

The hags cowered together, whispering amongst themselves, their foul breath only adding to the prevailing stench. Perseus saw that the three had only one crystal ball-like eye and one pointed tooth among them, which they passed between themselves as they spoke. "Why, boy, come closer!" the one holding the eye said. "We will give you just what you need! We welcome you!" The two other hags nodded and smiled through their rotting, toothless mouths.

"*Enough*! Your feminine charms died eons ago! Now, give me the location!"

"Oh, of course, you must go east.. "

"To the west…"

"Yes, to the north, over the water's edge to…" they babbled, quickly passing the eye and tooth between themselves.

"Enough! All three of you speak lies!" he said stepping closer, again banging his sword on the floor.

"No! I speak the truth… do not believe them!" the white-haired one said, slobber dripping from her gaping maw.

"No, no! *I* speak the truth! This is what you want to know…!"

Perseus sheathed his sword and began to encircle them as they huddled together as one, listening to the yarn they wove, each passing the globe and tooth to the next. Seizing his chance, Perseus snatched the eye from one filthy grip. Reaching out blindly in panic, they all moaned for its return, this being their only view into the world. Threatening to throw the precious globe into the unforgiving sea, the three quickly took turns reciting in detail precisely where Perseus must go. Satisfied they were telling the truth, he tossed the crystal eye onto the floor of their sickening cavern, threatening to return and slaughter them if they had lied. Then he swiftly made his way back to his ship and set sail for Hera's orchard.

It was as though the Fates were plotting against him as the wind died out before they reached their destination. His ship stood floating in a placid sea, lapped by the waves. As there was no time to waste, Perseus ordered his men to begin rowing the ship with its giant wooden ores. Perseus himself joined them as night fell and the men grew weakened and tired. However, even as Dawn arrived, no land could be seen in any direction. Exhausted, the men collapsed as Perseus finally gave the order to halt. Letting his men sleep, Perseus drank wine mixed with water to keep his senses keen, long enough to determine a course of action. *Did the Graeae lie to him? Or is the island of the Hesperides harder to locate than I had anticipated?*

Convinced that they were indeed on the correct course, Perseus resolved that stamina and patience were all that were needed to reach the fabled garden. *Surely, their destination was near!* As if by the blessing of the Gods, the wind began to pick up, so they raised their sails and in moments were cutting through the water like a sword through tallow and before long, seagulls began circling the tiny ship.

Now the wind had completely died down again; the silence around them eerie and unsettling. Rowing forward, they kept quiet, Perseus certain they were nearing the mystical land. The mist thickened until it enveloped their little ship like a thick, woollen blanket and they could not see the noses on their faces. Perseus, persistent and determined now, urged them to push forward. Then through the silence, they came aground on a soft, powder-like sandy reef. There, Perseus disembarked alone and without weapons or armour, set out to find the Hesperides and the orchard they guarded.

With only the Graeae and his instincts to guide him, Perseus made his way through the dense forests that ran along the shoreline. Then climbing high into the upper regions, he found his way to the heart of the island where he came to a massive green wall. The wall, at least twenty meters high, was made from tall reaching shrubs and vines that had enmeshed over time with towering trees, creating an impenetrable barricade. Quickly climbing the imposing barrier, Perseus saw before him a view like no other, the most vivid colours known to his eyes adorning the fabled garden; magnificent greens, reds, oranges and blues the hues of which Perseus had only imagined. What stood out amongst it all was a golden shine that the soft daylight now revealed to him. Entering the splendid garden, he walked closer to find the Tree of Immortality, where golden apples grew; fabled fruit that held the power to make one, young and immortal, like the Gods. Although legend carried great peril for anyone who went near the sacred tree, Perseus could not help but try to pluck a fruit from its bountiful branches. Just as he reached out, he was interrupted by a puff of steaming heat hitting the back of his neck. Startled, he turned to find himself standing in the shadow of Ladon, the serpentine dragon who lie coiled around the base of Hera's tree of golden apples.

The unarmed Perseus stood stock-still as the beastly Ladon towered over him with the look of Hades in his eyes. Forebodingly black as the dead of night, with eyes of fiery red, the dragon pushed forward and lowered his head to meet Perseus' sight. Perseus knew of the legend of the beast, and much to his astonishment, Landon spoke: "Perseus, do not continue on this quest; Medusa is not your enemy." Stunned at the deadly serpent's thoughtful words, Perseus was momentarily speechless. The dragon's soft-spoken voice sounded more like a wise man than a ferocious beast. Landon encircled Perseus with his long, cold body. "This will only end in tragedy for you, as for my sister," Ladon said.

"Your *sister*?!"

"Our burdens in this world are one and the same, Perseus. Know that Medusa is not alone and the forces of Night will not let this rest."

"And if I have no other choice but to finish my quest?"

"You are the son of Zeus, Perseus, and therefore, I cannot harm you. But know that there are others who can and are prepared to do so. Understand that there is always another choice, Perseus. Always another choice!"

Perseus pondered this mystical creature's words but resolutely stated "I have given my word in front of many, Landon. I would rather die than dishonour myself and my ancestors. This is something I *must* do!" As he spoke his last word the Hesperides approached; the three beautiful daughters of Night that seemed to float on clouds of colourful air. "Welcome, Perseus, we have been waiting for you," spoke the one beautiful Hesperida, her hair of red fire and eyes of fresh green leafs. She rested on Landon while she stroked his long, scaly neck. A second Hesperida with long blue hair and bright purple eyes came closer to Perseus and smiled as Ladon slithered around them and back to the golden tree.

"Come with us, Perseus. We possess the enchanted items which you seek."

Perseus stood cautious. "How do I know I can trust you?"

The third Hesperida with hair of long spun gold and eyes of dazzling white, floated towards him and took Perseus tenderly by the hand.

"Trust us, Perseus. Trust us."

Perseus turned to Ladon one final time as he followed the Hesperides and said in a low, solemn voice, "I am sorry."

The Hesperides did as they had been instructed by Athena, equipping the mortal Perseus with the weapons of the immortals: a pair of winged sandals to help fly him swiftly past the Gorgon, the Cap of Darkness of Hades to render him invisible, a special kibisis to carry his trophy, and a scimitar, a sword of enchanted adamantine to sever the Gorgon's head.

With a promise to return to the garden, Perseus embarked on the final phase of his quest, the high seas and the northerly winds ensuring that he would reach his destination at the speed of lighting. *Perhaps* he contemplated *my father, Zeus, has taken pity on me and offered some relief in the form of safe passage.* However, Zeus was not the only immortal keeping an eye on Perseus' progress as his brother, Poseidon, knew it was time to protect his lost love in the only way that he could. Unable to wield physical harm upon Perseus, he instead manipulated the elements around him. As

Perseus neared the island of the damned, the seas abruptly became hostile and unwelcoming, just as King Polydectes had faced. From clear blue and placid, the skies suddenly darkened and the waves slammed into the ship, knocking Perseus and his crew about like straw dolls. An ominous storm began to brew, far stronger and more vicious than the King had encountered.

Hail the size of grown men's fists rained down and veils of static enveloped the ship. Nearly knocked overboard, Perseus held on tightly. Staring down into the black waters, Perseus swore he saw Poseidon's scornful face staring back at him from the depths. His terrifying image sent shivers up Perseus' spine as he quickly ran and lashed himself to the middle mast. The Ocean below stirred and the monsters of the deep bellowed and cried mournfully as the men ran for cover. Armies of Hippocampi slapped their mighty, barbed tails into ship again and again, causing it to pitch and yaw. Perseus knew that if he stayed on board the ship a moment longer he would be responsible for the lives of his men. Reaching for the Cap of Darkness, he put it on his head and the very moment he did, he became invisible in sight and sound; neither mortal nor God was now able to sense his presence.

Slipping the winged sandals upon his feet, he let go of the ship's swaying mast and began to fly off into the raging sky. Covering himself with his shield, he flew to the island's calm shores. The men already had their instructions. As Perseus reached the island and began to climb the towering, jagged cliffs to the cavern where Medusa lie in wait, they rowed away from the island, headed for home. His winged sandals safely stowed away in a pouch, he made his way on foot; flying for him was for the Gods.

Taking considerable time to scale the mammoth structure, Perseus finally made his way to the top. He stood and watched his men sailing away, knowing that the more distance they put between themselves and the cursed island, the less that the wrath of Poseidon could affect them. As long as they were still in sight, danger could befall them at any moment. There, at last, at the entrance of his fate and his final opportunity to turn back, he set his jaw and cleared his mind. Bravely, he lifted his shield and entered the cavern knowing that there was no turning back now.

He could smell the burning of frankincense and dragons' blood as he walked through the dark and foreboding caves. Twisting and turning through one cave and then another, he felt a shiver as he looked at the archway ahead of him. Holding his shield to one side, he looked into its reflection to see his first image of the sleeping Medusa lying still on a bed of flat rock, her back turned towards him. All the dreams and visions she had experienced in her life were now manifesting before her, playing out as dramatic theatre and all she could do was lie back and watch.

As Morpheus showed her, Perseus had come for her. She knew he had his part to play for the Fates and she had hers. Rolling thunder echoed through the tunnels as Perseus crept closer and without a word, raised his sword and aimed for her neck. As the blade sliced through the stale air, Medusa instinctively moved out of its way, quickly springing to her feet and poising herself before him. As she stood facing him, he deflected her deadly gaze with his shield.

"Medusa, do not make this harder than it has to be. You know the Gods have plotted against you and will not allow you to leave this cavern alive! You know the task with which I have been charged!"

"I know Perseus. And, I feel sorry for you." Leaping forward, she mounted her attack, easily knocking his shield from his hand. The battle had begun. Like puppets, the two danced for the Gods' amusement. After all, what is the life of two semi-mortals worth to a God? But for a living creature, nothing is simple. Neither life nor death is simple; and if the ultimate goal is to find peace in either, one must struggle and toil beforehand. Nothing is expected to be easy; neither taking a life nor saving one. As they battled, Perseus and Medusa were both pieces that fit neatly together in a grand puzzle: Perseus the force and Medusa the reaction.

The storm outside was raging as night fell, but the claps of thunder were drowned out by the clashes of metal. The fight, a mix of hunt, chase and clash, lasted for hours. Both battling their emotions as they battled each other, Perseus knew it was time for it to come to an end before his energy was spent. As Medusa fired one deadly arrow after another at his young, shielded chest, he released his full force. Charging her, he pushed her through a crumbling wall that led to the crest of the mountain. There with nowhere to run, the rain poured down on them as the wicked winds blew powerful enough to create a raging wall of water around them.

"Medusa, this is it! There is nowhere to run! Nowhere to hide! Let it end here and now!" He screamed as he angled his burnished shield to catch her stark and ravaged reflection.

Soaked through, her cape draped down to reveal her serpentine locks that were ablaze within a writhing black ocean, the sight entrancing Perseus long enough for Medusa to seize the opportunity. Charging savagely, her feet gripped the cold, wet stones as the sword flew out of his hand. Cowering, he quickly held the shield over his body to protect himself from her dagger-like claws which she lashed out again and again. Attempting to crush him beneath his shield, she threw her weight upon it, with the shield's edge ripping into his neck. As she watched him writhing in pain, she knew she could easily end his life, but a voice deep within reminded her that this was not the path she had agreed to follow.

Screaming with all her strength, the ringing of her pain shattered Perseus' heart as Medusa released him from her deadly grip.

Standing tall and proud, she threw his sword at his feet as if to say, *Get it over with!*

Struggling to regain his footing, he picked up the sword, watching her turn away, a black ocean waved down her body as the serpents struck out in rage. Approaching slowly, he stood as sword's length watching her tenderly hold her belly. "I am sorry, truly sorry, Medusa," he whispered. Swinging his sword with all his considerable power, she turned and with one final scream, reached for his throat. A second later, her body fell limp onto the stone slab, her head rolling to his blood-soaked feet.

It was over.

The pupils of his eyes constricted to pins as her cry still echoed through his mind. As he picked up her head by its serpentine locks, the mysterious black sea dematerialized. He placed her head in his kibisis and secured it. Kneeling down, he held her ravaged hand in his. "I hope you find the peace in death you did not find in life Medusa."

Retrieving his cap, Perseus fled the island on his winged sandals as the storm quieted behind him. Two flying figures followed in pursuit, their bellowing screams haunting Perseus as he cloaked himself and vanished into the sea's rising mist.

CHAPTER NINETEEN

Medusa's body lay cold and pallid as the rain unmercifully poured down, washing away the blood she shed in sacrifice. She had bled her entire life; one tragedy after another, finally led her heart to turn cold. Fate, destiny, the future led her to this final resting place.

She had played her part well. Here, now upon this mortal earth, two groups of beings were left divided; the ones who live in fear, left to scurry and cower in the cold shadows of the merciless Gods. The others, those who see the multiplicity of truth through new eyes; the ones that would fight back.

Seven women emerged from the cave, all draped in black, carrying a golden litter which they placed beside Medusa's body. Six picked up her body and placed it on the golden bier. Each taking their place, they raised Medusa on high as they reverently marched into the cave.

The seventh knelt down and collected some of Medusa's blood in a golden vial. Entering the cave, Soteria took off her golden mask to reveal her flowing tears. Drinking the contents of the sacred vial, she spoke.

"Beloved Medusa, I await your return."

–The End–